Queen of Drattüjert

L. L. Nelson

Nelding & Michcomb Publishing

Contents

A mysterious young woman, an elven invasion, and the tokens of the High King

Haldrek Rodreksson has known his entire life where his future lies and what is expected of him. But on the eve of battle, soothsayers show him three visions of a different future: a mysterious young woman, a new invasion, and theft of the High King's tokens. Visions which make him question his future and that of his homeland, Lohikärra.

When the capital of Lohikärra falls, Haldrek's world is thrown into disarray and he must scramble to keep the young woman from his visions safe.

Injured, weaponless, and with little support, will Haldrek be able to save the woman and change the visions he was given? Or will he, his homeland, and his loved ones fall to their enemies?

❖

Get a free copy of the prequel
Visions of Lohikärra here:

https://www.llnelsonauthor.com/newsletter/

To my husband - For always supporting me, even when I doubted myself. You are more amazing than you know.

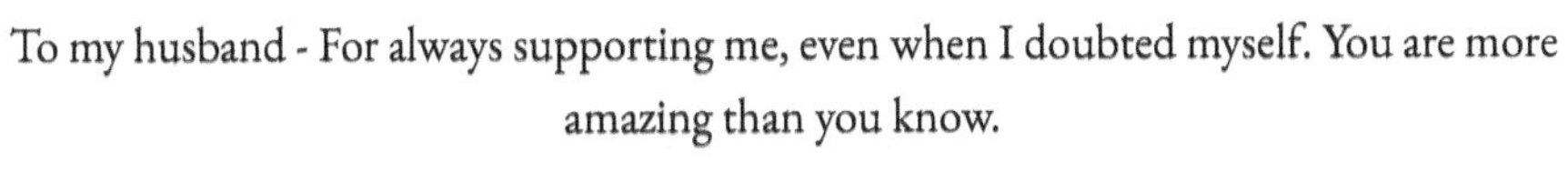

To my kids - For inspiring me to be a better mom and showing me what it looks like to have limitless confidence in yourself.

To my dad - For always believing I was an amazing writer and being my cheerleader.

To my sisters - For inspiring me and just being plain awesome.

Chapter One

Closing my eyes, I exhaled and tried to relax into the sounds and smells around me. One quick moment to center myself before more people came to say hello or gawk at me.

I was currently in Skarvollr, sitting at the far end of the main room in town's central tavern. On my right, Llamryl sat watching the festivities and trying to look tough. On my left, the gesith of Skarvollr sat drinking his newest tankard of mead and talking jovially with someone on his other side. The platform we three were on looked over the rest of the room, where the town was reveling in my arrival. Apparently my father hadn't visited Skarvollr too often during his time as thegn, so my visit was an occasion to behold for them.

"How are you doing, my thegn?" Llamryl's voice made me open my eyes. I turned to him, took a deep breath, and smiled.

"I'm fine. Just tired. Today has been long."

"The last couple of weeks have been long. I was worried you'd exhaust yourself when you said you wanted to visit the rest of your gesiths and the major towns here in Svartån."

"It's important. And your sisters are good healers." Thandes and Meri had tried every Hethurin restoration tonic they had known in the past two and a half months to restore both my strength and stamina to what it had been before I'd deep fried Seirye. Between them and Mattie's concoctions, I was almost back to normal. The only times I still felt effects from my overcharged lightning spell was when I forgot to pace myself. Like today.

"They are." Llamryl nodded. "I still wish Meri would have stayed at the estate. But I suppose that's of little import now."

I shrugged. "I'm not going to keep her in a place where she's lost so much. She needs to grieve in her own way." I had found out soon after my coronation that Meri and Ecaeris had grown close, after her return from Aldinnvollr and before Ecaeris's death. When she had asked to leave the estate again, I didn't take issue with it.

"Still..."

"Her leaving the estate gave me the idea to travel around Svartån. I needed to get out and explore just as much as she needed to leave. Different reasons, but—"

"May the dragons watch over our new thegn and her rule be long and prosperous for Svartån!"

A bard on the opposite side of the room stood on a long center table and jumped lithely between and over dishes of foods, strumming his instrument and launching into a new-to-me song about my victories over the Isillas. The townsfolk seemed to know and enjoy the song as I watched his acrobatics become more outlandish, waiting in apprehension for him to trip and fall. Instead, someone rapped a metal spoon against his kneecap as he drew near and a man's voice shouted:

"Get down, you drunken sot! Damn wench's done nothing worth singing about. If you must, sing about real heroes of Lohikärra!"

The bard stopped singing and the room's mood changed quickly. A few boos started and for a moment, I wondered if this man's open disdain had somehow changed things. Instead, he got jostled out of his spot and pushed from the tavern.

As soon as he was gone, the bard started up again, but this time with a new song about Bjornulf the Brave. A heavy, leathery hand landed on mine and began shaking it.

"Don't worry. Every town has their naysayers. As you can see, Skarvollr is very support-ive of our new thegn." The gesith smiled widely, revealing a tooth missing, but I could see a slight bit of panic in his expression.

I returned a smile instinctively, not wanting to sour the mood despite my own cheer fading. "Don't worry. I've had more than one naysayer before. And they were wrong." I cringed inside, the words sounding too cocky to me.

The gesith nodded quickly. "Of course. Of course. Are you still hungry, my thegn? Or thirsty?" He quickly gestured and a young boy popped out from the room's edges, a mug ready.

I took it, not wanting to be rude, and turned to see the bard finishing his song about Bjornulf. The people cheered more, but a heavy weight had settled into my chest. I knew the stories of Bjornulf, at least the ones that had been included in the video games in Fargo, and a thought struck me. I wondered whether or not songs like this would be written about Haldrek. I didn't want to be so arrogant as to think any of the songs about me would be remembered, but Haldrek...he was going to be the High King. There would definitely be stories about him. Just thinking about that made my spirits lift a little. Even if I was an outsider here in Lohikärra, I could still make sure he was remembered as well as Bjornulf or any of the other heroes of lore.

"Lady Ina?" Nudging my arm, Llamryl leaned toward me.

I smiled, trying to brush the heavy thoughts from my head. "Yes?"

"I hope you're not taking that man's comments too seriously."

I shook my head. "Why?" I wondered if my expression had betrayed what I'd really been feeling.

"You look less cheerful than before. I wanted to remind you that some people say things drunk that they regret when sober."

I opened my mouth to say something and then shook my head again. "I'm just tired. Pushed myself too much today."

Llamryl bobbed his head and looked out on the crowd for a moment. His face lit up and a light banter filled his voice. "I think I know something that would cheer you up."

"What?" I started to laugh from his tone.

"I'm sure no amount of naysayers would pull you down if Thegn Andrattür was here."

I grinned. "That's true. I miss Haldrek." Fingering my pendant, I said, "Talking with him regularly through this just isn't the same being around him." I paused for a moment to clap for the bard as he finished another song. "I'm sure you're missing someone right now as well." My smile turned impish as I cocked my head at Llamryl.

His cheeks flushed a little bit and he looked away from my stare. "I...I won't lie. That is true. Sometimes I wish I had a pendant to connect with Mattie like you and Thegn Andrattür do. But I know we'll be back at Svangendom soon."

"We will. One more town and then we'll be able to head back."

A few days later, we arrived in Sigreykir, the last town in my tour of Svartån. I knew the town had connections to Hardbein, so I was less than eager to visit. The day was less than welcoming as well. It may have been June and nearly summer, but this particular day was miserable and gray.

As we entered the city gates, the guards watched my group, me on my horse and my Thegn's Guard trailing behind me, with expressions ranging from wariness to disgust. I ignored the stares for the most part, focusing on the path in front of me and looking for the gesith's dwelling. Sigreykir didn't have any notable parts to it, as some of the other towns had. Though it sat at the southern crossroads of Svartån's easternmost valley, I didn't see much in the way of trade or markets. Instead, most of the city had iron shops, armories, and other businesses around the edge of town, and more residential areas toward the center. If the current gesith of Sigreykir and his forebears were anything like I expected, the gesith's manor would be in the center of town.

Within a few minutes, I rode up to a sturdy but ornately decorated building facing the square at the town's center. Standing outside was a group of men, one of whom wore finely made chainmail and more baubles in his hair and beard than I could count. In some ways, he reminded me of the former gesith of Katla. Except he didn't seem pleased to see me.

I stopped my horse. "Gesith Sigreykir, I assume?"

He looked me over for a long moment, arms crossed and disdain evident in his posture. Long enough for me to start feeling uncomfortable. "I guess you are the new Thegn of Svartån then. Yes, I am the Gesith of Sigreykir. Skarde Bosson."

I smiled in an attempt to warm up the conversation. "Maja Ingmar Svanunge." I'd found during my trip that many of the gesiths treated me with more respect if I used my full name instead of just Ina. The gesith said nothing, his posture still stiff. After a moment, I said, "Sigreykir looks like a very prosperous town. I'd love to see it."

The gesith waved his hand around him, gesturing to the center square and houses. "It is a good Lohikärran town. We mine much of the metal used by Svartån warriors and quarry much of the rock to make its buildings. You may wander around if you like, but I'm only here because it is part of my duty to welcome you and sign an oath of my allegiance to you. Nothing more, nothing less."

I grimaced and nodded. "Very well then." Trying to hide my annoyance and embarrassment, I got off my horse and gave the reins to Llamryl. "I'm guessing this shouldn't take too long. If you and the men want to find a place where you can rest, I'll be along shortly."

Llamryl nodded and the gesith cleared his throat. When I faced him, he wore a smirk on his face.

"Only *humans* are allowed to stay in Sigreykir's taverns and other establishments. If your 'men,' as you call them, want to find a place to rest, they'll have to do it outside the city walls."

My cheeks warmed up in anger, but as I opened my mouth to say something, Llamryl clasped my shoulder and said, "Don't worry, my thegn. We'll find something."

I nodded. Llamryl's tone of voice told me this wasn't a hill to die on. At least not yet.

As my men headed in the direction we had come from, I followed the gesith into his abode. Two of my guards stayed with me at Llamryl's behest and, while I didn't feel threatened by the gesith or his men, their presence made me feel better.

The inside of the gesith's home was warmly lit, showing off the beautifully carved stone and wood decorations. Images of dragons covered nearly every inch of the building and I couldn't help but smile. Even though it had been months since I'd spoken to Rhaegos in person, Sivath, another dragon who seemed to have a connection to Andrattür, visited

Svangendom regularly now. He mostly came to visit and train Mattie, but a handful of times he visited on behalf of Rhaegos, and I enjoyed those visits.

"Admiring Sigreykir handiwork?" The gesith's voice pulled me from my thoughts.

I nodded. "I am. Sigreykir has talented artisans."

The gesith stood next to me, staring at one particular dragon design. "My father took pride in making sure this place was decorated only by Sigreykir artisans while he was gesith. I remember running around here as a child with Hardbein, watching them in awe and looking forward to the day when we would become *haldragas*."

The brief bit of happiness I'd had from looking at the carvings of dragons disappeared. The gesith's last little jab hit its mark and I steadied my expression, careful not to reveal anything. I knew I was the only thegn right now who wasn't a haldraga. No dragon had yet bonded itself with me and I sensed this made me stick out. Most thegns were haldragas before they took the mantle and title.

The gesith continued. "I've heard that you are not a haldraga yet?" A lilt hung in his voice, as if he was leading me into some kind of trap. I stiffened up.

"Whether or not I am a haldraga is no one's concern except for mine and the dragons." I was repeating something Sivath had told both Mattie and I a few times when we had mentioned that concern to him.

"Huh. I wonder why the dragons chose you over my cousin then?" The gesith walked over to a table set with parchment and writing tools. My cheeks flared up again. "He's already a haldraga and a known son of Lohikärra. But I guess even the dragons have their traditions. Come. Let me sign this document and you can know of my continuing loyalty to the Thegns of Svartån."

I followed him, his underhanded insult still stinging. The document was written in Lohikärran runes, most of which I still didn't understand. It had been the same in other towns, but I'd had Llamryl or another person by my side to translate. The only parts I could read were the signatures and even then, only my father's and what I assumed was his father's. On the left-hand side there were another handful of signatures. I could decipher a corresponding gesith signature and thegn signature, much like the loyalty pledges the gesiths had signed in the other towns. The gesith quickly signed the document, at which point, so did I. After I signed, I heard a little laugh.

"You do not sign with your runes? Or you don't have them?"

My cheeks warmed up again. My signature hadn't been an issue anywhere else. "I choose to sign this way. That way people know my signature is mine."

The gesith bristled as he stood up. "Well, that is the document. I have heard of other gesiths holding festivities at your coming, but unfortunately, we have not been able to do anything like that here. Been busy with the upcoming summer solstice and all that." He crossed his arms and narrowed his eyes at me for a moment, re-emphasizing the feeling that my appearance here was an inconvenience. "If you are hungry, I'm sure any of the taverns would be happy to feed you for some coin." He gestured to the front door and I saw several other people in the room begin to leave, as if tending to other duties.

I hesitated, not necessarily wanting to take the gesith's lead, but to remind him of who was in charge. Haldrek's words about keeping gesiths in line popped up into my thoughts. While this gesith hadn't done anything yet to warrant a rebuke, I still had a feeling he might need a reminder of his position in the future.

"Tell me, Gesith Sigreykir... the warriors of your town, what are they noted for? Katla and Eldingheimr have sailors, Aldinnvollr fierce spearman. Should I need Sigreykir's aid in defending Svartån or Lohikärra, what should I expect?"

The gesith turned to me in confusion, cocking his head. "Do you expect to need Sigreykir's aid, Thegn Svartån?"

I shrugged. "We are still in the midst of a war with the Blodnar. There is a good chance Svartån will be asked to fight them once more."

Gesith Sigreykir nodded. "Did I not sign an oath to you just now?"

"You did, but certainly Sigreykir has warriors who are unsurpassed in some skill? Archers? Axemen? That's what I'm asking. Not if you'll send warriors when I ask for them."

He cleared his throat. "Of course. Sigreykir is known for its warriors as well."

We stood there standing for a few long moments before I nodded, realizing he wasn't about to reveal anything more.

I moved forward toward the door and said, "You don't seem too confident in the warriors of Sigreykir. I hope, for everyone's sake, they have some fighting skill worth mentioning and are better than you are implying."

The sound of fast, heavy footsteps made me turn quickly. The gesith got in my face, standing toe to toe with me. "My warriors are the best that Svartån has. Certainly better than the half breeds you keep around yourself. You may be thegn, but you are certainly no warrior and an outsider to boot. I give you six months before you're dead and Hardbein is named thegn. As he should have months ago."

I went cold, wondering how concerned I should be about his words. Stiffening up, I stared him down, trying to look as intimidating as possible. "I hope that's not a threat."

He smirked and looked past me, opening the door in one movement. "Of course not. *My thegn.*"

Chapter Two

Outside the western gate of Sigreykir, I tossed and turned most of the night in my tent. Llamryl and the rest of my guard had made a comfortable enough camp, but the gesith's words had left me with a cold foreboding. When I finally fell asleep, I found myself in the Realm of Ghosts. But what was normally a comforting visit—at least as comfortable as visiting the dead can be—felt more ominous. I didn't know whether the feeling lingered from my visit with the gesith or came from something new.

My dad sat on wide stone steps. After a moment, I realized it was the dais from the High King's palace. This was the throne room where my dad had first pulled me in to the Realm of Ghosts, but it was different now. It was darker, though I could see most everything around me. The room was also empty, where it had been filled with people milling around. The change made me nervous.

"Inka."

I turned toward my dad, surprised to hear his nickname for me. He only ever used it in somber situations. What scared me most though, was the sound of his voice. He sounded so exhausted. Or weak. As I got closer to him, I noticed how gaunt he looked, with bags under his eyes and his cheeks looking more hollow. His hand, which had had a hole in the flesh the last time we spoke, now had a larger gap in the skin. I gasped.

"Dad?" My voice squeaked and I tried to restrain my fear. What the heck was going on?

"I'm sorry to scare you, sweetheart. I wanted to check on you. Kalle thinks there is a necromancer in Drattüjert. There's no other reason for this." He gestured at himself and the room.

"What? A necromancer? Does this have to do with—"

My dad shook his head. "Don't worry about it. There's nothing you can do until the Blodnar are out...away...defeated." He groaned and I stepped toward him. The garish lights in the room revealed more decay on his exposed flesh and I stopped. "Tell me. How are the gesiths receiving you?"

"Uh... fine. As well as I expected. The Gesith of Sigreykir doesn't like me, but I would have been surprised if he did."

My dad nodded. "Hardbein is his cousin, and they grew up together. I'm sure he assumed Hardbein would succeed me and that would improve his status. Don't take his words personally, but... keep an eye on him. And don't be afraid—" He began coughing and something dark and slimy popped out of his mouth. His eyes widened at the blob. Then he asked, "Do you consider Lohikärra your home?"

"I...," I stuttered, trying to think of the right words for this situation. "Dad, I think you...we...have more pressing issues than my feelings—"

"Is Lohikärra your home? Will you stay here?"

"Yes. I'm the Thegn of Svartån. I feel more connected to Lohikärra than I ever did to Fargo. Whether I'm an outsider or not, I already made that decision—"

"Good." He took a ragged breath. "Home is where your heart is." He laughed weakly. "If that's true...then your home is in Andrattür right now."

I ducked my head in embarrassment. If I hadn't been in the Realm of Ghosts, my cheeks would have warmed up at the comment. "Haldrek has his duties and I have mine. We talk frequently. I'll see him soon enough."

My dad laughed again. "Have you two...?"

I froze. People assumed Haldrek and I had had sex ever since, well, since I got to Lohikärra, but the comments had increased since my coronation. Haldrek mentioned pressure being put on him to find his 'High Queen,' and rumors were beginning to go around that we had already done something on the night I became a thegn.

"Ina?" My dad's voice was low and hoarser this time. I looked up at him.

"We haven't had, you know, sex, if that's what you are asking." I sighed. "Haldrek has been getting pressure to get married or betrothed or whatever. I guess people think his hesitation is because the two of us...you know...but we haven't."

"Who has been pressuring him?" My dad shifted toward me, his attention now fully on me.

I shrugged. "Family members, I guess. He rattled off a few names. Other thegns, I think. One of them, Raynord, I remember. He was at my coronation. I thought he was suspicious, but Haldrek told me Raynord was an ally to Svartån."

My dad bobbed his head slowly. "He is. Though..."

"Though what?"

"It wouldn't surprise me if he wanted Haldrek to marry one of his granddaughters or another female relation. Even before Kalle's death, he was intent on making connections between Haldrek and his family members. Most members of the abthanry do that, though. If he has been trying to foster a relationship between one of his granddaughters and Haldrek, your arrival changed things."

"Should I be worried? Me and Haldrek being in a relationship...would Raynord turn against either of us?" I thought back to Gustav and the other thegns my father had mentioned as not being friendly to Svartån.

"I don't think so, but perhaps I should go have a little talk with Raynord. Remind him that there are bigger issues at stake right now than whom Haldrek ends up with."

I widened my eyes, imagining being thrust into a dream with someone who was currently dead and rotting. "How would he react to that?"

My dad smiled, revealing teeth stained dark with something I didn't want to think about. "I think I might scare him into backing off." His smile disappeared as he groaned. "I think I've kept you here too long. Be safe and know that I'm proud of you. Once Drattüjert is safe again—"

"I'll make sure you go off to Mirroth." The words popped out of my mouth before I could think.

He smiled sadly. "Find the necromancer."

A cold, sick feeling overwhelmed me as everything went dark and empty. The emptiness grew heavy and my eyes snapped shut.

When I opened them again, I was in my tent once again, the sounds of insects and rough whispers of the night watch filling the background noise. I exhaled, wishing for dawn break. There was no way that I'd be able to sleep now.

A few long and tiring days later, I returned to Svangendom with the small group of warriors that I had traveled with. I'd tried calling Haldrek a few times on my pendant, to no avail. I chided myself for contacting him, even though he had made no indication of being annoyed by our conversations through the pendants. But I knew we were busy. He with Andrattür and me with Svartån. Still, I missed him.

As I rode through the village, I saw what seemed like more and more people working on rebuilding places. For a moment, it felt like I was back in one of the Lohikärran games, with NPCs milling around. I frowned and shook my head as I returned to reality. Unlike the computer characters I was familiar with, the villagers here were all covered in dirt now and a few of them a little bit drunk still.

"Thegn Svartån!" One woman waved to me and then bowed deeply, dirt puffing out from her dress and hair. "Happy Solstice!"

I blinked for a moment and looked up at the sky. The sun was high above us, not quite at its peak, but still bright. Looking at Llamryl, he nodded.

"It is the summer solstice, my thegn."

Turning to the woman, I smiled. "Happy Solstice! I guess I've lost track of the days. Is there... Are there celebrations going on?"

She hesitated, her smile faltering into nervousness as she dusted some dirt from off her hair and then her dress. "There are, my thegn, if that's all right. The previous thegn... your father... encouraged celebration of the solstices."

"I'm glad to hear that. I don't know too many Svartån or Lohikärran solstice traditions."

"No?" Her eyes widened and I heard Llamryl clear his throat behind me.

"Are they doing the bonfire this year?"

The woman bobbed her head eagerly. "I think with all that has happened, people are eager for solstice traditions. Maybe even a visit from a dragon."

Llamryl laughed. "Then maybe the thegn will have to visit if she has a chance tonight."

I nodded. "I'd love to see what the solstice bonfire is like."

She bobbed her head again in excitement, then curtsied once more before hurrying off.

Llamryl strode up to where I sat on my horse. "I probably should have mentioned today was the solstice. To be fair though, I thought you knew."

"It's fine. Is there anything special I need to know? Like..." I jerked my head in the direction the lady had run off in. "What's with the dirt? It seems like people are more dusty today?"

Llamryl grinned and nodded. "That's a solstice tradition. Especially among the more rural people. To roll in the dirt as a way to welcome in the solstice."

I frowned. "That sounds strange."

He shrugged. "You can ask Skuti or anyone else about it. We roll in the dirt to remember the earth and the blessings it gives us, as well as to remember the cycles of life. From dirt and to dirt, so to speak. Each year is like a lifetime." We were quiet for a minute before he gestured toward the thegn hall. "We can continue on if you'd like. I'm sure Mattie or Master Skuti have news for us."

Inside the thegn hall people buzzed around, mostly servants, and I looked for a familiar face. Either Mattie or Skuti. Both for an update on what had happened while I was away, and also for what I need to do now. Neither were near the thegn chair and as I looked behind me, I noticed Llamryl hurrying up one of the staircases to the second level. I grinned, knowing exactly who he was looking for, and focusing my own search for Skuti.

Meandering into what I had dubbed the 'research room' off of the main hall, I looked over the many scrolls and books Skuti had on the various tables. Along the rear wall, the large thegn stone—which was in all reality a bowl with water in it and a stone on either side where you could lay your hands—sat temptingly empty. I wondered if Haldrek would answer if I called him now.

"Lady Ina!"

I jumped, my armor and chainmail clattering, as Skuti walk into the room. I sighed. Haldrek would have to wait. At least for now.

"How was your journey? I hope that the gesith all treated you with the respect they should have."

I nodded. "They did. Most of them. The others...my dad said those men were grumpy and rude with him as well."

Skuti laughed. "They may have been." His mirth disappeared as quickly as it came. "Not that they should be rude to a thegn."

I shrugged. "I expected more of them to be grumpy and rude to me, given how new I am."

"You shouldn't. Even if they are unsure of you or wished another to be thegn, you are their thegn. They should treat you as they would your father, or another thegn."

"I guess." We were quiet as Skuti looked over his scrolls and flipped through a few pages in a nearby book. "Skuti?"

He looked up. "Yes, my thegn?"

"Is there anything in those books about necromancy? And haldragas?"

He frowned, his hand stopping one of the pages. "Your ancestors studied a variety of subjects, so I'm sure there is something within your family's library. But what brings about your curiosity in necromancy?"

I exhaled. "My dad. He visited me again while I was traveling."

"That's not unusual for people in your family, I assume. Did he say something about necromancy?"

"Yes and no. Well, yes. But I noticed something before he said anything. He's rotting away. He had previously told me rotting wasn't possible, because he was a haldraga still connected to his dragon. The first thing he said during this last visit was that he thought there was a necromancer in Drattüjert."

Skuti groaned and then nodded, returning his attention to his scrolls and books. He asked, "Have you told Thegn Andrattür yet?"

I shook my head. "I've been trying to get a hold of him, but no luck. He's been busy, I'm sure, but—"

"This is important." Skuti took a deep breath. "If there is a necromancer in Drattüjert, that could spell disaster for those trying to re-take the city. Thegn Andrattür would know more about the hows and the whats in regards to fighting it."

I walked over to the thegn stones and placed my hands on the two stones while looking over the bowl of water.

"Mirratoft. Haldrek Rodreksson."

The water turned inky dark and tiny waves began to ripple from the center, as if someone had dropped a stone in it. After a few minutes, the movement stopped and the water went still again.

"Oh c'mon, Haldrek!" I snapped in frustration, trying to hide the sadness and worry creeping into my heart. Footsteps hurried behind me and I turned around to see Mattie enter the room. Her smile faded and her forehead furrowed for a second.

"What's going on?" She glanced at Skuti as he continued to go through his documents. "Did something happen between you and Haldrek, Ina?"

I sighed, more worry starting to creep up into my chest.

"No. As far as I can tell, no. I've been trying to contact him, either through my pendant or through the big thegn stones, but he hasn't answered. I don't think I did anything that would keep him from talking to me. I need to see if he knows something."

"What?" Mattie focused her attention on Llamryl as he entered the room. "Llamryl, did something happen with the gesiths?"

I shook my head. "The gesiths are the gesiths. My dad contacted me while we were on our journey and told me that there was a necromancer in Drattüjert. He looked terrible."

"Like no sleep terrible or zombie terrible?"

"Zombie terrible. He had chunks of flesh falling off of him, like both his body and spirit were rotting away. I just tried to contact Haldrek because Skuti said he'd likely know more than what is in our library, but he's not answering." I tried to hide the panic in my voice.

Mattie nodded. "Maybe he's busy? He was away for a long while even before we arrived."

"That's likely the case." Skuti muttered. He jabbed his finger at some runes in one of the books. "I think I know what is causing your father's ailment. Another Thegn of Svartån, your ancestor, wrote something his dragon told him. The one bonded to him. Haldragas and their dragons stay together after death. They only separate once the haldraga goes to Mirroth because of how dragons can be reborn and people cannot. But if the dragon and the haldraga are wedged apart, then bad things happen. Both begin to evolve? Devolve? I'm trying to translate this rune, but I'm guessing that's what is happening to your father. Did he say that others in the Realm of Ghosts were also afflicted?"

I nodded. "Not directly, but that is the impression I got."

Skuti sighed. "Keep trying to contact Thegn Andrattür. I can write a missive to his *husceorl* asking for information. It will take more time, but it is better than nothing." He returned to his books and began scribbling notes of his own. Mattie nodded her head towards the door and I left with her and Llamryl, more anxious and conflicted beyond what I had hoped for.

Chapter Three

That night, I found myself pacing at the top of the spire that rose up from the thegn's hall. In the distance, I could see a bright light coming from the edge of the village. Music and laughter drifted toward me on the wind. I wished I could join them, but the thoughts of my dad, the news that the necromancer might hurt more people, and my inability to get a hold of Haldrek would have kept me from enjoying the festivities. Next year I would celebrate with them. If there were celebrations next year.

I shook my head to get away from the gloomy thoughts. Squeezing my pendant once more, I whispered, more to myself than anyone, "If you don't answer, Haldrek, I swear I'm gonna…"

The pendant grew warm in my palm and I eagerly flipped it open. Haldrek's grin greeted me. All of a sudden, my anger and irritation disappeared.

"Happy solstice, Ina."

"Happy solstice. Have you been busy?" I wanted to blurt out everything on my mind, but I held back, not wanted to overwhelm him or freak him out. I missed him and I wanted him near right now. My chest squeezed tight with that feeling. Longing? Desire? Whatever the word was, I wanted Haldrek next to me and the distance between us physically hurt.

He nodded. "You'd think that Jaonos, my *husceorl*, was new to his position for all his questions." Haldrek groaned and then laughed. "I thought I'd get a break for my birthday, but no. At least he's wanting to do things the right way instead of just guessing. A lot of things have changed since I left for Drattüjert."

"Yeah… that's good, I guess. Wait. Is today your birthday? I don't remember you mentioning that. If you did, I'm sorry. Happy birthday." My cheeks warmed up with embarrassment and I tried to recall if he'd ever mentioned when his birthday was exactly.

"Thank you. I can't remember if I did or not. Not that it matters. I tried to get Jaonos to partake in some of the solstice celebrations, so I could get a break, but…" He shrugged. "I'm over it now. He's trying to do his best. I'm going to need a *husceorl* who can do things right the first time when I head back to Drattüjert. I know Aallotar won't wait forever to avenge her uncles and grandfather."

I nodded, all of my wants and emotions feeling less important now. There were bigger things to deal with. Not that a possible necromancer wasn't a big thing to deal with. My stomach churned with the familiar anxiety and I pushed my emotions aside for the moment. I didn't want to ruin or stress out Haldrek further on his birthday.

"How have you been? You look distracted."

I returned my focus to Haldrek. "Sorry. The past few days have been interesting. Weird. I tried calling you on your pendant but you didn't answer. I know you're busy there and I didn't—" My voice faltered.

"What's going on?" Haldrek's expression turned somber.

"Nothing major. Well, maybe. I dunno. I got back from meeting and greeting my gesiths. Some of them were grumpier with me than others. I expected that and that's not the big thing. It's a dream I had after leaving Sigreykir. My dad pulled me into the Realm of Ghosts. He thinks there might be a necromancer in Drattüjert."

"What?" Haldrek's eyes widened. "When? What exactly did he say? What makes him think that?"

"All the people in the Realm of Ghosts, at least the ones who died in Drattüjert and haven't had their rites done, are rotting away. Like their spirits are rotting away. My dad. My dad had chunks of flesh..." My face scrunched up as I fought the urge to cry.

"Ina..."

"I'm sorry. I'm supposed to be tougher than that. I didn't cry when I saw my dad, but I was more in shock. Like, he didn't look good."

"He said it wasn't just him?"

I nodded. "He said Kalle and the rest are rotting too. When I talked to Skuti, he referenced one of my ancestors saying something about the dragons and their souls being pulled apart?"

Haldrek nodded. "A dragon's soul will stay with a haldraga's soul until the person goes to Mirroth. If the two are forced apart, then that person's soul will start to decay in the Realm of Ghosts."

"What about people who aren't haldragas?"

"Their spirits begin to slowly decay as soon as they reach the Realm of Ghosts."

"If they don't get sent off to Mirroth or another place, what happens to them?"

Haldrek shrugged. "That would be something your family knows more about. However..."

"However what?"

"Lore has it that undead creatures can be created by raising the spirit of a completely decayed body and joining it with that body. But the body has to be partially decayed and, I guess, the spirit as well."

"So zombies can be created if both the body and the spirit are decayed?"

"In a way. I'm assuming you're talking about the undead when you say zombies, but yes. If a necromancer wants to raise an army of them, he or she can do so, even with people who have been long dead. I'm guessing a decayed spirit doesn't necessarily disappear in the Realm of Ghosts. It just exists?" Haldrek exhaled and looked away from his pendant. I winced, hating the fact that I was ruining his birthday.

"I'm sorry."

He focused on the pendant once more and smiled. "Don't be. I needed to know this. I'll have to start searching my library for information on fighting necromancers." He laughed. "Maybe I'll have my *husceorl* do it." His amusement faded a little. "I miss you. A part of me wishes we could be together today. Not only because of my birthday, but because I'd love to show you the solstice festivities we have here in Andrattür."

"I'd love to see them with you." I smiled and glanced up at the bonfire light off in the distance. "The people here at the estate seem to be having a good time."

"They're having a bonfire as well?"

I nodded. "I feel like a bonfire would be more of a winter thing though."

"We have bonfires at the winter solstice too. Perhaps we'll be able to have one in Drattüjert come then. My uncle..." Haldrek's voice dropped off.

"This isn't such a great birthday, is it?"

He shook his head. "A lot of heavy things have happened since my last birthday. But many good things as well. Like you." His expression lit up and I couldn't help but smile.

"Who knows where we'll be a year from now? Wherever we are, I hope we're together."

"I will drink to that. May the Blodnar be gone for good and may we be together in Drattüjert. If I am High King, I hope you'll be by my side as High Queen."

My neck and cheeks heated up as I nodded, my smile widening. The thought of being with Haldrek made me warm and tingly on the inside. Although I never mentioned it to anyone, I'd had dreams about him. And me. Being physically intimate. I enjoyed those dreams. As for being the High Queen, as exciting as that thought was, I was just barely figuring out how to be a good thegn. If I was by his side in Drattüjert a year from now, that would mean many things, including more expectations as High Queen.

"If you're High King and I'm High Queen in a year, they're going to expect us..." My cheeks started to burn with embarrassment even to talk about having kids. I mean, I was barely eighteen and Haldrek, only twenty-two now. We were technically adults, but I still felt like a kid.

"They're going to expect aethlings. I know. I'm well aware." His tone sounded less than thrilled.

I frowned. "Why? What's been going on? Has your uncle been pestering you again?"

"Raynord? He's always pestering me. But yes, he continues to get me and one of his eldest granddaughters, Quenby or Kamira, together. But a few of the other thegns have been calling on me through the thegn stones. Bjorn Susi had his daughter Freygerd contact me through the thegn stones once. Supposedly to apologize for Hardbein's behavior, but the conversation was strained and she kept asking me questions that seemed forced. And then there was Gustav."

My eyes widened. "Gustav? Why?"

"He said it was to talk about matters concerning Drattüjert and his lands. He brought up his daughter, Sibila. Someone he's never spoken of before."

I frowned. "Did you know of her before this conversation or...?"

Haldrek nodded. "I'd seen her once or twice when I was younger and visiting the palace. Gustav brought both her and his son Rorik for some event. Even then, she was strange, though."

"Strange, how?"

"People called her elf-touched. Obviously that's not true, but she'd speak to people or things no one else could see. As if under some enchantment. There was plenty of gossip about her when they were at the palace, and it was evident Gustav favored Rorik over her."

"Why'd he bring her up? Did he say anything about the vampire he sent my way? Or at least that I think he sent my way."

Haldrek shook his head. "Part of me wanted to say something to see how'd he react. But he was more focused on trying to arrange something between me and Sibila."

"What?" Secondhand annoyance started to grow in my chest.

Haldrek shook his head. "I didn't entertain the conversation long. I told him that my main focus right now was on taking Drattüjert back and kicking the Blodnar out of Lohikärra. He grumbled at that and our conversation ended soon after."

I sighed. "You'd think the other thegns would be focused on fighting more than romance."

Haldrek shrugged. "I think they are focused on both. At least Raynord and Bjorn. Gustav... I still think he has ties to the Blodnar. It wouldn't surprise me if he was trying to ensure his position regardless of how the war goes. That said, Aallotar sent me a messenger as well. She's already planning how to retake Drattüjert. She wants to avenge her grandfather and uncles as much as I do."

I nodded. "Do you think...?" My mind swirled with questions. Part of me wanted to fight alongside Haldrek if he was returning to Drattüjert, but I also didn't want to be a weak link or waste of space if I couldn't fight like him or the other thegns.

"Do I think what?"

"Aallotar is heading up the attack to get Drattüjert. Do you think she'll need Svartån's help?"

A teasing smile spread across Haldrek's face. "Are you already itching to fight again?"

I laughed. "I dunno. Maybe. Part of me is. I want to fight with you. And the others. But I don't want to be a waste of space. Or a distraction."

Now Haldrek laughed. "If Aallotar sends you a messenger, it's because she needs your help. She's always been very practical about fighting. Very good at strategy. But she also knows about the Isillas and how hard Svartån warriors fought under your father. As for distractions..." His expression sobered up. "I know how to focus when I need to."

I bit my bottom lip and nodded. Of course Haldrek would know how to focus. He'd shown that when Seirye had attacked Andrattür along with Svartån.

"How is Mattie doing?"

I returned my focus to the pendant. "She's doing well. Helping to keep things organized here at the estate. Sivath's been coming around frequently to train her on dragon things? I guess? Sometimes I'll join them in the trainings."

Haldrek nodded. "He's preparing her to become a haldraga. Teminth did the same with me before we bonded."

I sighed. Beyond the one time Rhaegos visited her shrine months ago, I had yet to see her or be visited by any other dragon. My mind returned to what the Gesith of Sigreykir had said.

"Do you think I'll become a haldraga soon?"

Haldrek opened his mouth, then closed it. After a moment, he nodded. "Of course. I've yet to hear of a thegn who didn't eventually become a haldraga. If the dragons chose you to be thegn over Hardbein, then you'll become a haldraga when they see fit."

I sighed, still not satisfied but too tired to press the issue.

"Ina..."

I focused on his smiling face and couldn't help but smile myself. "Yes?"

"I love you. You'll be a haldraga soon enough."

"I love you too. I hope so. I'd hate if me not being a haldraga impacted my ability to be a good thegn, or us." The thought popped up in my head that a High Queen might need to be a haldraga as well.

"It won't. I promise. Go to bed. I'll call you on the pendants tomorrow. I'm going to see what information my ancestors might have on necromancers and haldragas. If I find anything, I'll let you know."

I nodded and watched as the pendant glass darkened again, the number eight shining brightly against the inky blackness.

Chapter Four

The next morning, Mattie and I found ourselves in the library, studying with Skuti. I continued practicing my runes, like a child, as Mattie continued researching one of a variety of subjects she'd taken up. Skuti stayed quiet, with the exception of a few mumblings about necromancers and haldragas.

"Ina...?"

"Hmm?" I looked up at Mattie, unable to focus on my runes any longer.

"Remind me about that person you saw in the dungeon when Seirye had you down there."

"My dad?"

"You said it wasn't your dad, but it looked like him?"

I nodded. "It chewed me out. Told me I was being mopey and that people in my family never gave up. Why?"

"It's been bugging me. Because I don't think it was anything bad, but if it's something good, we could figure out how to harness it. Anyway, I think it might be an aspect."

"An aspect?" I frowned. "What's a—"

A loud screeching wail interrupted me, and all three of our heads jerked toward the sound. Skuti jumped up and the three of us ran into the main hall.

Servants and other people who had been milling around, stood stock still, their attention either on us or large main doors. I spotted Llamryl in the midst of the hall. He had his weapon ready as another bellow shook the walls.

"Sivath..." Mattie whispered, terror filling her voice. She bolted down the stairs and toward the front door. I followed as she scrambled to pull them open. Llamryl helped her. As they opened one, a large dragon shuddered, its snout at the bottom of the outside stairs. He was covered in blood, his wings torn. Pieces of wing skin fluttered weakly in the wind, and a few arrows protruded from his hind quarters.

"Sivath?" I gasped as Mattie and I ran to him. Mattie reached for him and he pulled away. She stopped as he made some kind of grunt. He shifted as if to morph into his human form, only to shudder again.

"He says he has a message for you from Rhaegos."

I stared at Sivath's dragon form and nodded, still in shock. He voiced a few more grumbles and grunts, with Mattie nodding every few seconds. When he finished, Mattie turned to me. "He says Rhaegos awaits you in Drattüjert. He wishes he had more time to train us both to be haldragas." Mattie turned to Sivath, her voice cracking, "You're not...? I mean...?"

Sivath rumbled and Mattie hesitated. She glanced at me, then stretched her hand out to touch him.

"Mattie?"

As soon as her hand rested on one of the scales behind his eye, the air around all of us began to shimmer and expand.

"Llamryl! The thegn!" Skuti shouted from the doors behind us.

Llamryl latched onto my arm and pulled me inside the thegn hall before I could react. The door slammed shut as the hall shook once more. My face ground into the wooden planks of the floor as Llamryl covered me with his body. As soon as the shaking stopped, he pulled himself off me. As we sat up, we found Skuti standing above us.

"What the—"

"Sivath was binding with Mattie just now. A bit unconventional, but..."

"Is she okay?" I stumbled to my feet, grabbing the door and pulling it open alongside Llamryl. Everyone in the courtyard had been knocked to their feet, but were slowly getting up. Mattie still lay on the ground, groaning and moving slightly. Where Sivath had once laid, ash and a few bones covered the ground.

Llamryl ran over to Mattie and gently cradled her in his arms. I followed and stood behind him. Mattie didn't seem worse for the wear, just stunned.

Mattie smiled, looking at Llamryl and me. "That was a trip. Not as scary as I thought it would be."

"Are you all right?" Llamryl's voice was barely discernible.

She exhaled. "I'm tired. Very tired." Closing her eyes, she relaxed into Llamryl's arms.

"Mattie!" I reached for her as Llamryl put his ear to her chest.

"She's still breathing." Llamryl sat up and tried to rouse her. Nothing.

I turned to Skuti in a panic. "Is she going to be okay?"

He nodded. "She'll need to rest, but if she survives, she'll wake up in a few days."

"*If she survives?*" I spun around, my focus on Llamryl. "Take her to her quarters, and then go find Thandes or one of the other healers."

Llamryl nodded, lifting Mattie with ease. She was fully unconscious, limp in his arms. As Llamryl took her inside, I stared at Skuti. "What do you mean '*if she survives*'?"

He straightened up, looking very somber. "I was under the impression Sivath would have mentioned it. On very rare occasions, the haldraga ceremony will overpower a person, killing them during the process. I'm sure Lady Mattie will be fine. I only meant to comfort you in saying her current condition is temporary."

I bit my bottom lip in an attempt to focus on something other than the panic threatening to overwhelm me. I wanted to yell at Skuti. Sivath had said nothing about Mattie—or me—possibly dying when we become haldragas.

"My thegn, if it would comfort you, I would suggest calling Thegn Andrattür and letting him know what has happened. He might be able to help you in ways I cannot. Given that he has gone through the haldraga process."

I nodded and made my way inside without another word. Haldrek could help. And I knew that if I spoke at all right now, I might end up in tears or screaming at someone.

Once inside Mattie's quarters—I had made sure hers was within what Skuti called the family quarters and close to my own—I pulled my pendant out and tried to collect my emotions. Mattie lay resting on her bed. As unruffled as I tried to appear, internally I only felt chaos. My stomach churned with worry and every muscle was tense, as if ready to jump into action at a moment's notice. Tears threatened to spill over as I took a deep breath to calm myself. At the edge of my mind, a voice whispered that I was somehow to blame for the current predicament. I brushed it away angrily, knowing how ridiculous it was. Had Mattie or Haldrek felt this chaotic after I'd electrocuted myself?

Pressing my thumb on the glass, I said, "Haldrek Rodreksson."

The black inky background began to shimmer for a moment before Haldrek's face came into view.

"Ina?" His eyes widened in alarm and I guessed I looked like a wreck. "What happened?"

"Sivath came and... he looked beat up, but he made Mattie into a haldraga and... is there a chance she's going to die?" The last few words came out in a panicked squeak.

He exhaled and nodded. "A tiny chance. Possibly because you and she are partially from another world. Skuti asked my opinion on the subject before you became thegn. He worried one of the dragons might make you a haldraga while you were still recovering and how that might affect Svartån. But the last time someone died was years ago. Long before I, or my father, was born. Keldan once said he remembered hearing one of his peers dying from it, but he didn't seem too concerned about it."

"Like he didn't care or...?"

"Like most people are fine, but there was something uncommon about this person. I don't know the full story, but I wouldn't worry. Did anything strange happen when they bonded?"

I stared at him in disbelief. "The whole event was strange. Sivath arrived bloodied and beat up, arrows sticking out of him, and told Mattie that he had a message from Rhaegos for me."

"What message?" Haldrek's expression darkened with concern.

"Something about Drattüjert. That I needed to meet her there. Then he said something to Mattie and she put her hand on one of his scales and the air started to shimmer. Skuti told Llamryl to grab me and next thing I knew, I was inside the thegn hall with the door shut and there was a boom. When we went back outside, Sivath was gone except for some bones and ash. Mattie was talking a little bit before she passed out, but... am I going to have the same experience as Mattie? If I ever become a haldraga?"

"You'll become a haldraga. Don't worry. I'm glad to hear Mattie was talking after Sivath merged with her. That's a good sign." He sighed. "The fact Sivath arrived bloodied and with arrows in him doesn't bode well for Drattüjert. Normally, man-made arrows bounce off dragonskin. The fact that he came with a message from Rhaegos...I've never known the dragons to send messengers of their own kind. That makes me think..."

"Things are grim in Drattüjert?"

Haldrek nodded. "I should probably tell Aallotar what happened. She'll want whatever information she can get her hands on. In the meantime, keep an eye on Mattie. I think she'll be fine and I think she's in good hands there at Svangendom, but..."

"But what?"

"I've rewritten my heirship papers. Should something happen to me, whether I become High King or die, Mattie will become the next Thegn of Andrattür."

I nodded, trying to keep the sense of foreboding from weighing me down.

Haldrek smiled somberly. "I love you, Ina. I'm going to let Aallotar know what you told me."

"I love you too." I went to say something else, but my throat tightened up to keep from crying. The pendant went black and I closed it, moving over to where Mattie lay. Taking a deep breath, my emotions flooded over me and, for once, I let myself cry.

I spent the night in Mattie's room, curled up either on a nearby chair or the room's solitary window nook. Every few hours I'd wake up with a jolt, usually after a dream about Mattie dying from the haldraga ceremony. Thandes, Llamryl, and a few other Hethurin took turns watching her with me as well.

In the morning, I woke up to the smell of food on a nearby table and Llamryl curled up on Mattie's bed. I cleared my throat and he immediately jumped up, eyes wide.

"I... my thegn..."

I waved off whatever he was about to say and asked, "Is she...? How is she doing?"

We both watched her chest as it rose and fell slowly. "She is still alive. Which is good. I'm sure she'll wake up soon."

I nodded. "Let me know if anything abnormal happens. On the estate or in the hall. I plan on staying with Mattie for at least this morning." I felt awkward sending him away, but I also needed to clear my thoughts and let Haldrek know how Mattie was doing. That would be awkward as well if I had an audience.

"Of course." Llamryl bowed and quickly left the room.

I looked at my food, then at Mattie. My anxiety hadn't lessened, so my appetite was nowhere to be found. Walking over to where she lay, I sat in the chair next to her bed. She looked normal, as if she was just sleeping and would wake up at any moment.

"I wish I knew how to read Lohikärran better. I'd be searching the library from top to bottom." Reclining into the chair, I let my mind wander. Why hadn't Sivath mentioned anything about this during the times he was teaching me and Mattie about haldragas and the ways of the dragons? Was this something she already knew? Was the possibility of Mattie dying so rare that it didn't cross his mind? I tried to let that thought comfort me. Maybe Mattie would be fine. Maybe the fact that we were from a different realm wouldn't matter. But what if Mattie didn't pull through?

"Mattie." My voice cracked, even as I kept it soft. "Mattie, you better come through this. I know I've always said I'd love to live in Lohikärra, but I don't know what I'd do if you weren't here by my side. This place... there's still so much that I need to know and learn and if you don't make it through this, what chance do I have?" I blinked back my tears.

That thought had been scaring me for a while now. If a dragon decided to bond with me, how would I survive the haldraga ceremony? Was it hard? Mattie didn't seem to be in any pain currently, but she'd been knocked off her feet. I wondered if it would be like when I had killed Seirye. Would I be weakened again, having to regrow my skills once more?

Worse yet was the other worry I had. What if the dragons deemed me not worthy of becoming a haldraga? People here seemed to put a lot of weight on the idea. It didn't seem like those outside of the abthanry normally became haldragas, but for people like me, it was a given. So if I didn't become a haldraga, how would that affect me as a thegn? Or... I thought about my relationship with Haldrek. When he became the High King, would me not being a haldraga affect us?

I focused on Mattie. My worries threatened to overwhelm me and I tried to ignore them. It wasn't like I could do anything about Mattie or being a haldraga right now, right?

My pendant grew warm, and I flipped it open. Seeing Haldrek's face made me smile despite my heavy heart.

"How are you doing? How's Mattie?"

"Mattie's doing fine. I think. She doesn't seem to be in any kind of distress. Just looks like she's sleeping. I'm stressed out, but trying not to think about it. I definitely didn't sleep well last night. How are you doing?" The background was noisier and more chaotic than normal. Haldrek's attention was elsewhere, even as his eyes were focused on me.

"All right. I got a messenger from Aallotar this morning. She's asking for aid in taking the fight to the Blodnar, so I'm rounding up whoever I can and heading south. The messenger said he wasn't the only one sent out, so..."

"Should I be expecting a messenger?" My chest tightened at the idea. As much as I wanted to fight and help push out the Blodnar, the timing was bad.

Haldrek nodded. "I don't know if it'll be today or tomorrow, but soon. It may be worth putting your men on alert or sending a few messengers out to some of the towns in Svartån."

"Did Aallotar mention how many warriors she's expecting?"

"No." Haldrek shook his head. "I already had a few sattars with me before the battle of Drattüjert. I expect those who survived will have returned to Andrattür by now. I plan to visit a few of the towns here and see who is willing to fight. I expect I'll have a couple of sattars by the time I get to Aallotar's camp."

I nodded, then looked up as a knock came at the door. Thandes poked her head inside. "My thegn. Skuti told me to come find you. You have a visitor waiting for you. From another thegn?"

I returned my focus to Haldrek. "I guess that might be the messenger from Aallotar?"

"I would assume so. I'll let you go then. Let me know what he or she says."

"Will do." I watched as the image in my pendant faded to inky black, then stood up.

Thandes slipped inside the room and took my place next to Mattie.

"I'll watch her and let you know if anything changes."

"Thank you, Thandes." I grabbed a piece of bread from the now-cold plate of food, slipping out of the room and heading for the main hall.

Chapter Five

When I arrived in the main hall, Skuti was speaking with an older man wearing a tabard with an unfamiliar insignia. Not that I was well-versed with all of Lohikärra's insignias. It bore what looked like a tankard with a handful of small flying creatures surrounding it.

"Thegn Svartån!" Skuti hailed me as I walked over to the fire pit. The fact that Skuti used my official title versus a more familiar one told me this individual was here on official business.

"Yes?"

"A messenger from Thegn-heir Heidrunefoss has arrived. He's asking to speak with you in person."

I nodded, surprised that Aallotar hadn't been crowned Thegn of Heidrunefoss yet. Though, if Heidrunefoss still had Blodnar within its borders, perhaps that was more reason for her to get rid of them.

"Thegn Svartån, Lady Aallotar of Heidrunefoss asks for your aid in eliminating the Blodnar threat. She hopes Svartån will be able to bring two sattars to aid Heidrunefoss and the rest of Lohikärra."

I nodded. "Of course. I should be able to bring that many at least. Is there a day she needs us to be there by? Or wherever she's wanting us to aid her?" If I had to recruit warriors from places more than a day's journey from the estate, it could be a few weeks before I had two sattars ready to go.

The messenger grimaced. "As soon as possible, my thegn. The longer the Blodnar are in Heidrunefoss, the longer it will take to get rid of them and the longer it will take to recapture Drattüjert. She wishes for those aiding her to join her at her camp on the border of Heidrunefoss and Svarhestån."

I thought back to my father and his warning about the necromancer in Drattüjert. "I'll pull together warriors as quickly as I can."

"Thank you, my thegn." The man bowed and turned to the doors of the hall, seeming eager to leave. I frowned and turned to Skuti.

"Is that normal?"

"For him to leave like that? I suppose so. He..." Skuti nodded. "You've never travelled to Drattüjert from here, have you? Or even Heidrunefoss. You were hoping he'd stay as a guide?"

I nodded. "If Aallotar wants my warriors and I to meet her at her camp, I need to know where it is."

Skuti hesitated, then nodded. "I suppose '*the border of Heidrunefoss and Svarhestån*' is a bit vague if one didn't grow up in Lohikärra."

"Is there a particular pass or something between the two thegn lands?"

Skuti nodded again. "There are a couple. The one I believe the thegn-heir of Heidrunefoss is referring to is the southernmost one. There's a map in the library I can show you later. If you wish. If the thegn-heir is calling for other thegns to aid her, I'm assuming..."

"Haldrek is already on his way. He called me this morning." I tugged at my pendant, remembering Mattie was still upstairs. Resting? Healing? Transforming? Whatever was going on now that she was a haldraga.

"That would make sense. If Haldrek is on his way, you could always ask him where exactly the camp is." Skuti paused. "How is Lady Mattie doing, by the way? I'm assuming she is still resting?"

"She is. Still breathing and alive. In a coma of some sort, I guess."

"Coma?" Skuti cocked his head and frowned.

"It's when you're unconscious, but still alive. The longer you're in a coma, though, the less likely you are to wake up."

"Ah. Sounds very similar to what happens when one becomes a haldraga. At least from what I've seen and heard."

"How long are people in...I guess...a dragon-induced coma? I mean, is there a point where I should be worried?"

"Most, I heard, wake within a few days of binding with a dragon. I've never heard of anyone going more than a week's time."

I nodded. Calculations began to form in my head. I hoped Mattie would wake up before I had to leave, but if she didn't...

"My thegn?"

I focused on Skuti as his voice brought me out of my reverie. "Yes?"

"Would you like me to send messengers to some of the southern villages to rally recruits? Perhaps see if some of the local villages have people wanting to fight as well?"

"I'd appreciate that, Skuti. Maybe some of them will be familiar with where we need to go."

"More than likely." He bowed and left me alone in the hall to focus on the embers. They were giving off a little heat to keep the morning chill away. It may be summer, but there was still a brisk sharpness in the air until mid-afternoon.

I thought about whether or not I'd bring warriors from Svangendom. The estate and village were still recovering from Seirye's last attack. Though more people arrived every day, there was still so much to do.

"My thegn."

Llamryl run up behind me, his voice making me jump.

"What's going on?" The last thing I needed was some other calamity.

"Was there a messenger from Heidrunefoss just here?"

I nodded. "Yes. The thegn-heir asked for aid. I'll be sending people."

"From the estate?" Llamryl's eyes widened, and I couldn't tell whether or not he was excited or frightened.

"I was thinking about it. Why?"

"I... I just..." His head fell. "My apologies, my thegn. I ran here without thinking."

"What?" I cocked my head as I remembered seeing him curled up next to Mattie this morning. "Wait. Are you...? Are you wanting to go to Drattüjert? Or are you wanting to stay here?"

"My desires are not important, my thegn. I apologize for running in here like this."

I grimaced. "Llamryl, talk to me like a friend, not like thegn and subject."

He lifted his head and smiled weakly. "I'm sorry. I keep forgetting my place. With you as thegn and Mattie one day being thegn.... But we're friends as well."

"You and Mattie are more than friends." I crossed my arms and tried not to laugh. Maybe I'd never had a boyfriend, or kissed a guy before Haldrek, but I wasn't stupid.

"We are. That's true. Only because Mattie accepts my affection. I..." His cheeks reddened and he looked away. "I guess I wanted to know whether I and the others should prepare to leave."

I shook my head. "Svangendom can't be left defenseless. Not that I think the Isillas are going to launch another attack, but I need people to stay here." I smiled. "I need someone to watch over Mattie and let me know how she's doing after I leave." My heart twisted a bit at the idea of her still being passed out while I was gone. I had no idea what I would do if... I brushed the thought away. "If she's still unconscious. But even if she wakes up before I leave, I need warriors to keep Svangendom protected."

Llamryl nodded and smiled. "I thank you, my thegn. And..."

"And?" I smiled a little bit.

"I thank you as a friend. I love Mattie dearly. I'm glad that you're not angered by that, given both of your statuses as abthanry."

"Since when have I been a stickler for being part of the abthanry? Six months ago, all of Lohikärra was still a fantasy. As long as you and Mattie are happy, I don't care."

"I'm glad to hear that. Still, in the future, you may need to be a stickler for the abthanry, as you say."

I cocked my head. "What do you mean?"

Llamryl shrugged. "I know a lot of Lohikärrans put pride in their social status. Many at Drattüjert would be upset if a member of the abthanry was with a commoner, much less a 'half-breed' like myself." He sighed. "Which could affect Mattie. As for you, if others know that you aren't upset about those kinds of things, they could use that against you in the future. I don't want that to happen."

"Neither do I. "

Llamryl bowed. "If you'd like, I'll return to my duties. But thank you. Again."

I nodded and he left.

After checking on Mattie a few more times and dealing with a few minor tasks, I made my way to the library. Even with my minimal knowledge of the Lohikärran runic alphabet, I could read a map. I knew what Lohikärra looked like, roughly, from the games and I knew where cities and towns in Svartån were now. When I made my way into the room, I was happy to see a table covered in maps.

The table next to it, however, caught my attention before I could get to the maps. It was where Mattie had been studying yesterday before Sivath arrived. Most of the documents on the table, both books and scrolls, were in runes. I ignored them. Instead, I saw some notes Mattie had been writing down.

Aspect - Realms - Realms inside people? Theory by Thegn XXX of Svartån. (1330-1397) Aspects are inside everyone, parts of us and our perceptions. Inner voices? Similiar? Aspects can manifest in the presence of lots of magic. Ina's dad in dungeon —> Aspect?

Subconscious?

Unconscious?

How common are aspects? Check with Skuti, Haldrek, or Mirratoft husceorl for info from Mirratoft

"Looking over Mattie's notes?"

I jumped and my heart squeezed tight as my feet slipped out from under me. Landing butt first on the ground, I groaned. Skuti put his hand out to help me up.

"Apologies, my thegn. I came in here to grab some more notes on necromancers and haldragas. I'm trying to make sense of what might be happening in Drattüjert. Especially if you are headed there in the near future. Did you come in here to look at the maps I found earlier?"

I nodded. "I figured I might as well. Maps can be read without much in the way of writing, runic or otherwise. But now I'm curious about the aspects Mattie was researching before, you know..."

Skuti glanced over the materials laid out on the table. "Aspects. I'm not too familiar with those. Or that subject." He turned to me. "Do you know the reason Lady Mattie was interested in the subject? May I ask?"

"Yeah, I saw my father when Seirye threw me in the dungeon. Only it wasn't him."

Skuti frowned. "What?"

I nodded. "He pulled me into the Realm of Ghosts soon after I killed Seirye and said it hadn't been him. Not that the entity was menacing; it just wasn't him."

"What did the entity say?"

"It basically chastised me for sulking. Told me I was a Svanunge and that our family never gives up. That I could defeat Seirye if I tried."

"And you did." Skuti pursed his lips thoughtfully. "Lady Mattie may have been on to something then. Perhaps you two can find a way to use these aspects to your advantage in the future?"

I nodded. "Maybe." I folded the note and put it in my pocket. "As for my other concerns..."

"Necromancers and Drattüjert?"

I nodded. "What have you found so far?"

Skuti meandered over to the table with maps on it and tapped on one with the full map of Lohikärra. "Do you know why Drattüjert is so important to the people of Lohikärra? And why it was such a blow for the Blodnar to take it?"

I shook my head. "I know Bjornulf and Freya are connected to it. And I know about the dragon's mound that is below it or next to it? Supposedly Tenelth's bones reside there?"

"They do. Never said 'supposedly' in regards to that. It is a firm belief and knowledge that Tenelth's bones are there. The shrine built into that mound is also where the new High King or Queen is accepted by the dragons. Either way, there is great amounts of dragon magic imbued in that area. Some say it's because of Tenelth and Bjornulf's bond, others say the magic was there before, but either way, there is a lot of dragon magic there."

"Dragon magic?" I thought back to the dragon stone that had brought Mattie and I here.

"Yes. The elves and other magic creatures can manipulate various forms of elements, but dragons go beyond that. They can shift into other realms." He frowned thoughtfully. "I wouldn't be surprised if dragon magic was involved in your father's travels. Or your arrival here." He shook his head. "I'm meandering, though. Necromancers and Drattüjert. If there is a necromancer in Drattüjert, I would bet my gold they are channeling dragon magic into their spells. If they're pulling dragon magic from the city, the easiest source would be dead bodies of haldragas or dragons themselves. Of course, this is all just my theory."

"It sounds plausible. How powerful would a necromancer who is doing that be? Like, would armies still be able to take the city?"

"Physically, yes. A necromancer won't necessarily be able to stand in the face of an army of trained warriors. But if they gained control of enough dragon magic, they could…" Skuti's face whitened.

"What?"

"They could do some terrible things. They could control the dragons themselves. Or worse."

"What's worse? If Haldrek…" If Haldrek and the others were potentially facing a necromancer… "If *I* was potentially facing a necromancer, I wanted to know worse case scenarios."

"Well, there's always the chance of raising an army of undead warriors. Not that they'd be *ruumii* by any means. But dragons can travel between realms. If a necromancer gained enough dragon magic or controlled the dragons themselves, they could open a hole between realms and bring in creatures or things we have no ability to fight."

I nodded and sighed. "That would be bad."

"Good news is it would be difficult for one necromancer to gain that much power. The dragons don't particularly like it when humans, or any creature for that matter, takes more power than they are bestowed." Skuti walked over to another stack of scrolls. "I'm looking into whether or not any of your ancestors experienced what you did with your father. A haldraga rotting away in the Realm of Ghosts. So far I haven't seen anything, but I don't want you to worry. You have plenty to worry about with preparing for your march to Drattüjert. Or at least Heidrunefoss."

"Thank you." My heart felt heavier than before, but I was glad for Skuti's honesty. He bowed once more, this time with the stack of scrolls, and hurried out.

Chapter Six

I slept little that night. After checking on Mattie once more, I headed outside, hoping some fresh air might clear my thoughts.

Instead I found small groups of men scattered around the courtyard, armed, and a few bickering with each other.

"What is going on?"

A familiar face popped out of one of the groups.

"Thegn Svartån!" Modolf bowed deeply, his beard jewelry clinking together.

I smiled. "Are you here to help drive out the Blodnar?"

"Of course! Eldingheimr answers your call, my thegn." He grinned, showing off a few darkened teeth. "I was saddened that I did not personally get to give some Isillas scum a thorough thrashing when they took the estate. When your messenger called for warriors to fight the Blodnar once and for all, I rallied some of my men." He looked at the men behind him. "I think there are more than a few of us itching for a fight. I love my wife, but I was an adventurer in my youth, and sometimes you have to heed the call."

"The call to adventure?"

He nodded. "My wife tried to persuade me to stay in Eldingheimr. Told me that they didn't need to lose two gesiths in one year." He sighed. "But what kind of gesith would I be if I didn't fight with my men?" He turned to me. "I suppose the call to adventure will be a call to Mirroth one of these days, but today is not it." His smile returned and I couldn't help but smile myself.

"I'm glad to see you in better spirits. And more energized." Some loud voices from one of the groups caught my attention. "I have a feeling I'll be proving myself as thegn once more. It's good to have allies." I walked over to the loud voices and saw one man shove another to the ground.

"Thegn don't need no half-breeds fightin' for her! Go back to wallowing in the shit piles or wherever you're from."

I cleared my throat and the two men looked at me. The one standing straightened up as Modolf walked up behind me. He looked to be about my age, and part of me wondered how seriously he'd take me. But I ignored the thought and focused on acting as confident as I could.

"What's going on?"

"Half-breed is saying he's gonna fight the Blodnar along with us. Told him you don't need no half-breeds fightin' for you."

"Did *I* ever say that?" My chest tightened with irritation as I gripped the hilt of my sword and stared at the man. The last thing I needed was discord between my warriors right before we headed to Drattüjert.

The man kept his mouth shut and looked away.

"Answer her!" Modolf barked. The warriors straightened up at the sound of his voice. Even I straightened up at his tone.

"No, my thegn." The man still refused to look me in the eyes.

"I don't care whether someone is Hethurin, Lohikärran, or anything else. I only care that they follow my instructions and will fight the Blodnar with me. My father died trying to protect Drattüjert, Lohikärra, and by extension, Svartån." I paused, trying to figure out what I'd say next. "Every warrior under me needs to work together. To avenge my father and push the Blodnar out of Lohikärra once and for all. No exceptions. Any one not interested in that, they can go home now."

The group in front of me was silent. I noticed other groups had also stopped talking and started watching us. When the silence became palpable enough, I said, "Are you all willing to work together? To destroy the Blodnar?"

More silence. Frustration bubbled up inside of me, and I wondered how well I'd be able to lead these warriors. These ones in particular were from Eldingheimr. As far as I knew, Eldingheimr was one of the more welcoming towns for Hethurin. What would I do if warriors from other towns, less friendly toward the Hethurin, joined up?

"For Pete's sake! Do you really hate fighting alongside the Hethurin more than defeating the Blodnar? They're like the Isillas. If we're divided, we're easier to defeat. Do you really want that to happen?"

A few grumbles came from the group and Modolf cleared his throat.

"The thegn is right. When was the last time a Hethurin, or someone of Hethurin descent, was untrustworthy? Failed to protect Svartån and our towns?"

One of the older warriors snapped, "I heard Bolvo—"

"The Hethurin of Bolvo gave their lives to protect it." I snapped. Guilt over the Hethurin who had sacrificed themselves for that ungrateful city still lingered, and I wouldn't allow those warriors to be insulted. "Even when the gesith there wanted nothing to do with them. Same goes for Katla. Don't tell me Bolvo suffered because of the Hethurin. It's still around *because* of the Hethurin."

The man shut up and I looked around, anger now fueling my words. "Anyone else?" Silence. I continued, a thought popping into my head. "How many of you are fighting for glory?"

A few of the men frowned, then mumbled, "Yea."

"How many of you are fighting for vengeance?"

More of the men called out, "Yea!"

"Then if you're not willing to fight alongside your Hethurin neighbors, you can go home. You can *forget* about glory or vengeance. You won't get either if you refuse to work with your Hethurin neighbors. When we're fighting the Blodnar, I don't want to fail because the warriors of Svartån are unwilling to fight together."

A few of the men looked away as I stared around at them.

"Who is willing to fight with me and the Hethurin?"

Silence. I relaxed my grip on the hilt of my sword and exhaled, trying to contain my frustration. I was getting sick and tired of the contention between the non-Hethurin and the Hethurin. Or rather, the non-Hethurin animosity.

"Who here is willing to fight alongside the thegn in defense of Lohikärra?" Modolf's voice boomed behind me once more. A majority of the men cheered in response. "Then do not make her question your loyalty."

The crowd bobbed their heads in reluctance. After another moment of awkward silence and with a deflated wave of my hand, they dispersed.

"I wish I had your orating skills, Modolf."

He laughed. "That's only because I've fought with many of these warriors. And thrashed them soundly in combat. They know I mean what I say."

"I don't?"

He shrugged. "You are new to Svartån and to your title, my thegn. I mean that as no insult. Only fact. I think after we fight in Drattüjert, they will respect you much more." We turned to the thegn hall. "Many here disliked your father's sympathies for the Hethurin, but they fought alongside him, or alongside those who respected him. They were loyal. But he grew up with them as well."

"He had time to gain their trust."

Modolf nodded. "So will you. Already stories of your battles with the Isillas and Hardbein travel across your thegn land. People are learning that you aren't a weak thegn. That trust and respect will continue to grow as you get older." He paused. "How old are you? If that doesn't offend. I was under the assumption you were at least eighteen years of age, given you had your official thegn ceremony, but I don't remember hearing anything else."

I shook my head. "I'm only eighteen."

"Then you will have plenty of years to show Svartån—and Lohikärra—how worthy you are of their trust and respect. In the meantime, I'll keep at least the warriors of Eldingheimr on their toes and respecting you."

I grinned. "Thank you, Modolf."

I waited a couple more days before leaving, both to allow more warriors to join up at the estate, and to hopefully see Mattie wake up before I left. On one hand, I was more successful than I had expected. By the afternoon before I planned to leave, warriors from near half of the biggest towns in Svartån had arrived, including, to my surprise, at least fifty men from Katla who had previously fought off the Isillas with me. Even with only the gesiths and a few other veteran warriors, the hall was loud and chaotic. Yet, as much as I enjoyed the camaraderie, it worried me that Mattie hadn't woken up yet. Five days had passed since Sivath and she had been bound together and, while she was still alive, nothing else had changed.

"My thegn?" Llamryl hurried over as I ate at one of the tables set up for the influx of new warriors. I had sent him to check on Mattie in hopes that she had awakened.

"How is she?"

"Still sleeping. Thandes is tending to her."

I sighed, still anxious. Maybe she'd wake up tonight. Or tomorrow. "Thank you, Llamryl."

He nodded. I gestured for him to sit next to me and get some food. As he did, a shout came from the other end of the table.

"Why's that half-breed eating with us?"

I looked up to see the Gesith of Sigreykir staring at me.

"He's the head of the Thegn's Guard and he's been doing a lot of work to help me today." My nerves began to prickle as I sensed a confrontation brewing. Not that it mattered. "Why does it matter if he eats here or not?" I was in my territory now and the gesith was a guest in my house.

"Never eaten with a half-breed before. Do they know how to eat at a table?"

Laughter came from the men at the far end of the table, including the Gesith of Sigreykir, but I could see Llamryl gripping his silverware as he paused before sitting.

"I don't get the joke," I responded flatly. Of course the Gesith of Sigreykir would say something nasty about the Hethurin. All of the stress of the past few days began to simmer into a desire to fight. I wanted him to feel as awkward as he was trying to make Llamryl feel.

"You... It's a... It's not a joke. It was a question."

"Then why are people laughing? Why were you laughing?" I tried to keep my voice level. Calm. Rational.

"I... I... You're overthinking this." He began stumbling over his words as they got louder. "Your father wouldn't have been this way. Or Hardbein." He huffed as if that settled the discussion.

The accusation of overthinking hit hard, but I pushed it away as soon as he mentioned my dad. I straightened up, as all the worry and tension I'd been feeling over the past few days hit a breaking point. If he wanted a fight, I'd give him a fight. One that I could win.

"What exactly would my father say, Gesith Sigreykir? What would he say if he was sitting here right now?"

Gesith Sigreykir opened his mouth, but said nothing for a long time. When he finally spoke, he said, "He wouldn't let a Hethurin mingle with true sons and daughters of Svartån. Even if he did like them. It's like letting a cow or a horse eat at your table. You might be fond of them, but they aren't the same."

"I don't believe my father would have barred Hethurin, the same *people* who were willing to fight and risk their lives for him, from eating with him."

"The thegn is right." Modolf spoke before the Gesith of Sigreykir could open his mouth again. "Her father ate quite frequently with the Hethurin here. At least those he put in leadership positions."

"How would you know that, Modolf? The only reason you're gesith is because the man before you was too weak to fight the Isillas. When did you have a chance to mingle with the current thegn's father?"

Modolf put his tankard down and slowly brushed mead from his facial hair.

"The late thegn was often in need of people who are discreet. People who knew how to handle themselves, could disappear into a crowd. As I had gained those skills in my youth, I was one of those people for him. What about you? Have you done anything special to earn a thegn's trust? Or are you merely the gesith of your village because your father was?"

The Gesith of Sigreykir stood up abruptly, glaring at Modolf. "Have you done anything to earn the title of gesith except be in the right place at the right time? I've defended Sigreykir and fought for Svartån my entire life. The only reason you're where you are is because the last gesith thought you had his back. You let the Isillas kill him."

"I was bringing reinforcements, from the very estate that gutted the Isillas in Eldingheimr. I know how to defend my city. When was the last time you did that?"

The entire table exploded into argument, some taking Modolf's side and others taking the Gesith of Sigreykir's side.

"Enough!" I stood up from my seat, rattling the bowl and cup before me.

The men went silent. The thought of how Ottkatla would have settled this came to mind.

"If we keep bickering among ourselves like this, how on earth—how in Sethys—are we going to fight the Blodnar? This," I gestured to the table, "this is why it took so long to get rid of the Isillas. People bickering and being prideful. It's stupid. This is why the Blodnar are still in Drattüjert! Our enemies see us fractured and come in to feast. I've said this before, and I'll keep saying it. It doesn't matter if a warrior is Hethurin or non-Hethurin. We work together. We fight together. If you can't handle that, go home."

The Gesith of Sigreykir glared at me, eyes narrowed with hate. "You would have me take my one hundred men home in order to appease some half-breeds?"

I focused on the table, realizing what he was doing. When I finally looked up, I held his stare. "I never said your men had to leave. If they want glory and vengeance, and they're willing to fight beside the Hethurin, they are welcome."

"If I were you, I wouldn't try to manipulate the thegn." Modolf snapped. "You don't know in whose ears those words might land."

The Gesith of Sigreykir scoffed and returned his focus to me. "You will regret this."

"Will I?" My anger pushed me forward. Responding to him might not be the best thing to do, but I wanted him—and the others— to know I wasn't someone to be bullied. Not anymore. "Or will you?"

He shoved his bowl and tankard off the table, letting them clatter loudly to the floor, before stalking out of the hall.

The rest of the people at the tables sat silently as I watched him depart. Once he had left, I heard Llamryl whisper, "I'm sorry, my thegn."

I shook my head and sat down. "You don't need to apologize. I'm thegn and I demand the warriors under me work together. A house divided..." I couldn't remember the quote, but it didn't matter. A few of the other people nodded and returned to their meals.

"The Gesith of Sigreykir is just bitter Lady Ina is the thegn and not his cousin, Hardbein." Modolf added. He turned to me. "If you wish, you can stop his men from leaving with him. You are in your rights as the thegn to do that. Call on them to preserve Svartån and Lohikärra, regardless of their feelings or their gesith's feelings."

I nodded and turned to Llamryl as he took a bite. Before I could say anything, he shook his head and stood up.

"I suppose the gesith wouldn't be happy to see me, but I know someone who can deliver your message to the warriors of Sigreykir."

"Thank you, Llamryl."

He bowed and hurried off. I focused on the rest of the warriors. The mood of the room had lightened up significantly. I was glad for that; however, a worry dug itself into my thoughts. Would my confrontation with the gesith come back to bite me in the future?

Chapter Seven

The next morning, I woke up before the sun rose. Today, I would be riding out with the warriors of Svartån—at least those who had heeded my call thus far— and head south to the camp Haldrek's cousin Aallotar had set up. I had asked Thandes and the others who had been tending to Mattie to wake me if anything changed, good or bad. There had been nothing. As I changed into my gambeson and armor, a knock came at the door, making me jump. I spun around as one of my servants—something I still felt weird about calling anyone— opened the door.

"My thegn?"

"Is Mattie okay? Did she wake up?"

The girl shook her head. "She's still sleeping, last I checked. I came to see if you were awake and needed anything. There's a meal ready for you, if you wish."

I exhaled, trying to conceal my disappointment. "No, I'm fine. I'm not too hungry right now, but I might be later. Is the food something that can be packed up?"

The girl nodded quickly and shut the door. I shook my hands and arms out, hoping to relieve the pinpricks of anxiety coursing through my limbs. My father—or one of my other ancestors—had procured a full-length mirror. It stood near the fireplace, tinted dark on the edges with time and, I guessed, soot. But I could still see myself in it for the most part. My thegn armor was shiny and near brand new. Flexing my fingers, rolling my elbow and shoulder, I focused on the joints in the armor. I looked like a strong and mighty thegn. I had moments when I felt I acted like one. Like last night. But right now, I felt terrified and overwhelmed. Terrified for what lay ahead—fighting, blood, guts, and gore—and overwhelmed by the responsibility of being in charge of so many warriors.

When I'd been fighting the Isillas, I had only been in charge of one hundred warriors. As of last night, before the Gesith of Sigreykir's outburst, there had been between four and five hundred. Much more than I'd expected. Even if he took all one hundred or so of his warriors back to Sigreykir, I'd still have more than Aallotar had asked for. More than I'd ever handled before.

Taking a deep breath, I pushed those worries from my mind and headed down the hall to Mattie's room. Maybe she'd woken up while the servant was trying to find me? But then Thandes or Llamryl would have come find me, unless something else had happened.

I opened the door and found Mattie still sleeping. Llamryl slept by her side and Thandes stood at a nearby table, measuring something into a small wooden cup. Next to the cup was a mortar and pestle, filled halfway with something brightly colored.

"She's still resting, my thegn."

"No change?" My throat tightened. I had really hoped Mattie would have woken up by now. If she couldn't survive the haldraga ceremony, what did that mean for me?

"She takes the nourishment tonic when Llamryl or I give it to her, but she hasn't opened her eyes yet."

"What do you mean?"

Thandes gestured for me to follow her. She placed the tonic on Mattie's nightstand and adjusted her head so it was at an angle. Using a syringe-like instrument, she drew some of the liquid she'd been measuring into it. Without a word, she put the syringe into Mattie's mouth and gave her whatever tonic she had been working with. Much to my surprise, instead of the liquid dripping out of Mattie's mouth or otherwise making a mess, the muscles in her throat moved as if she was swallowing.

"Lady Mattie showed me how to make this type of tube," Thandes said as she continued to give Mattie the tonic. "I made a few adjustments, but this is how we fed you while you were unconscious."

I nodded. "I guess if she's still breathing and getting nourishment, that's a good sign." It still worried me that she'd been unconscious for nearly a week, though.

Thandes finished and smiled. "This is a good sign. Skuti said that the person he'd heard of who didn't survive their haldraga ceremony started wasting away after a few days of this. Lady Mattie is still strong, I think. Even if she's been in this state for a week."

Still staring at her, I nodded once more. "You know how to use the thegn stones? Or Mattie's pendant?"

Thandes widened her eyes in surprise as I pulled my own pendant out.

"If she wakes up or anything changes, I want to know as soon as possible. If you need Skuti to help you with anything, tell him what I told you."

"Of course. Though I don't think Skuti will fuss." Thandes hesitated before speaking again. "How long do you think it will take you to get to your destination?"

I shrugged. "Modolf is expecting it to take a few days to get to the border of Svartån and Svarhestån with as many warriors as we have. Beyond that, I supposed another few days. Maybe a week?"

"I'll keep that in mind. When Mattie wakes up, we'll be sure to let her know what is going on." Thandes hesitated again, then gave me a quick hug. Despite my armor, the tight hug felt good. She pulled away and bowed more respectfully.

"Be safe, my thegn. May the dragons watch over you in your travels."

I smiled. "Thank you. I hope to return here soon." Part of me wanted to say something lighthearted. Something to lessen the heavy mood. But nothing came to mind that I didn't think I'd mess up. With one last glance at Mattie, I left.

Outside, the men were organized into nine equally sized groups. Modolf was standing by one of them, but approached as I walked down the stairs.

"Four hundred and fifty-nine, my thegn. It seems that the Gesith of Sigreykir took a few dozen of his men back to their hovels."

I exhaled. That was to be expected. Still, we had more than twice what Aallotar had asked for. That would improve our odds, I hoped.

"How are you feeling? You look nervous."

"I am nervous. A little bit. A lot." I focused on the men in front of me. "Mattie is still recovering from becoming a haldraga. She'll be fine. I'm sure. I'd hoped she would be awake before I left."

"And?"

I turned to Modolf. "And? What?"

"This is your first war march. Not to say that what you did against the Isillas wasn't tough, but this is different."

I nodded. Now I was aiding other thegns in Lohikärra. I was marching back to face the same people who had tried to kill me when I first got here. While I trusted in the strength of Svartån's warriors, Modolf was right. This was new.

"You'll do fine. Every thegn is nervous about this. Thegn of Andrattür especially. At least, that's my guess. What happens in the next few months could change the course of Lohikärra's history." He paused, as if realizing the gravity of what he'd just said. "I think it'll be for the better. I think Thegn Andrattür will become High King. You'll be High Queen—" He nudged me and I grinned. "And Lohikärra will become stronger than ever."

"How confident are you in that?" I asked as Modolf helped me up onto the horse that had been brought out for me.

"Confident enough to say when you and Thegn Andrattür are crowned High Queen and High King, I will be there to cheer you both on with the finest Svartån mead."

I laughed and looked behind us at the men and women waiting for me. Taking a deep breath, I headed out.

A few days after we left Svangendom, we reached the western border of Svarhestån. Mountains created a natural border between the two thegn lands and it took us an entire day to bring everyone through the pass. Modolf and one of the other gesiths had mentioned a good, secure spot at the bottom of the pass where we could break for camp with enough space for everyone.

As the sun began to set behind the mountains, I found myself in that spot, struggling with my tent and trying not to make myself look any more inexperienced than I felt. The last few days had been spent in or around villages in southern Svartån, so I'd been able to sleep in manmade buildings for the most part. But tonight was the first time since leaving Svangendom that I'd had to create my own shelter. Back in Fargo, I'd never had the opportunity to camp, and even here in Lohikärra, other people had offered to set up my tent in the past. It had looked simple when Haldrek or any of my warriors had done it. So now was my time to do it. Yet I struggled to attach the fabric between the poles that had been included. I had finally figured out how to balance some of the poles when they all collapsed at my feet.

Behind me, I heard a loud laugh.

"Apologies, my thegn." Modolf smiled widely, showing off one of his gold teeth. "Can I help you?"

I nodded and let him take my place. I was too tired and sore from riding today to deal with this stupid tent.

"I hate that I can't pitch my own tent. I'm sure Haldrek and the other warriors can."

Modolf laughed again. "Don't worry. Many men can, but only because they have practiced since their youth."

I folded my arms and looked around crossly at the other warriors setting up camp with ease. "I hope I can pitch my own tent soon enough. I hate..." I hated having to rely on others. Being the weak link.

"You hate having others pitch your tent for you?" Modolf chuckled softer this time, still entertained by my predicament.

"I do. I may not have had the training that others like you and Haldrek had, but I want to learn."

He began to wheeze with laughter as he finished tying the last of the leather cords and shook his head. After taking a deep breath, he said, "I wouldn't worry if I were you. I'm sure you will gain many skills before this campaign is over."

I sighed. "Probably. Thank you, Modolf, for your help." My thoughts returned to the estate. Hopefully, Mattie had woken up while we were traveling through the pass. "I'm going to check on Mattie and Svangendom."

He bowed. "Glad to be of help." With that, he wandered off toward where the Eldingheimr warriors were setting up camp.

Slipping inside the small tent, I pulled my pendant from my gambeson. "Mattie Gunvald." The last few days, when I'd tried to reach her, either there had been no response or Llamryl had popped the pendant open. As nice as it was to see someone at Svangendom and get updates, I hoped it would be Mattie today. Anxiety swelled inside me, rising as the black ink rippled within the pendant.

Then a pair of brown eyes were staring at me. The image pulled back and Mattie frowned, still looking exhausted. "What's going on? Where are you?"

"Mattie!" My throat and chest tightened up with joy. "I'm marching with the warriors of Svartån to help Haldrek and the other thegns kick out the Blodnar. I'm so glad you're alive though. How are you feeling?"

Mattie smiled. "Good. Tired. Sivath is happy to hear you are acting on his message."

I cocked my head, confusion flooding me. "He...? How...? I'm glad you're okay. But what do you mean about Sivath?"

"He likes to talk a lot." Mattie laughed. "After we initially bonded, I got...transported? Somewhere? He was in his human form and told me a bunch of stuff about being a haldraga and everything it entails. It's actually not too different than what the lore in the video games makes it out to be."

"Other than you were unconscious for over a week and could have possibly died?" I blurted out before wincing.

"Sivath said that if I were to die, it would have happened in the moment we bonded. But it freaked me out at first too. I mean, that was my first thought."

"It took him a week to teach you everything about being a haldraga?"

"I guess. He mentioned that time for dragons is different than time for humans. It felt like we were talking for a few hours, kinda? I don't know. It didn't seem like I was unconscious for a week."

"Ten days to be exact." Llamryl poked his head into the view of the pendant and bobbed. "My thegn."

"Hi, Llamryl." I smiled. "Thank you for your updates, both on the estate and on how Mattie was doing."

"More than happy to aid you. How goes your march?"

"Good. We're in Svarhestån now. Some of the gesiths who have traveled this way before mentioned that it shouldn't be more than a few days until we arrive at the southern pass where Aallotar—Thegn-heir Heidrunefoss—has her camp."

"That's good. Things are still quiet here. Other than Mattie waking up. Thandes has the kitchen preparing a host of food to help her fully recover."

I smiled broadly, my whole body feeling lighter and more relaxed. Mattie cocked her head to the side. "Any word from Haldrek?"

"Since you bonded with Sivath? A little bit. He's bringing a few hundred Andrattür warriors with him to help Aallotar. Once we're done, I should probably call him on his pendant and let him know you're awake. He seemed more confident that you'd be fine, but he wanted to know you were all right as well."

"I bet you are looking forward to seeing him again." A teasing smile crossed Mattie's face.

My cheeks warmed up and I nodded. "I am. It'll be good. I know it won't be all fun and games because we're going to be fighting the Blodnar, but I've missed him." I exhaled, thinking about the near future and what would happen once we arrived at Aallotar's camp. Part of me was excited. I couldn't wait to see and be with Haldrek again. But part of me was terrified. One way or another, I and the other thegns would have to face the Blodnar. "We'll see what happens when we get to the camp. I expect it'll be a lot of practice and stuff. Not too much free time. As much as I would love that."

Llamryl nodded. "It'll be a good place to work with your warriors either way. Practice with them and get them to show you different moves. I think many would appreciate that. A thegn who can lead them but also fight alongside them."

"True..." I failed to suppress a yawn and Mattie laughed.

"Go talk to Haldrek and get some sleep. We can talk in the morning tomorrow, and I'll tell more about what Sivath told me. If you want."

"Okay." I yawned again and smiled. The pendant went dark before a bright number eight popped up again, lighting up the darkness in the tent. Evening had set over us. Though it didn't get pitch black at night here during the summer months, it was still dark enough inside my tent. I listened to the warriors outside talking and singing. I couldn't hear much of what they were saying, but those who were singing... The sounds reminded me of the background music on the Lohikärran video games. It soothed me.

Focusing on my pendant, I put my thumb on the glass and said, "Haldrek Rodreks-son."

The inky blackness rippled for a moment before Haldrek's face popped up. He looked bleary eyed and his beard was scruffier than usual. The thought of it brushing against my cheek and neck popped into my mind and sent a thrill through my body. I grinned in spite of myself.

"I hope I didn't wake you..."

He shook his head. "I closed my eyes for a moment to relax, but I should be awake right now. How are you doing? Is everything all right?"

"It is. We're in Svarhestån now. And Mattie woke up today, which makes me feel better. A lot better."

"That's good." He yawned and shook his head more vigorously this time. "My men and I got to Aallotar's camp earlier today, so I've been training and helping them set up camp. We also encountered some Blodnar yesterday, so I didn't sleep well last night."

"Are they still out there?" It hit me that my men and I might end up in a fight with Blodnar before we arrived at the war camp.

Haldrek shook his head. "No. My men and I destroyed the small group we encoun-tered. And if you're in Svarhestån, I doubt there are any Blodnar near you. My cousin, Hrimfax, and his men would have found them." He paused. "Maybe a scouting party, but that shouldn't be an issue for your men. Which reminds me," Haldrek yawned again. "Aallotar said she sent a messenger to Hrimfax as well. You and your warriors may run into him before you arrive here."

"Do you think there will be enough space?" I had no idea how big Aallotar's war camp would be, but if it was too big, wouldn't that alert the Blodnar?

"There will be plenty of room. Aallotar is expecting plenty of warriors. The Blodnar have captured her thegn hall, and our camp is within eyesight of the hall and village. She wants the Blodnar to know we're here and ready to fight."

"All right. Well, we'll be there in a few days, barring anything unforeseen."

"I'm glad." Haldrek smiled ear to ear and stroked his beard as if trying to tame it. "I'm looking forward to see you again. I've missed you."

My cheeks grew hot and an excited, jittery feeling grew quickly from my stomach and into the rest of my body. "I've missed you too. But I know this is more business than play."

"So was dealing with Hardbein and Seirye, but we still had time to enjoy each other's presence, didn't we?" His smile warmed me up even more and I wished we were already at the camp.

"We did." He was right. Despite the dilemmas we'd had to deal with, we had certainly had time to relax and get to know each other during that time.

"I love you, Ina. I look forward to seeing you in a few days." Another yawn. "But for now..."

"Go get some sleep, Haldrek. I should probably get some as well. I love you."

He laughed and his face disappeared from the pendant. I yawned myself, fatigue hitting me like a pile of bricks.

Chapter Eight

The next couple of days were peaceful as we made our way through Svarhestån. I realized how much it reminded me of the massive farms in North Dakota. On rare occasions I'd left Fargo, there were miles and miles of crops. Sunflowers, corn, wheat, pretty much everything you could think of over some of the flattest looking land. Svarhestån was the same, but without the sunflowers. At least as far as I could see. Did Lohikärra even have sunflowers? Probably. Or something like them. But still, the land reminded me of home and for a short time, I felt nostalgic.

Our third night along the acres and acres of wheat, we made our way to a wide grassy area that seemed to have been left for marches like this. It was handy, but I cringed at the idea of camping in some poor farmer's field, even if it didn't have crops in it this season. I also felt uneasy being in the open. I pitched my tent toward the center of the space as quickly as possible—trying to remember how Modolf had shown me—then watched some of the warriors begin sentry duty as the last of the warriors came into view.

"It looks like you figured out your tent, my thegn." Modolf's voice caught my attention and I turned to look at the small tent. It was still saggy, but it stood with enough space for sleeping.

"I don't want to be the only warrior or thegn to not be able to pitch their own tent in Aallotar's war camp."

Modolf chuckled loudly, surprising me. "I don't think you have to worry about that."

A strange feeling came over me and I nodded. "I suppose." Looking over the camp as the sun dipped beyond the horizon, giving the sky a deep reddish hue, I asked, "What are the chances there are Blodnar around?"

Modolf frowned and looked over the wheat fields stretching before us. "I suppose the closer we get to Drattüjert, the better the chance is. Why?"

I shook my head. "I just got an odd feeling. Like we're not alone. Which, I mean," I gestured to the large camp around us, "is probably nothing."

Modolf shook his head. "If there is something I learned while adventuring, odd feelings are there for a reason. Should we add to the night guard?"

"I don't know. I suppose those who are on guard duty tonight should be on higher alert than normal." I shook my head. "It's probably nothing. I don't want to scare anyone."

"We're warriors of Svartån. It takes a lot more than a possible night attack to scare us. I'll talk to the gesiths and we'll let our men on guard duty know to be more alert tonight."

I nodded. "If anything happens, let me know. I don't care if I'm asleep. Wake me up."

"Understood." Modolf bowed slightly. "Hopefully nothing happens and we all sleep well."

"Same." With that, I slipped into my little saggy tent.

"My thegn, wake up!"

I woke to someone pulling my tent flap open. My tent poles wobbled and I ducked through the opening, sword and shield in hand, to see flames licking the air on the far side of camp. The sounds of shouting pulled my attention toward the area as a few other warriors hurry over.

"What's going on?" I glanced at the warrior who hurried alongside me.

"We're being attacked! The guards sent up a warning."

"The fire?"

"I don't know, my thegn."

I looked ahead, scrambling to the edge of the camp. Across from me was a field with several small fires in it, burning the crops. A handful of my men fought in the shadows of the flames. I ran to join them, jumping into the waist high wheat. A few fighters came my way. As I blocked one with my shield, I swung at the other man's sword arm. My blade cut through his armor easily and his arm went limp, dropping the blade. He swung at me with his good arm and I blocked it with my sword as someone from behind me tackled him.

Focusing on the other man, who was locked in combat with another one of my men, I swung my blade at the back of his knee, cutting through it. He screamed and collapsed, my warrior jumping on top of him.

"My thegn!"

I turned to see Modolf wading through the wheat toward me, his voice recognizable. He held what looked like torch until he got closer and I realized it was just burning chunk of wood.

"My thegn!" he gasped as he stood before me. "There's something you need to see."

I followed him away from the main conflict as my men began to douse the larger flames. We reached a darker part of the field, only lightly illuminated by the moon and a handful of wandering ghosts. My foot hit something solid, and it groaned.

"Die already, you Blodnar bastard." Modolf kicked the body and it went silent.

"What are we looking for?" I did my best to walk around the body and not think about what lay at my feet. My periphery was covered in a bluish haze from the number of ghosts meandering about.

"This. One of the bastards I killed."

Modolf reached down with one hand while keeping his makeshift torch high in the air. Fabric ripped as Modolf pulled the man's cloth armor cover from him.

"Look what's on his tabard."

I squinted, trying to make out the insignia on the piece of clothing. It had a dragon flying above a mound of round things, like a stylized bunch of grapes, but upside down. On one side was what looked like a bag with more round objects flowing from it.

Money. Coins. A horde of gold?

I racked my mind for which thegn land was connected to money and trade in the Lohikärran games, then gasped.

"Etelaranikä?"

Modolf nodded. "I have some of my men checking to see if any of the other raiders wore Etelaranikän garb. This man's tabard was covered by Blodnar armor, but when he fell, the armor dropped away, revealing this."

"This is important." I looked up as the Etelaranikän man's ghost ran toward me. He stopped on the other side of his body. There was no anger emanating from him, at least not toward me. Instead, an sense of betrayal overwhelmed me.

"What are you looking at, my thegn?" Modolf asked.

"The ghost of this man."

"You should send him to Lyrroth for what he's done." Modolf kicked the man's body and the ghost reacted by lunging at him. Modolf twitched, but nothing more.

"I'm not so sure Lyrroth is the right place for him." I watched the spirit as it turned to me. Much to my surprise, it knelt to one knee, head bowed and hands clasped if asking for mercy.

"I wonder how many of the rank and file warriors know exactly what they are doing?"

"You think this man was just following orders? Whose orders?"

"If he's from Etelaranikä..."

"Then the Thegn of Etelaranikä? That's a heavy accusation."

I turned to Modolf. "Only as heavy as some of the others I've heard recently."

His eyes widened.

"This man seems remorseful. But he did try to kill warriors of Svartån too." I exhaled, new thoughts coming over me. Did spirits end up in whatever realm they were sent to? Or was there movement in the afterlife based on other things?

"You would have mercy on this man, then? Send him to Mirroth?" A hint of disbelief colored Modolf's words.

"Maybe not Mirroth. But if he was just following orders, he doesn't belong in Lyrroth, either." I thought back to my decision with the elf I had sent to Lyrroth months ago. He had had much more animosity and intention. "Camroth. He did what he was told to do, right? Obedience and whatnot, but he didn't question the orders to attack his fellow Lohikärrans and aid the Blodnar." I focused on Modolf, looking for his reaction.

Modolf nodded. "It makes sense. You are a far more merciful person than me."

I spread my arms wide and tried to remember the incantation for sending a spirit to Camroth. In my mind's eye, the Etelaranikän man groveled, and I hoped I was making the right decision. Once I had finished, his spirit faded from my view and a weight fell over me. I had no idea if it was from the ritual or from guilt.

"Modolf?" I opened my eyes and looked around the many spirits.

"Yes, my thegn?"

"Have your men gather our dead if they haven't already." I took a deep breath, trying to steady myself. "I want to do their rituals before we leave camp. As for the rest..." I really didn't want ghosts to be haunting this place. At least not Blodnar ghosts. "Have one of your men fetch some priest of Tenelth from a local village so their rites can be done as well."

"Are you sure, my thegn?"

I nodded. "Others may not see them, but I'd rather have less ghosts haunting Lohikärra if possible."

Modolf chuckled humorlessly. "As you command, my thegn." He began walking and I followed him, exhausted and not looking forward to the next few hours.

The sun began to rise by the time I returned to my tent. I knew I should start packing up, but I was too exhausted. It was going take an hour or two before everyone else would be ready, anyway. Today would be miserable, but a few hours of sleep would make it easier.

When we finally did get on the road, I grabbed an 'energy tonic' stowed in one of my saddle bags. As soon as I chugged it, I felt more awake and coherent. Miles and miles of wheat fields lay ahead of us, but in the distance, I could see the peaks of mountains steadily growing bigger.

"Modolf?"

He pulled his horse next to mine. "Yes, my thegn?"

"Are those the mountains we're headed for?"

He squinted, then nodded. "They are. This is a good sign. One more night on the road and we should be to the pass into Heidrunefoss."

I smiled, my shoulders relaxing with relief. "It'll be nice to join up with the other thegns and their sattars."

Modolf glanced behind us. "They'll be happy to have the warriors of Svartån with them. You brought a decent sized army."

"Hopefully it will be enough to take back Drattüjert."

"I think it will." He returned his gaze to the horizon in front of us. "You see that?"

Halfway between us and the mountains, wheat waved in the summer air, except it was only moving in one direction. I cocked my head. "That's not wheat, is it?"

Modolf laughed. "No, it isn't. It's people. Warriors, I'm guessing."

My thoughts flashed back to the previous night. "Blodnar?"

"I doubt it, but you could send a scout or two to check. Or wait until we cross paths with them."

I looked around and saw a few scouts perk up. When I nodded, they dashed off, slipping through the wheat with ease. After a few minutes, they returned.

"The Thegn of Svarhestån sends his greetings."

"Thank you." I turned to Modolf. "You were right. I'm glad to see a familiar face. I mean, outside of the warriors here."

"Of course. I wonder how many he's bringing as well? I'd be surprised if the Blodnar weren't pressing Svarhestån as well." He gestured to the crops around us. "This is a mighty tempting prize."

I nodded. "We'll have to see."

A few hours later, our bands finally merged at a large, but fairly empty crossroads. Hrimfax waved to me.

"Hail, Thegn of Svartån!"

I returned his greeting. "Hail, Thegn of Svarhestån." I felt both weird and official at the same time, saying that. Hrimfax brought his horse in line with mine and I watched as his men began to blend in with my troops.

"How have you been since your coronation?"

"Pretty good. Exploring more of Svartån, studying up on what my father did while he was thegn, interacting with gesiths."

"Sounds like you've been busy. It'll be good that you're fighting alongside us though. The warriors of Svartån were renowned for their devotion to the High King and Lohikärra. I'm sure it'll be no different with you." He looked over our combined warriors and smiled broadly. "Aallotar will be pleased when we arrive. How many warriors do you have with you?"

"Almost five hundred."

Hrimfax whistled. "The warriors of Svartån do come when called. I have three sattars with me. But I also have many wagons of supplies for Allotar's camp. Her messenger came requesting not only men, but foodstuffs as well." He gestured behind us and I saw a long line of covered wagons. I assumed they held the supplies he mentioned.

"Svarhestån is the land of horses, right? I remember you having a connection with the horses at that Blodnar war camp."

Hrimfax nodded. "I can talk to horses, much like Haldrek can speak to the dragons while they are dragons. But Svarhestån is also a very fruitful thegn land. The soil is rich and we have plenty of animal droppings to keep it that way." His smile faded away. "Most years, we have more than enough to feed all of Lohikärra."

"Even with all the fighting?"

He nodded. "Kalle—the late High King—was wise enough to keep most of Svarhestån's men in the fields. An army is easier to command when they are well fed. But between the lingering war and the Blodnar raiding the southern parts of my lands, the harvest this year will be less than normal. Svarhestån will not starve, but we won't have as much to spare either."

"Hopefully, we can get rid of the Blodnar once and for all. Then Svarhestån can return to being the bread basket of Lohikärra."

Hrimfax's smile returned. "I hope for that. While I was trained to fight as much as the other thegns, like Aallotar and Haldrek, I am more comfortable with growing things. Plants, animals, prosperity. We've been fighting the Blodnar since I was a young man. I'd like to focus on other aspects of being a thegn." He laughed loudly, making me and a few others around us jump. "I'm sure that's not expected from a thegn of Lohikärra."

I shook my head. "It's fine. A people constantly at war, there has to be balance. You know?"

"I understand. If you're always fighting, there's no time for growth. If you're not growing, you're dying."

Our conversation lulled and I returned my attention to the world around us. It was as if we were in a sea of wheat. I wasn't a farmer, but Svarhestån seemed to have plenty to go around. At least here. Not that I doubted Hrimfax.

"Svarhestån reminds me a lot of where I grew up." I blurted out.

Hrimfax cocked his head. "Really? How so?"

"I grew up in a city. A large town, I guess. But it was surrounded by fields of wheat, corn, and everything else as far as the eye could see. It's very flat. I could go hours without seeing another person or village. Some villages weren't really villages either. Just a family who worked the land and sold stuff to travelers as they pass through."

He laughed. "We have those too. How do you like Svartån compared to where you grew up? That Fartogo place?"

"Fargo? Fargo was...Fargo. Not terrible. But I don't have much of a connection to it. It's just where I grew up. Before Mattie and I arrived here, we'd been talking about leaving Fargo. Svartån always felt like home, even before I arrived here."

Hrimfax cocked his head again. "That's interesting. And who is...Mattie, you said?"

I realized that he may not have known who Mattie was, though he was at my coronation.

"Mattie is my friend. I assumed you had met her. She arrived from Fargo at the same time as me, but we got separated at first. We only met up again when I arrived at Svangendom."

He nodded and looked as if he was trying to remember something. Then his face lit up and he smiled again. "Lady Mathilde of Sea Castle? The dark-skinned woman who is Haldrek's half-sister?"

I nodded. "We've known each other for a while now. I trust her almost more than anyone. She's pretty much like a sister to me now."

"I understand. You two have known each other long enough to create that kind of bond. There are a few of us thegns who are like that as well. Haldrek, Aallotar, and I all grew up together. Though we are cousins, I trust them as though we were siblings. Hence why I am quick to bring aid when either asks. Not that I wouldn't do it for Lohikärra in general, but I know Aallotar and Haldrek's intentions."

"That's good to know." I hesitated, new questions swirling in my head as I tried to figure how to ask them. "I know we're going to fight once we get there, but..." I lowered my voice. "How long will it be before our first battle?" I'd been practicing my swordplay and magic wielding as much as my strength allowed, but I still felt so far behind even the youngest of my warriors.

"Eager to get your vengeance on the Blodnar?"

I shook my head. "I'm just trying to figure how much training I'll be able to get in before, you know, getting into a big battle. The one big battle in Katla against the Isillas taught me a lot, but I have more warriors now. I wasn't in charge of everyone at Katla."

Hrimfax nodded. "Battles don't happen on a set schedule. They happen when one side sees an advantage over the other. We could be fighting the Blodnar tomorrow or two weeks from now. But whenever we do, I'll be cutting down as many of those bastards as I can. I've seen the damage they've done to Svarhestån. Innocents slaughtered for nothing more than being in the way. If I had my way, anyone with even a single drop of Blodnar blood would be exiled from Svarhestån and Lohikärra."

Hrimfax's passion and anger pricked at me and anxiety crawled over my skin like ants. My thoughts went to those who didn't choose their bloodlines or their heritage. Like the Hethurin behind me, I wondered how many people in Lohikärra or even Svarhestån had ancestry that wasn't fully Lohikärran. I wanted to figure out how deep Hrimfax's animosity went, but at the same time, I didn't want to agitate him. We'd have to fight the Blodnar together and the number of thegns who I felt comfortable in challenging right now was less than the fingers on one hand.

Still...

"I hope you aren't put off by fighting alongside the Hethurin."

"If they have proven their loyalty to Svartån, I have no qualms. They are your warriors, not mine. Though the chances that I personally will be fighting next to a half-elf is slim. Unless the forces of Svartån and Svarhestån get mixed during battle for some reason." We were quiet for a moment. Then he turned to me. "Why do you ask?"

"I just know that sometimes people don't like to be excluded or judged because of their heritage. It's not like they had any choice in the matter."

Hrimfax laughed somberly. "That is true." Silence resumed between us. I wanted to say something, but the heat and my anxiety made my throat dry.

Instead, I grabbed my water bag from my saddle. Taking a swig, I looked ahead to more fields of wheat. The mountains signaling Aallotar's camp were still far in the distance.

Today would be a long day.

Chapter Nine

Our travels slowed considerably once Hrimfax's warriors and mine joined together. Our band of almost eight hundred spent a few more nights in Svarhestån, and I made sure to practice more with my men each night, just in case we ended up fighting the Blodnar as soon as we got to Aallotar's camp.

It was near midday when Hrimfax and I stopped in front of a massive camp. We had moved through the mountain pass splitting Heidrunefoss from Svarhestån early in the morning, and had spent the next few hours making our way to the camp. Gently sloping hills surrounded it. In the distance, near the southern horizon, I could see signs of more human activity. Given what Hrimfax had told me over the past few days, I assumed it was Aallotar's estate and the surrounding village, now occupied by Blodnar. Still too far away from the camp to endanger it, but close enough that I could see us fighting the Blodnar soon. I wondered what kind of preparations they were currently making. Here, however, male and female warriors milled around—just like in the games, and small plots of dirt outside the rough perimeter of the camp had been turned into practice areas.

"Hail Thegn of Svarhestån and… Svartån?" One of the sentries squinted at me, then smiled widely, showing a mouth full of darkened teeth. From dye or decay, I didn't know. "It's good to see the Thegn-heir's call has been answered. Thegn Andrattür and Thegn-heir Heidrunefoss have been waiting for you." He leaned to the side to assess the warriors behind us and nodded. "The northern edge of camp is still empty. Thegn-heir Heidrunefoss has been sending those arriving to that part."

"How many people…?" I tried to gauge how many people were in the vicinity, but that got me nowhere.

He shook his head. "I dunno. Thegn-heir Heidrunefoss had a handful of warriors with her when she set up camp here, but now…" He gestured behind him. "All I know, and all I care about, is that Thegn-heir Heidrunefoss and her allied thegns bring the Blodnar to their knees once and for all."

Hrimfax raised his fist in agreement. "To Lohikärra!"

The rest of those around us repeated his cheer, and I joined in a half second after the rest, caught off-guard by the sudden shout.

"Thegn-heir Heidrunefoss gave orders to tell any newly arriving thegns she wants to meet with them as soon as they arrive."

Hrimfax and I nodded as the sentries returned to their duties. Hrimfax sent back orders among his ranks. I did so as well and the massive group of warriors began to shift northward. Hrimfax began heading north, so I followed him.

"How many warriors do you think are here?" I looked past the training areas and into the camp. How exactly were the logistics of this whole thing going to work? I didn't know how many Aallotar had, but if Haldrek had brought a minimum of two hundred with him and Aallotar had just as many, Hrimfax's forces and mine could easily enlarge the camp size by two or three times. If it wasn't already, it would become a large town in and of itself, just in regards to the warriors.

Hrimfax looked over at the camp. "I wouldn't be surprised if there were five hundred here right now. This will be a large camp when all is said and done. Probably nearly as many warriors as fought to defend Drattüjert." He exhaled. "But we will win this time. I hope."

I was surprised by his tone. "Are you not sure?"

He shrugged. "We had many warriors last time, but some betrayed us. I saw it with my own eyes and heard whispers of similar actions from other thegns. I don't think Aallotar sent messengers to those she deemed untrustworthy after the battle at Drattüjert."

A small amount of relief coursed through me to think that I was considered trustworthy. Or at least not untrustworthy.

"How long do you think it'll be before Aallotar and Haldrek know we're here?" I wondered whether it would be better to attempt putting my tent up and assisting my warriors or to wait until after we met with Aallotar and Haldrek.

"They probably already know." Hrimfax laughed. "You've been keeping in touch with Haldrek since your coronation, haven't you?" He pointed to the chain on my neck.

"I have. I'm just wondering if they—or more so, Aallotar— will be mad if I'm not prompt in arriving to wherever they were."

Hrimfax laughed again. "I doubt Aallotar will upset if either of us takes our time before meeting with them. Haldrek might be, but not because he's mad." He raised an eyebrow and I just shook my head, trying not to smile. He continued, "I know my cousin well. Even in the state we were all in, bloodied and bruised, I saw how he looked at you."

Now it was my turn to raise an eyebrow. "Really?" I knew Hrimfax was teasing me, but to what extent, I didn't know.

Hrimfax nodded. "You couldn't tell?"

"I was in the middle of trying not to die." I retorted, trying to keep the conversation light. "There were more important things on my mind at the time. Like survival."

He laughed, as if aware of how his question sounded. "Fair enough."

I shook my head and looked around to see if we were close to the north side of the camp. I had no idea why the conversation had turned in the direction that it had. Not that I didn't care dearly for Haldrek, and Hrimfax was a nice enough person, it seemed. But part of me didn't feel comfortable talking about that stuff with anyone other than Mattie or Haldrek.

"Where is the north edge of the camp? This place seems to go on pretty far."

Hrimfax pointed to where people were milling around a few yards from us. "I'm guessing that's it. That's where the Andrattür tents and flags end. You can have your warriors set up on the eastern side and I'll have my warriors on the western side. That way it'll be easier," he grinned at me, "if you and my cousin have to go over strategy or more training."

My body heated up from embarrassment under my armor, but before I could say anything, Hrimfax was off with some of his men, heading for the far western side.

Behind me, I heard someone clearing his throat. Modolf and a few other gesiths were awaiting orders. I gestured to the space between us and Hrimfax's group.

"This is where we'll set up camp while we're here. Thegn-heir Heidrunefoss said the northern side."

One of the other gesiths waved to the warriors behind us. "You heard the thegn!"

Warriors began to move quickly around me and the gesiths moved along with them, taking charge of their particular troops. I got off my horse and began walking into the large space.

"Would you like some help, my thegn?" Modolf followed me while gesturing to some of his warriors.

Looking around, I nodded. "If you mean helping put up my tent and organizing everything, absolutely." I sighed. "No one ever mentioned how to set up a war camp to me."

Modolf waved me off, shaking his head with a smile. "I doubt that is part of any thegn's book training. The other gesiths and I will take care of building up the camp." Modolf turned to me with a chuckle. "Show me where you'd like your tent to be set up and I'll have one of my men do it. That way, you can meet with other thegns and see your beloved."

My body warmed up once more. It would be nice to see Haldrek again. Modolf grabbed a young warrior who was passing by and stopped him.

"Go with the thegn and set up her tent where she tells you to. She has to meet with the other thegns. Understood?"

The young man nodded and I looked around for a suitable spot. Not that I really knew what I was doing. I walked forward a few yards and watched as the warriors began setting up their tents, creating little pathways.

"Would you like me to set it up here, my thegn?"

I looked around, seeing no better spot. "Yes. This will work." Within a few minutes, he and another warrior began to pull up a larger tent than I had used on the trek here. As soon as the tent was up and stable, I was able to carry my supplies into it. The young warrior stood by my horse.

"Would you like me to take your horse to where the others are, my thegn?"

I nodded. "Thank you."

He bowed and slipped away without another word, leaving me to my next task: finding where Haldrek and the other thegns were.

I began wandering through the camp, looking for what might be a central location. I got the impression Aallotar had different areas for the other thegns and their men, but I had no clue where she or Haldrek might be.

"Thegn Svartån!"

I spun around to see Hrimfax jogging up to me. "Thegn Svarhestån."

"Looking for the others?"

I nodded and he gestured for me to keep following him.

"How do you know where to go?"

"I know my cousins. And this isn't my first war march. You'll quickly find there is a method to this chaos. Aallotar is the one in charge for now. This is Heidrunefoss, her thegn land, and as you saw, she is the one who sent messengers for aid. But I wouldn't be surprised if, now that Haldrek is here, she'll have him take charge. Or at least help her."

"Why?" If this was her campaign, why give control to someone else?

"Because he will become the next High King once the Blodnar have been destroyed. Once we get Drattüjert back, the push to rid Lohikärra of them will fall on his shoulders, and she will only need to deal with Heidrunefoss's issues. That shift may take place quickly, so it would make sense for them to work together at this point." Hrimfax shrugged. "At least, that would be my opinion. It's what warriors and thegns before us have done."

I nodded and continued to look around at the camp. It was massive, more so than the re-imagined war camps in the video games. I didn't know if this was just because we were within the area where the Heidrunefoss warriors had been camped, but there was a sense of organization within the chaos.

"I'll be honest. I didn't expect a war camp to be this big. It feels like it would be a huge target for the Blodnar."

Hrimfax shook his head. "Only as much as Aallotar's thegn hall is to us. For as evil as they are, the Blodnar aren't stupid. They know it would take a lot to stage a direct attack on a camp this size. Even without the warriors of Svartån and Svarhestån." He gestured at the camp around us. "Aallotar was raised to be a warrior. I mean all of us were, but after her uncle named her his heir, even more so. Living in Heidrunefoss and so close to Drattüjert, she's been in war camps her entire life. I'd be more surprised if she didn't know how to run one."

He guided me further into the center of camp, until all I could see were tents and flags for what I assumed was Heidrunefoss.

"Here we are." Hrimfax opened the tent flap and ushered me in. It took a moment for my eyes to adjust to the darkness. When they did, I saw three people standing at a table with maps and tokens a plenty on it. The three people looked up and for a moment, I felt as overwhelmed as I did on the first night I had been in Lohikärra.

Across from me stood Haldrek, in a set of thegn armor that was very impressive and imposing. I gasped a little as my chest lightened with excitement and I became more aware of our surroundings. Everyone here exuded strength and confidence, but he stood out, even among his peers. He'd looked powerful when wearing the armor borrowed from Svangendom, but now the small plates of leather and metal laced into horizontal rows resembled impervious dragon scales. I smiled, despite wanting to look impassive. On Haldrek's left was a woman who wore similarly styled thegn armor and an interesting hair style. Half of it was buzzed short, but the other side was combed over and cropped just below her ear. Lastly, there was an older man on Haldrek's right side. He also wore thegn armor, though more worn and beat up, and a loose ponytail of salt and pepper colored hair with a beard to match. His glare made me stand straighter. He was familiar, but it took me a moment to realize from where.

"Uncle Raynord!" Hrimfax's voice boomed and the older man's attention was diverted. I took a step toward the center table, giving Hrimfax room to enter the tent. Haldrek's face was alight with the biggest, toothiest smile I'd ever seen and even the woman I assumed to be Aallotar looked happy. She reached out and shook my hand. "It's a pleasure to finally meet, Thegn Svartån. Though it is strange to say that name and not see your father."

I smiled and shrugged. "I'm still getting used to the title myself."

"We'll see if you manage to hold yourself to a tenth of your father's capabilities, or show yourself to be an embarrassment to the house of Svartån."

"Uncle Raynord!" Haldrek, Aallotar, and Hrimfax all shouted at the same time as I focused on Raynord myself. Irritation and embarrassment replaced my initial emotions. He straightened up and crossed him arms over his chest.

"I am only saying what I'm seeing. She is young, green, and seems to be more aligned toward other pursuits. I don't know why you sent a messenger to her, Aallotar."

My cheeks flushed in the dimly lit tent. I was glad for the darkness.

"If I remember correctly, Uncle Raynord, my grandfather and my uncles often used those three descriptions for you. Svartån is known for its warriors. You can't deny their strength and valor," Aallotar retorted.

Raynord ignored the jab at his past. "I have no qualms with the warriors of Svartån. They have been proven time and again. *Her* though," he jabbed a finger in my direction. "I'd prefer not to fight with someone so inexperienced. If we are to win back Drattüjert, we need thegns who are able to fight, not just be a distraction. On the battlefield or off."

The accusations hit hard, digging into my insecurities, though I knew they weren't true. I was frozen. Part of me wanted to flee, but I knew that would just reinforce what Raynord was saying about me. I didn't want any more reasons for the other thegns to think I was a weak link or unable to fight.

"The only distraction right now is you," Aallotar snapped. "I don't know what your issue is with Thegn Svartån, but it needs to stop. If we start bickering, there is no chance of us taking back Drattüjert."

Raynord said nothing, choosing to look away instead.

Haldrek's smile disappeared and he looked between Raynord and Aallotar for a few moments before facing Hrimfax.

"It's nearly midday, cousin, is it not?"

Hrimfax nodded. "Yes, why?"

"I suggest we each take time to eat and rest. Not all day, but enough that we can think clearly again. I know I've been staring at this map for hours and I'm hungry." He turned to Aallotar. "What do you think?"

She nodded. "Food will serve us all well. Fresh air and sunlight too. We can return here in an hour or so and perhaps we'll all be in better moods." She glanced up at Raynord, who scowled. He said nothing, but moved toward the tent's door flaps.

Hrimfax opened a flap and moved outside, Aallotar following him. My heart sank. I had wanted to spend some time with Haldrek, but after the scene with Raynord, I was afraid staying in the tent would cause more trouble. As I turned around and moved toward the tent flaps, a familiar hand grabbed mine, pulling me further into the tent.

"*You* don't get to leave so quickly."

"*You* don't get to leave so quickly."

Chapter Ten

I smiled and let Haldrek pull me into his embrace. His beard tickled my cheek as he went to kiss my jawline and neck. I laughed a little as my body heated up. The thought of pulling his armor off flashed through my mind.

"You don't know how much I've missed you." He kissed the bottom of my earlobe, making me shudder as the nerves all over my body came alive with excitement. Even in places I didn't think they would.

Wrapping my arms around his neck, I whispered, "I've missed you too. But I thought you were hungry?"

He laughed, hot air hitting my neck. "I am hungry. I'm hungry to see you." He sat on a stool that I hadn't seen, pulling me into his lap at the same time. I straddled his waist to keep my balance while staying close. Despite our armor, being this close was electrifying.

His lips reached mine and began to explore them as I did the same, savoring the sweetness of honey that was still on his lips. How long had it been since we'd seen each other? Not just on our pendants, but in real life? Pulling him closer, I took in his smell, enjoying the familiar scent of campfire woodsmoke and sweat.

The tent door flap slapped open and I pulled away in surprise. Haldrek's hand tightened around my waist, holding me in place. In the sunlight pouring in, I saw Aallotar staring at us, lips pursed as if stifling a laugh. She held up a metal pot and some bowls.

"We had extra portions in my camp." She glanced at me. "I figured you and your warriors would be busy setting up camp, so I sent a little their way as well."

I nodded as she placed the food and bowls on the table.

"Thank you."

She nodded and looked at Haldrek. "I'll do my best to keep Raynord out of your hair. Just don't exert yourself too much, cousin." With that, she disappeared.

After a moment, Haldrek started chuckling. "Aallotar has always had the best timing."

"Is she going to be mad?" I pulled myself off his lap as my stomach grumbled. He reluctantly let me get up.

"Aallotar? No. She understands. As long as we fight hard alongside her, she doesn't care. She, Hrimfax, myself…We've been in too many battles and campaigns together." He began dishing up food into the two bowls and took it to a nearby box that seemed to serve as a makeshift table. "She has her own partner here at camp. So she understands."

I nodded and took a seat on one of the stools Haldrek had also brought over. It wasn't cushy, but I was able to relax. Just being in the same room as Haldrek made me feel better. More energized.

"How have your travels been? The last time we spoke, you had just joined up with Hrimfax."

"Pretty calm. I finally figured how to pitch a tent. Or at least a basic travel one."

Haldrek chuckled at that. "A very good skill that has served many a warrior well. I'm surprised that you didn't meet with any resistance. I know Svarhestån has been getting hit almost as hard as Heidrunefoss."

I stopped eating, my spoon mid-air as the night attack returned to my mind. Haldrek cocked his head as he watched me.

"Something happened?"

"Yes. I'm surprised I didn't tell you. I thought I had. We were attacked just after we got into Svarhestån. I mean, it was a small skirmish, but the attackers weren't all Blodnar."

"What do you mean?" Haldrek returned his spoon to the bowl, but continued to hold it.

"Modolf brought me to a man he'd fought and killed. The man wasn't Blodnar though. I could tell that from his spirit easily enough."

"What was he then?" Haldrek straightened up and put his bowl on the box.

"He wore the insignia of Etelaranikä. That's…"

Haldrek's jaw slackened and he stood up abruptly. "Curses to Lyrroth."

"Are you mad at me?" I stood up as well, my stomach clenched as I realized how much of an idiot I was for not being more concerned about the attack. I knew it was strange, but I hadn't thought it strange enough to mention, or give second thought, apparently. "I'm sorry."

Haldrek shook his head. "I'm not mad at you. This just complicates things. And it confirms my suspicions. *I* should have seen it coming." He began pacing around the tent. After a moment, he looked up at me. "You weren't hurt, were you?"

I shook my head. "By the time I was awakened, the skirmish was mostly over."

"How many people attacked your warriors?"

"At least a dozen. It wasn't just a scouting party; that I know."

Haldrek shook his head. "No, more like a raiding party. Like what hit my men and I. Only those who hit us were all Blodnar, at least as far as the armor went. Was this man wearing the Etelaranikän insignia, or was he trying to hide it?"

I shrugged. "I'll have to ask Modolf. He was the one who killed the man, so he would know. But the spirit seemed unusual."

"What do you mean?"

"Anger emanated from him, but not at me, or even Modolf. It was anger in general. Like at the situation. And betrayal. Modolf wanted me to send him to Lyrroth."

"You should have." Haldrek grumbled, still pacing.

"I got the impression that the man was only following orders. Yes, he probably would have tried to fight me had he gotten that far, but it wasn't personal. I sent him to Camroth. I felt that was a good compromise."

Haldrek shook his head. "You are merciful. The man betrayed his own people and fought alongside the Blodnar. Most thegns would have sent him to Lyrroth."

I paused, trying to form my question the best I could. It didn't seem fair that someone could be sent to a miserable afterlife because of orders they may or may not have agreed with. Or because the person doing their rite hated them. "Lohikärra has had many civil wars, hasn't it?" I thought back to the video games. At least in the lore, Lohikärra had more times of fractiousness than peace.

Haldrek nodded. "Why?"

"So warriors, who were otherwise good people but on the losing side, were always sent to Lyrroth?

He opened his mouth, then hesitated.

"The dragons deal with the realms of the afterlife, don't they?"

"To an extent. They can travel between them and give the dead that ability. But they don't necessarily watch over those realms."

"But if someone was given the wrong rites, or unfairly judged...like, is it permanent? Or is there an appeal process?"

Haldrek laughed. "An appeal process? I don't know what that means, but I can guess from the context." He shook his head. "Not that I know of."

"Then I guess it is better to err on the side of mercy." Images of my father flashed through my mind and I shivered.

Haldrek nodded. "Perhaps." He came over to hug me and exhaled. "I'm just glad you're safe. And I plan on doing everything I can to keep you safe. Until you're a haldraga, you're still fragile."

I groaned. "Am I the only thegn to not be a haldraga?"

He nodded, his beard tickling my ear. "I wouldn't worry though."

"Why not?" My heart sank as I realized that, though I figured it was true.

"You'll become a haldraga soon enough. You're important. At least the dragons think so. If you weren't important to them, then they wouldn't make you a haldraga. It's just a matter of time."

He guided me to our stools, encouraging me to sit.

"Let's continue our meal. We have much to do, both short term and long term. But it's been too long since we've spent time together and I'm not about to let that slip away."

The next morning, I woke up feeling as if I had a great weight on me. Hot air flowed across the back of my neck as I realized where I was. Haldrek's tent. As cozy as his body was against mine, the heat radiating from him was now stifling. Popping my head out of the fur blankets, I found myself in a cot with Haldrek curled up behind me. I brushed my hand behind me, feeling his undershirt and trousers.

I thought back to yesterday, or even last night. It was all hazy and my head throbbed, much like it had when I'd first tried mead. Yesterday had been an eventful one. While I'd been thrown into the logistics of war planning after lunch, after that, Haldrek and I had spent time together under the guise of him helping me orient myself to the camp and the area. We had returned to his tent and the Andrattür warriors for the evening meal, but beyond that, everything was hazy. I slipped my hand over my body, relieved to feel my pants, long shirt, and gambeson firmly in place. The anxiety that had begun to flood me receded, and I was grateful I hadn't done anything too crazy. At least that I could remember. I groaned and heard footsteps coming toward the tent. My panic returning, I dove under the blankets.

"Haldrek!"

The tent flaps snapped open and I held my breath, an easy feat given the smell of sweat and funky animal skins permeating the blankets.

"Haldrek! What are you doing? Why aren't you up?"

Haldrek groaned and grunted as he rolled from the bed. I grabbed tight to a fur blanket, hoping it's keep me covered. The last thing I need was more antagonism from Raynord. Before I could do anything more, the rest of the blankets dropped on top of me.

"I overslept. It happens from time to time. What are you doing in my tent, Raynord?"

"Getting you up. It is well past breakfast and Aallotar is waiting for you. And apparently Thegn Svartån as well, though I don't know why. Her time would be better spent doing other things."

Haldrek grunted again and I heard him dust himself off. "Like what?"

"If she must fight, she should be training now with her own warriors. It's not like she will have anything of value to say in the tent."

"You don't know that."

"I've lived and fought far longer than you, Haldrek. I've seen much, and I want to help you. As pretty as Svartån may be to you, there isn't an ounce of common sense in her head. Trust me. And trust me when I say she won't be a good High Queen. You will have a lot on your plate once you are High King. You need a strong woman by your side. Not just a pretty face."

Hot tears bubbled up in my eyes and I squeezed my chest tighter to keep from making a sound. I knew I wasn't going to be on friendly terms with every thegn. I mean, one had sent a freaking vampire to kill me. But I didn't expect this amount of animosity from people in Haldrek's family.

"No. It doesn't speak well of you to disparage Thegn Svartån. Once I am High King, the last thing I'll need is thegns bickering with each other." Haldrek's tone was low, irritation evident.

"That is why you need to choose your alliances—and your High Queen—with caution. Whoever stands with you will set an example for how Lohikärra will be led in the near future. You need someone who is savvy with the politics of Drattüjert. Not just a pretty face."

"Why recommend your granddaughters to me, then? In all my experience, they've been merely pretty faces fawning over Kalle's grandsons. I've yet to see them guide armies or outwit our enemies. As it is, we have not yet won back Drattüjert. I'm not yet High King. And Thegn Svartån has brought near five sattars with her. For someone whom you think so poorly of, she brought more warriors than you did. Knowing the warriors of Svartån, I'm guessing it isn't because she's a pretty face."

Raynord huffed. "Kamira and Quenby have traits better fitted to Drattüjert than Thegn Svartån ever will. They were raised there and know the subtle nuances of court life and dealing with emissaries. They also know how to fight. Perhaps not to the level that you or I do, but enough to defend themselves and those around them."

"Did you not see Drattüjert after the last battle there? It will be a long time before court life and emissaries will be like they were under Kalle. Drattüjert will need to be rebuilt." There was rustling on the dirt floor, as if someone was pacing around. Haldrek spoke again. "I'll be to the main tent soon. If Aallotar is in such a rush to speak with all of us, I should get ready and not spend my morning dealing with this. Give me a moment to get dressed, privately. I'll see you there."

Raynord grumbled, but said nothing. The tent flaps slapped back and forth, indicating that he'd left. A moment later, some of the animal skins were pulled off me gently. Haldrek's head popped into view.

"Rise and—" He exhaled and frowned. "I'm sorry you had to hear that. My uncle's rudeness is not warranted."

I popped out of the bed and wobbled as I stood up. Whatever we'd been drinking, the hangover wasn't fun. Not as bad as my first time, but still miserable. I wiped the tears from my face, embarrassed to be caught crying.

"I didn't expect Raynord to loathe me so quickly. He seemed standoffish at the coronation, but..."

Haldrek shook his head. "He is just eager to place one of his granddaughters in a position of power. All the thegns—at least those with children and grandchildren—do it. But his reasons don't sway me. I've known Kamira and Quenby too long to be attracted to either of them. As you and Mattie have mentioned before, marrying one's kin may not be such a great idea." He turned his back to me as he began getting ready for the day. He was right. Both Mattie and I'd mentioned briefly stories about royals intermarrying in the past and how that had affected those royal houses. Now with Raynord's insistence and current loathing toward me, another question popped into my head.

"How many of the other thegns have tried to arrange matches with you? You mentioned a few before, but have they all been like this?"

Haldrek nodded. "Most all of them with unmarried close kin. Even Gustav. Which," Haldrek pulled his gambeson on and grabbed his chainmail shirt, "if he's sending some of his warriors to aid the Blodnar in attacking fellow thegns..."

I helped him pull his chainmail over his gambeson. "Makes you less inclined to deal with him."

"I was never inclined to deal with him in the first place. Especially with my hunches about where his loyalty was during the battle for Drattüjert." Haldrek sighed. "I fully believe he betrayed us there. With the attack on your men, I think his loyalty is all but gone. He may have tried to match his daughter with me, but that was entirely a power move."

I sighed, my head still throbbing. "If we end up together, is that going to make it harder for you as High King?"

Haldrek wrapped his arms around me, squeezing me tight into his armored body. It clinked against my gambeson and I grunted.

"No matter who becomes my High Queen, there will be people who are upset that I didn't choose their relative. Yes, you may not have the court skills of Raynord's granddaughters, but you have the rebuilding skills and," he pulled away, "you and Mattie have knowledge from another world I think will help Lohikärra going forward. Aallotar was telling me about the weapons the Blodnar have started using. As much as I enjoy swinging a sword, I have a feeling we'll need to adapt to whatever the Blodnar are now using. The world is not how it was in our fathers' time."

He kissed me on the forehead. "We should probably get going. Aallotar is patient, but if we wait much longer, she may come looking for us herself."

Chapter Eleven

I took a long, roundabout path through the Andrattür camp, earning a few laughs and impish grins along my way. It made me wonder what rumors swirled about Haldrek and me, even before last night. We hadn't done anything, but no one knew that, and I wondered how much people assumed about us.

When I arrived at the main tent, the other four thegns were there. I gave Aallotar a feeble nod.

"Sorry for being late."

"Tardiness is the sign of a weak thegn," Raynord said behind me.

Haldrek and Hrimfax both glared at him, but Aallotar kept her focus on me.

"You're fine. Just be more prompt in the future. I like to converse with all the thegns at least once a day, usually just after breakfast."

I nodded and stepped up to an open space between Haldrek and Aallotar. It surprised me how tall she was. I wasn't short by any means, but she was easily a head taller than me. Looking between her and Haldrek, I guessed she was even taller than him.

"As I was saying, I've received more information about what the Blodnar are doing at Gunnsteinar," She looked at me. "I don't know if Haldrek mentioned it, but Gunnsteinar is the thegn hall in Heidrunefoss. I'd say it was mine, but I have yet to step foot in it since I became the thegn-heir."

I nodded, but said nothing as she returned her attention to the map and tokens in front of us. Near Aallotar's hand was a small leather bag that smelled like a mix between rotten eggs and manure. I wrinkled my nose and tried to focus on the conversation.

"The Blodnar use Gunnsteinar as a supply station for keeping their soldiers in and around Drattüjert. My informants have overheard word that while the Blodnar are in the city and are harassing those still there, they aren't able to get into the palace, as that is still physically protected by the dragons."

"One good piece of news," Raynord muttered. "Not much else."

My mind returned to the last dream I'd had with my father. He'd looked horrible. *Necromancer.* At least one person had gotten into the palace, if those whose corpses were still in the palace were being turned into zombies.

"Are…" I looked up and all of a sudden, everyone's attention was on me.

"It's not polite to interrupt, Thegn Svartån." Raynord sneered.

"A question. I had a question about that." I turned to Aallotar, hoping she wasn't as mad as Raynord. But she looked more curious.

"What?"

"Do the dragons ever leave the palace? To go on the attack or do other dragon things?"

Aallotar shook her head. "I don't know. My informants haven't gone directly to Drattüjert. Only to Gunnsteinar. Why?"

"I… I spoke to my dad recently and he said something bad is going on in the palace."

"You spoke to your father?" Raynord snapped, disbelief heavy in his tone.

"Ingmar had the same gift, uncle. Remember? Ina has mentioned as much to me." Haldrek replied. "He said there was a necromancer in Drattüjert."

Aallotar gasped and stared at me. "Are you sure?"

I nodded. "That's what my dad said, and he didn't look so good. Normally people in the Realm of Ghosts don't decay. Especially haldragas." I looked around for confirmation, but the other thegns shrugged and Raynord continued to glare at me. "Haldragas don't decay because of their connection to the dragons. At least that's what my ancestors wrote down. But my dad looked like he was falling apart, literally. Skin falling off, rotting, everything." I grimaced as I thought about it. "There's something going on inside the palace."

"Impossible." Raynord snapped. "The dragons would never let a necromancer in their midst. I doubt your vision was more than a delusion."

"It wasn't a vision. My father brought me to the Realm of Ghosts and we spoke. Like we had plenty of other times after he died. That's why I wondered if there were times when the dragons were away from the palace."

Aallotar grimaced and nodded. "I will send some of my people to see if they can get into the palace. If there is a necromancer, that will change our plans for Drattüjert. That said, we need to work on removing Gunnsteinar from Blodnar hands. The longer they have it, the more entrenched they will be and the longer they can use it for supplies." She looked over at Hrimfax. "My informants mentioned that they've been receiving large wagons of grain. I'm guessing it's from Svarhestån."

Hrimfax nodded. "There's a reason I could only bring three sattars with me. Most of my warriors are fighting the Blodnar in the south. They have done a lot of damage in the past few months."

Aallotar nodded. "If we can take back Gunnsteinar, we'll put the Blodnar on the run and without a place to store all of their stolen grain. We'll also regain that stolen grain for our warriors."

"But." Raynord paused to clear his throat. "If we go after Gunnsteinar first, those who escape may very well make their way to Drattüjert. Taking it would become even more difficult."

"But if we have Gunnsteinar, we'll have better quarters and supplies for our warriors." Aallotar countered.

"If we destroy the Blodnar at Gunnsteinar, there will be fewer fighters to steal from Svarhestån. We just have to kill as many of those bastards as we can when we get there," Hrimfax added.

"If they make their way to Drattüjert, the dragons can kill them," Haldrek added. He scratched his beard. "You know...we could try something."

"What?" Aallotar looked up from the map.

"How many warriors do we have now? Between the five of us?"

Aallotar tapped her finger on the map. "Almost fifteen sattars. Why?"

"We could try a diversion. Some of our troops ride for Drattüjert while others ride for Gunnsteinar. If the dragons start fighting while we are near Drattüjert, the Blodnar will think we're headed for the city and pull their soldiers from Gunnsteinar."

"What if they see the ruse and we have our warriors spread too thin?" Raynord snapped.

Haldrek turned to him. "If we fight alongside the dragons, we won't have to worry."

"We were fighting alongside the dragons when we *lost* the city, *nephew*. If you don't remember."

"I remember, *uncle*. I was in the palace when Kalle fell. I have every intention of taking the city back. But if we can get the Blodnar to leave Gunnsteinar, we'll lose fewer warriors in that battle and have a higher chance of taking the village and thegn hall."

"How many Blodnar are at Gunnsteinar?" I asked, ignoring Raynord and focusing on Aallotar.

"Five hundred at least. Which means if we came at them with our full force, we'd be evenly matched."

"Which is why it would be a mistake to split our forces. Because if the fighters at Gunnsteinar didn't leave, it would be too late to pull the other forces back and we'd be destroyed. I'll not have my warriors die in a fruitless battle."

"Then what would you suggest, Raynord?" Aallotar leaned across the table, staring him down. "Because it's been months since the Blodnar took Drattüjert and Gunnsteinar. It's been months since my people have had an easy night's rest. I know Drattrede doesn't have to worry about that, but some of us would like to remove the Blodnar from Lohikärra sooner rather than later."

"I suggest we find a less foolish plan."

"Can…" I hesitated and Raynord glared at me again. "Haldrek, are you able to speak with any of the other dragons? Whether through Teminth or through riding to where they might be?"

"It would be foolish for Haldrek to ride out alone searching for one of the dragons."

"He could take a squad of men with him." I snapped. Raynord was beginning to irritate me with all of his naysaying. Part of me wondered if he was always this bad tempered.

"I can speak with Teminth. Perhaps gaining his guidance will help us decide which plan is better—to take Gunnsteinar alone or try and trick the Blodnar into pulling their forces toward Drattüjert."

Aallotar nodded and put her hand on the hilt of her belt. "Good. Then it is settled for now. I need to practice with my warriors and figure out what in Sethys this stuff is." She grabbed the mysterious bag in front of her. "If we're done?"

The rest of us nodded and she left.

I left the tent and made my way back to where my warriors were training. Before I reached the edge of the Heidrunefoss camp, a hand grabbed my arm.

"Thegn Svartån. May I speak with you?"

I froze as my nerves started to burn with anxiety. Turning around, I saw Aallotar staring at me, her expression unreadable. In my mind, I thought about all the reasons she would have to stop me. She had said she was going to train with her warriors. Why stop me? Had I done or said something wrong?

"Sure?"

Aallotar laughed lightly, a smile lighting up her face. "I didn't mean to frighten you. I was just curious about some things. Come. Let's talk." She let go of my arm and we walked together, but I let her lead the way.

"I thought you were going to train with your warriors?"

"I am. Later today. I use that excuse to get out of gatherings that might go on longer than necessary. Uncle Raynord has been in a foul mood for a while now and he needs to get over himself."

"I think I have a little bit to do with that." I mumbled.

"Because of you and Haldrek? Probably. But still, we're in a war camp preparing for battle. If Raynord is focused on wedding one of his granddaughters to Haldrek in order to have more political control, he needs to stop. Focus on what's important right now. Which is taking back Drattüjert."

"I agree." I started jogging to keep up with her quick pace. Despite moving through both Andrattür's camp and mine, we were quickly in the grasslands outside of the perimeter and moving toward a patch of green trees that nestled at the base of the mountains.

"That said, I'm curious about some things." Aallotar had stopped on the path now that we were a fair distance from the camp and even far from where a few groups of warriors were training outside the camp. My anxiety shot up again. I placed my hand on my hilt to steady myself and Aallotar laughed.

"Probably shouldn't do that unless you're trying to intimidate someone. You don't intimidate me. Also, I didn't bring you here to beat you up. I want to get to know you better. Find out more about the mysterious new thegn who has completely smitten my cousin. You've been here less than six months and he's head over heels for you." She paused, scrutinizing me. "You don't seem to be intentionally beguiling him. It's just strange. A man who has devoted his life to his people and country, who has never had a lover as far as I know, now is enthralled with someone." She shook her head and sniffed. "Come on, I want to show you a place. It's hard to stay clean when you're in a camp full of men who could care less what they smell like."

I frowned and followed her. "Are you mad at me for being in a relationship with Haldrek?" Her actions confused me and I kept my distance, wondering if she'd turn into another person who tried to 'help' me as a guise for controlling me.

She shook her head. "I've known Haldrek since we could both barely walk. He's a brother to me. I've beaten him up and he's done the same. I just..." She laughed softly. "I just don't want him to get hurt."

I nodded. Aallotar wasn't trying to 'help' me or control me, per se. She wanted to protect Haldrek. And I guess, make sure I wasn't doing anything shady. Or have any secret motives. Honestly, I could understand that.

"I have no intention of hurting Haldrek. Ever. I..." I could say 'I love you' to Haldrek easily, but it felt weird to say it to someone else. Like they would laugh at me or dismiss me for it.

"You what?" Aallotar stopped as we reached the top of a tree-covered ridge. Below us was a large pond with a naturally tiered waterfall at the far end. Several groups of people, mostly women, gathered around the edge of pond, working on various tasks or bathing.

"I love him." Turning to her, I continued, "It probably sounds childish. I know he and I have only known each other for a few months, but he's been there for me since day one here and that's more than what I can say for a lot of people I've known during my life. Here and in Fargo."

"Do you love him, or do you just appreciate what he does for you? There's a difference." She turned to me.

"I love him. If he asked me to do the same things for him that he's done for me, I'd do it in a heartbeat. I trust him. I want him to be happy."

Aallotar smiled. "I'm glad to hear that." She began walking down the path that zigzagged to the large pond. "This is one of the reasons I chose this area for our camp. It's a bit unusual, but the pond here is fed by fresh mountain water every summer, making it the perfect place to bathe, wash, clean, and gather water for the camp."

"Hopefully you gather the water before people bathe in the pond." The words slipped out of my mouth and I froze. Aallotar nodded. "We're aware that drinking dirty water can make one sick. That's why the bathing and washing area is at the farthest point from the waterfall." She pointed downstream. "This place has been used like this for as long as I can remember. Who knows? Maybe Bjornulf and Freya used it as well."

Continuing down the path, I watched those working and saw how organized they were in their tasks. "I guess it takes a lot to keep an army camp from falling in on itself with disease and muck."

Aallotar nodded. "Do they have things like this where you're from? Fargo?"

"Not in Fargo, but around it. I mean Fargo is one city in a much larger place."

"How big?"

"I don't know the numbers, but it's basically fifty thegn lands combined together."

That made Aallotar stop. "*Fifty*? How do they stay together? I would think that many would always be bickering. It's difficult here with twelve."

"They do bicker. A lot." I didn't want to get into politics, but it hit me: Now that I was a thegn, politics would be my life. "But they have a strong central government. Not a High King and his court, but something like that. And it's worked so far."

"Does your High King, or his equivalent, rule for a lifetime?"

I shook my head. "At most, eight years. But much of the people around that position, and those who run the 'thegn lands,' usually are in their positions for a long time."

We made our way to the bottom, the sound of the waterfall much louder here. Aallotar leaned over from where she'd stopped. "Do you think you could be in a position like that your entire life?"

"I guess. I mean I'm the Thegn of Svartån now. I already made that choice."

She shook her head. "No. I mean if you and Haldrek end up together, you will be the High Queen. You two will be the face of Lohikärra and whom everyone, even the thegns, look to for guidance. People will constantly be watching you. Everything you do, you say...It's a difficult mantle. It was for my grandparents. Do you think you can handle it?"

The subtext of the question hit me hard. I knew what Aallotar was asking. Once they reclaimed Drattüjert, Haldrek would become High King. If he and I ended up together, if we got married at any point in the future, I would become the High Queen, along with being the Thegn of Svartån. I would need to support him in that position. It was something that had been in the edge of my mind for the past few months. Something I'd ignored for more pressing matters.

Before I could say anything, a woman came running over to Aallotar and tackled her with a hug. Aallotar started laughing and kissed her on the lips. Heat rushed to my cheeks and I looked away. A whiff of my own body odor escaped my armor and I grimaced. While Aallotar was busy, I slipped away to where a few other women were bathing and began to take off my armor. I figured I could bathe in my shift and underwear, so I didn't have to get completely naked and vulnerable. It would be like swimming, right?

As soon as I was waist deep in the chilled water, I plunged below the surface, letting the water close in around me. The coldness drew my focus from the thoughts and feelings swirling in my head and for a split second, everything was calm.

I re-emerged from the water to find Aallotar's face next to mine. I jerked away from her, trying not to scream. She held up her hands, eyes wide at my reaction.

"Did I scare you back there?"

I stared at her for a moment, then looked back at the woman on the small beach watching us.

"No. I just figured you wanted a private moment. I'm not one for public displays of affection, and I realized how much I stunk." Weakly, I laughed to ease any tension.

"Oh. No worries." Aallotar waved the woman over. She quickly began undressing and Aallotar turned back to me. "Vilde is my partner. My lover." She hesitated. "What do people from Fargo think of women lovers?"

My cheeks warmed up again despite the icy cold water. "Uh, Fargo in particular, or my world in general?"

"Either. I ask because there are some here in Lohikärra who frown on lovers like myself and Vilde. There are others who only care if there is no offspring to account for."

"It depends on who you ask, honestly. Younger generations are more accepting of it, I think. I had a friend back in Fargo. He had a boyfriend. I didn't care. They were some of the few people who were nice to me, even before they got together."

"I'm glad to hear that." Aallotar replied as Vilde joined us. "Vilde is one of the few people, outside of my cousins, whom I trust with my life." She smiled at Vilde for a moment. "I have no intention of fighting my cousin for the title of High King. If anything, I hope he has someone like Vilde by his side." Aallotar smiled again, this time at me. "If you end up with him, perhaps he will."

That evening, after the interesting conversation at the watering hole and after training with my warriors to the point where I was just as sweaty and gross as before, I found myself in Haldrek's tent again, eating a hearty and filling war camp stew with him. The food was enjoyable, and after a day full of mental, emotional, and physical exertion, it was nice to relax with Haldrek. As I ate, Haldrek rubbed some knots out of my shoulders and we talked about my conversation with Aallotar. As he went over one particularly hard one, I groaned and he laughed.

"Aallotar has always been fiercely protective of those she is close to. She is a good friend and ally to have. I probably should have told her to be easier on you."

I flinched and moaned as he dug his thumb into my shoulder. The nerves in my left arm and hand tingled like they had fallen asleep.

"I'm used to people not trusting me. And I don't blame her." I gasped as the knot in my shoulder popped under Haldrek's thumb. "I know…it's hard…to trust…new people."

He began to rub my upper arms as the pins and needles sensation went away and my muscles felt more relaxed.

"You never seemed like an untrustworthy person to me. And I've met my share."

I took another bite of my food and washed it down with some water from the waterfall. "I was considered the weird kid growing up. Other children wouldn't play with me. Weird equaled untrustworthy. One time they made up a rude song about me and how I wasn't allowed to play with them. Until Mattie arrived, my only two friends were Henry and Alex. They were big into the Lohikärran games as well." I sighed.

It'd been years since I'd talked to either of them. Around the time Mattie had arrived, they convinced us to come over to play one of the games. We'd had fun and nothing happened, but my mother had been livid, telling me that she was "breaking up our friendship" because Henry was such a bad influence. After that, neither Henry nor Alex talked much to me.

Haldrek placed his hands on my waist and began kissing my neck. My nerves surged with electricity, in a good way, and I giggled as his beard rubbed against my jaw and chest.

"Well, the past is the past. And children can be very immature. If anyone tries to exclude you, they'll have to deal with me."

"Like your uncle?" Our meeting replayed in my head as I tried to figure out how to tolerate Raynord. The man was never going to like me as long as I was a threat to his political plans, but I still had to work with him in order to help Haldrek and Aallotar.

"Mmhmm." Haldrek nibbled my ear a little, then sat back. "Raynord needs to realize that I'm not going to marry either of his granddaughters. Even if you weren't around, or had no interest in me, I still wouldn't marry Kamira or Quenby. Not just because they're related to me, but because I don't think either of them would do well as High Queen. They have been trained to work in the circles of Drattüjert, talking to emissaries and gossiping. Those circles no longer exist, and it will be a long time before emissaries return to Drattüjert." Now it was Haldrek's turn to sigh. He got up and grabbed a bag from off a small crate near where he slept.

"Aallotar brought this to me this afternoon. Her informants brought it to her from Gunnsteinar. It's something the Blodnar are hoarding, but they haven't used it yet. We don't have any alchemists in camp, so we've be trying to figure it out, to no avail."

I took the bag in my hand. It was the same stinky substance I'd seen Aallotar playing with earlier. Rotten eggs and manure. Opening it, I was surprised to find a dry, grainy substance instead of the sticky sludge I expected.

"Is this...?" I didn't dare taste it, but it looked familiar. Like something from in Fargo. "Is this gunpowder?"

Haldrek shrugged his shoulders.

I took a few grains and created a small bowl of dirt to surround the grains. Then I lit a nearby stick from the candle that Haldrek had for light and carefully placed the fiery edge of the stick next to the grains. They exploded with a loud pop and Haldrek pushed me away from the small explosion. He stamped on the pile, grinding it into the dirt.

Looking at him in surprise, I asked, "No one checked to see if it exploded?"

Haldrek shrugged. "Aallotar gave it to me to see if I knew what it was. How did you know it was...what did you call it? Gunpowder?"

I nodded. "It's used in my world for a lot of things. Mostly guns. It's a type of weapon. Like a bow and arrow, but handheld and faster, more deadly." I sat up and grabbed the bag, tying it up again. "I knew a few kids in my school who would come to class smelling like gunpowder. Not this exactly, just the rotten egg part. They'd make their own ammunition for hunting animals."

"Somehow, I don't think the Blodnar are using this for hunting food."

I shook my head. "Guns can be used for hunting, but mostly people use them for fighting. Like in wars and such. But I'm confused how the Blodnar got this. It makes sense that they are hoarding it. They're obviously using it for some kind of weapon, but where did they find it? How did they make it? Why now?" I hesitated. "Gunpowder was a game changer in my world when it came to fighting." I picked up Haldrek's chainmail shirt. "Armor like this was made obsolete. Instead of arrows, guns have little metal bullets and the gunpowder goes behind it and punches right through most obstacles." I gestured to the smothered gunpowder grains. "This gunpowder is rougher than the stuff I saw in Fargo, but..."

"It's still explosive." Haldrek said softly. "I'll have to let Aallotar know what you've told me. Maybe the next time we meet over strategy tomorrow, you can help me explain."

"If Raynord will stop staring daggers at me."

Haldrek laughed and pulled me onto his lap, so we were facing each other. He moved my legs so they wrapped around his waist. "I can't stop him from staring at you, but if he gets rude again, I'll tell him to knock it off." Haldrek nuzzled his nose and mouth into the crook of my neck. He began kissing me again and I moaned a little bit. After the stress of today, it was nice to just relax with him.

"I'm glad you came," he whispered in between kisses. "And not just because you brought the most warriors of all of us. I missed you."

"I missed you too." Pulling his mouth to mine, I brushed my tongue against his lips. He smiled and began to kiss me more eagerly. Because of the heat of the day, we were in our linen shirts and leather pants, having left the armor aside. Haldrek's hand stroked up my side and back, tracing my ribcage and just below my breasts. My skin craved his touch with every passing second and I enjoyed the caress, but at the same time, anxiety pulled my thoughts from the pleasure of the moment. I began to focus on where his hand was. I suddenly felt very naked without my armor. Taking a deep breath, I tried to focus on his lips and take his hand in mine. Still, it went lower as he stroked my belly button. That sent chills up my spine, so I shifted off of his lap and onto his knee, my thoughts torn between increasing panic and my desire to not hurt his feelings. He pulled me back on, his kisses getting hungrier as his hand brushed down to my hip. He began caressing my thigh, rubbing and kneading it as I leaned backwards and he leaned with me. His hand stroked the inside of my thigh, gently tugging on it as I hit the ground.

"Haldrek!" I pulled away from him as the Fargo house flashed in my mind's eye. Instead of Haldrek, I felt Robert touching me.

As quickly as the image came, it disappeared. I found myself staring at Haldrek, my chest thumping hard. He stared at me, eyes wide with confusion. His pants were a little tight and as he caught my stare, he placed his hand over his crotch. Tears began to blur my sight as I scrambled to sit upright.

"I'm sorry, Ina."

"I... I..." My cheeks were hotter than before, and while part of me wanted to curl up in Haldrek's arms, the other part of me wanted to flee. "I'm sorry." Thoughts flooded my mind of how stupid I was, how Haldrek and I were too close, how slutty I was being, how I wasn't focusing on being a fighter and a thegn. My mother's voice echoed in my head, louder than it had been in months, telling me how I was a whore and frigid at the same time. That I was leading men on. Why was it okay that Haldrek could touch me and not Robert?

I didn't realize I was shaking until Haldrek touched my shoulder. He knelt in front of me.

"I'm sorry. I wasn't thinking."

I shook my head and wiped my nose. "I enjoyed the kissing, but when you touched my leg, I got flashbacks of home. Memories from Fargo I didn't want to remember."

He nodded and grimaced as he shifted. "I shouldn't have been so eager."

"I don't blame you." I laughed weakly to ease the tension. "Just... I'm stupid. I'm... I dunno. Do you hate me?"

Haldrek laughed, his tone much lighter. "No. I don't hate you. Would I like to do more than kissing? Yes. But I would never force you to anything you're not comfortable with." He sighed. "I may have to take care of some stuff tonight though, so maybe we should part for the evening."

My heart constricted. I knew I'd have to leave at some point. After the first night, I had returned to my tent every night. But I didn't want to leave on such an awkward note.

"I'm sorry."

He shook his head, groaning a little bit while not looking at me. "You don't have anything to be sorry about." Taking a deep breathe, he added, "I love you, Ina."

"I love you too."

He gestured to the tent entrance with his head.

"I'll see you at the thegn meeting tomorrow, all right?"

"All right. I...I hope you feel better." Inside, I cringed, feeling responsible for his sudden change in mood.

Slowly, I left his tent with my armor, hating myself a little more with every step.

Chapter Twelve

The cacophony of metal, wood, and feet pounding in the dirt around my tent, woke me up the next morning. Quickly, I put on my gear, wondering what was going on outside. My thoughts flashed back to the surprise raid in Svarhestån and I grabbed my blade and shield. As soon as I left the tent, I saw my warriors rushing around, gesiths and *skjarals* frantically throwing out orders. Modolf ran by me and caught my eye. He stopped, relief flooding his face.

"You're wake, my thegn! The Blodnar, they approach!" His face lit up a little and he hurried off, charging after a group of warriors.

"What?!" I looked around, having no idea what to do, but knowing I was supposed to be guiding my men. No one had mentioned what exactly I should be doing in this situation. Why hadn't anyone woken me up?

A warrior came running up to me with my horse. He bowed quickly. "My thegn, they'll want you at the far edge of the camp. We'll follow behind you." I took the reins from him and nodded, still having no clue what to do. At least I had a destination and my armor on.

As I made my way through Andrattür's camp, memories of the previous night hit me like arrows, piercing my heart. What happened if Haldrek or I got hurt or killed during this battle, skirmish, whatever was going on? I didn't want last night to be the last memory he had of the two of us.

Following the warriors from the other thegn lands, I found myself on a ridge, with warriors of Heidrunefoss on my right and warriors carrying the insignia of Svarhestån on my left. A few yards away, Hrimfax sat on horseback, directing both his foot soldiers and calvary into various formations. I got on my horse and began mirroring his body language.

After a moment, he caught sight of me and nodded. Guiding his horse through his warriors, he smiled enthusiastically.

"Your first battle, Thegn Svartån! May we meet at battle's end with blood-stained blade and mead in our hand!"

"*What?*" My heart seized for a split second.

He laughed. "It's an oath we say to wish victory on one another." He gestured to where my men were forming a shield wall on the edge of the ridge. "The Blodnar are in the valley below us. Their commander is hurling insults at Haldrek, demanding he submit. When Haldrek gives the command, we attack."

"And?" I had no idea how Haldrek wanted us to attack.

Hrimfax's smile faded as he turned serious. "Keep your warriors at a slow march coming down the hill. Then they need to charge. Once we're on the field, we'll be within range of their archers and catapults."

My eyes widened as Hrimfax turned around to stand with his own men. My stomach tightened into a knot. If I'd eaten anything this morning, I would have thrown up right then and there.

"My thegn!"

I turned to see Modolf waving to me. "We await your leadership at the ridge."

Nodding, I led my horse through my men as they shifted around me. As soon as I reached the ridge, I stared into the valley. Sure enough, there were three square formations of Blodnar. Their shields created a tight shell around the warriors and archers in the center. Behind them were three tall catapults, ready to launch. In between the catapults were two shorter, more squat launchers. The launchers held what looked like massive arrows. I knew little about warfare, but those catapults and launchers had the ability to do more damage to our forces than anything else.

Looking to the other forces on the ridge, it baffled me that the Blodnar had pulled their troops away from the thegn hall and village. Why attack us here when they could just hole up in the thegn hall and we'd have to fight them there? Wasn't the thegn hall heavily defensible?

"My thegn, what are your orders?"

I looked down to see one of my gesiths staring at me. Turning to the valley below, I wondered if the other gesiths had a cohesive plan. If they did, I didn't know about it.

"Ignore the Blodnar in front. Go after the catapults and those launchers between them."

"Ignore the Blodnar fighters, my thegn?" He raised an eyebrow.

I pointed to the catapults and launchers. "I mean, we'll need to fight through them, but those catapults will kill more Lohikärran warriors than any group of fighters. Trust me. If we destroy those things, then we can sweep up and destroy whatever Blodnar soldiers are left over."

The man glanced into the valley and nodded. "I'll let my men know."

"Let the other gesiths know, too. Chances are the Blodnar will try to protect those things at all costs."

He nodded and disappeared into the sea of warriors behind me. A shout to my right got my attention, and I turned to see Haldrek shouting at a man in the valley. A knot pushed up into my throat. Andrattür's warriors began to rustle, their shields and weapons moving with a nervous energy. They were ready for a fight. Many of them had likely fought at the battle of Drattüjert. That energy made its way across all of the warriors, mine included, and I straightened up, preparing myself to ride with one hand on my horse's reins and the other on my sword hilt.

"For Drattüjert!" The anger in Haldrek's voice made his words louder and clearer than before.

Everyone began moving down the ridge. I rode with them, my horse gaining speed as it kept in line with my first row of warriors. I unsheathed my sword and ducked my head as arrows sped over it. My horse made a beeline for the left-most Blodnar soldier box just as it shifted to our right. Surprised, I glanced up to see a far-right chunk of the Lohikärran warriors pull away, the Blodnar shifting to fill that hole.

And then we hit. I turned just in time to see my horse jump over some shield bearers and land on Blodnar archers, taking them to the ground. Screams and war cries echoed all around me as the square pulled apart and I began swinging my sword, cutting and stabbing anything that came near me with a spear or blade.

The Blodnar continued to shift right as something grabbed my foot, trying to pull me off my horse. My saddle slackened underneath me and I tumbled off, landing face first into the dirt and mud.

A blade stabbed the mud next to my neck as I was pulled up by the back of my armor. I was greeted by a Blodnar soldier with a spear head sticking out of his neck, blood pouring from the injury. The spear pulled back and the man fell to the ground in front of me, only to be replaced by another Blodnar face. The man thrust a dagger in my face as I blocked it with the shield still miraculously attached to my arm. The chaos around me was disorienting, and made me want to scream. I shoved forward into the man, knocking him to the ground and sticking my sword through his armor as I moved forward.

"Calvary!"

I turned to my left to see a handful of Blodnar calvary coming at me. The lead horseman grinned maniacally as we made eye contact, his sword raised high in attack. I raised my shield and braced for his attack. As soon as I saw his horse's leg, I slammed my blade into it. The horse's shriek hurt my ears as both man and beast fell to the ground.

Someone pulled me away as the other horsemen stampeded over the man, crushing him before he had a chance to get up. I gasped, then was pushed forward.

"Into the gap!" I shouted, my voice louder and more guttural. It sounded nothing like it had ever before.

My warriors surged forward and I with them. Blodnar soldiers came at us from the right as we aimed for the catapults and other siege weapons, some of which were already being attacked. One of the smaller weapons twisted toward my men and I saw the bolt in it get pulled back.

"Attack!" I shouted, hoping the warriors closest to it would prevent the bolt from launching. But as I spoke, the bolt released and I watched it hurtle toward me. My legs refused to move, as if I was in a dream. Someone shoved me to the left as the bolt grazed past me and I felt the air from it hit my armor. I tumbled into the dirt and twisted around to see where the bolt had landed. It lay embedded in the ground, Modolf slumped over it like a rag doll.

"Modolf!" I screamed, my voice raw with pain. Had he just…? No. He had to be okay. He couldn't die. Why wasn't he moving?

Another warrior picked me up and shouted, "He's dead, my thegn. But we've got the hall! And look! The dragons!"

I looked around to see the siege weapons all but destroyed, the fields now hazy and thick with blue fog. Dragons sailed in from the right side of the village, and I wondered if they had just arrived or if they had been waiting for all of us to slaughter each other. A few Blodnar stumbled around, but most of the fighting was done.

We had won. But at what cost?

My warriors helped me through the village. Despite the fact that my body was only mildly sore, I had a hard time walking straight. As we reached the hall's courtyard, there were warriors laying on the ground, being tended to, and bluish Blodnar ghosts scrambling as if still fighting.

Outside of my thoughts, I could hear voices, but they felt distant.

"Where are the thegns?"

"In the hall proper. Some of them got pretty messed up." Someone stared at me, but I didn't have the strength to look back. "She might be in charge soon. Hope she isn't messed up too."

The warriors helping me walked up a set of stairs and through the massive doors. The smell of something metallic overwhelmed the air and made me wrinkle my nose. I looked around at the mass of bodies. Were they dead too? No. Some were moving. They were injured.

"Thegn-heir Heidrunefoss." The man next to me bowed and I turned to stare at Aallotar, her face, hair, and armor discolored with red and brown. I blinked and tried to focus on her.

"I'll help her from here. I know that look when I see it."

I frowned, confused about what they were talking about. What look? Did I look weird? Aallotar walked with me as I stared directly ahead. She didn't say anything as we moved into a smaller side room. People were bustling in and out, but they looked far less injured than the warriors within the thegn hall. Aallotar sat me in a chair with arms, and despite the lack of fabric or padding on it, I sank into it, letting my muscles relax.

"Curse our luck. *She* survived."

I looked up at Raynord scowling at me. What the hell was his problem?

"Were you wanting me to die out there?" I snapped. "Sorry about that."

He sneered. "You may be a thegn, but you're expendable. It's not like you've trained your whole life for this. How many of your warriors are left standing? A handful? Did you even know what you were doing?"

Before I could say something, Aallotar turned to Raynord and jabbed him in the chest. "Shut up. I could ask you the same thing. You peeled off your warriors as soon as we were off the ridge, leaving Haldrek's flank exposed. If Haldrek dies, you are the one I'm holding responsible."

I turned to her, stunned. "Where is Haldrek? And Hrimfax?"

Aallotar grimaced. "My cousins are still with us, for now. Hrimfax is about as beat up as you. Haldrek, on the other hand..." She turned to glare at Raynord. He straightened up under her stare. "He had to protect his right flank and nearly died for it." Raynord looked away.

"Haldrek is..." Panic flooded me and I stood up before my knees gave way. Aallotar grabbed me and sat me back down.

"Haldrek will be fine. He's a haldraga. We're more durable than most warriors. You need to rest. I have my best healers tending to Haldrek and I'll have others help you."

I stared at her for a moment and then nodded. Healers. We'd need a lot of healers for all the injured that we had. Had any of my Hethurin warriors survived? Would they be treated here or left to die? Could they help Haldrek?

Footsteps rushed toward us and I twitched. Aallotar glanced at me before focusing on the young woman who had come running over. Her clothes were covered in blood nearly as much as Aallotar's, but she wore no armor. She looked familiar as well, but I couldn't remember her name. Almost as if it was just out of reach within my brain.

"Aallotar, Thegn Andrattür keeps refusing to let any of us healers touch him. He keeps saying 'Svartån'."

Aallotar grimaced. "My cousin is a stubborn one. Tell him I have Ina and she is alive. I'm assuming that's what he's worried about."

Raynord huffed and Aallotar gave him a death stare. When she returned her focus on the young woman, she hugged her. "I'll bring Ina upstairs, and then I need to tend to my warriors and check on the estate. I promise I'm fine."

The woman nodded, then scrutinized me. She glanced at Aallotar and said, "I'll bring something for Thegn Svartån as well."

"No need." Raynord snapped. "Let the fittest survive."

Aallotar spun on him, her face hard as stone. Raynord was stupid if he thought trifling with her was the best thing right now.

"You may stay in the thegn hall long enough to be healed. But as soon as you are in fighting condition, you can set your camp *outside* the village walls. Understood?"

Raynord gaped, then scowled at her. "Tread carefully, Aallotar. It's not wise to alienate your allies." He said nothing more, hurrying off into another room.

Aallotar turned to me, the edges of her eyes sagging with exhaustion. She was tired. I was tired. We were all tired.

"Do you understand me?"

I blinked. "Huh?"

She grimaced and helped me up. "Let's go see Haldrek and Hrimfax. I'll let my cousin know you need rest as well."

We left the room and walked up a set of stairs to the second floor. This hall looked somewhat like Svangendom, but certain things were different. More stone, less wood. The smell from downstairs permeated this area, as did the moans and cries of the injured.

"I'm going to take you to the same room as Haldrek, but he was pretty badly hurt. I need you to be calm when you see him."

My gut twisted and grew heavy, like I'd just swallowed a stone. "He's going to be okay, right?"

"He'll survive, if that's what you mean. But he may not have the same pretty face." Aallotar laughed, but I could sense the anger and bitterness in it. "If we didn't need Raynord and his warriors right now, I would have railed on him to Lyrroth and back. Whatever is going on in his head...I dunno. He was a mighty fighter when I was a child. I respected him. But after today, we'll see."

"Do you think he was intentionally trying to get Haldrek killed?"

Aallotar shook her head. "I think he was trying to show off. Pull the Blodnar's attention away. I dunno. But I don't think he was trying to kill Haldrek. If that had happened, you would be High Queen and his power moves would all be foiled."

We arrived at the room as a healer left, her hands covered in blood. She bowed to Aallotar. "We're doing as much as we can, but it may be up to the dragons now."

I straightened up, looking between the grim expressions on both her and Aallotar's faces. "Go find where the Svartån warriors have gathered. Ask for one or two Hethurin. If they are still alive, they'll be able to help."

The healer frowned. "But we've done—"

"Do as she says." Aallotar snapped and the woman ran off. She turned to me. "What are you thinking? That the Hethurin know more than my healers?"

I hesitated, not wanting to alienate Aallotar. "They're more in tune with healing and growth magic than anyone I know. A few at Svangendom healed me when I nearly killed myself."

Aallotar nodded and ushered me into the room. "I hope those who came with you are able to help."

I nodded as I watched the crowd of people in the corner, hovering over what I expected was Haldrek's bed. One of the people looked up and smiled. Hrimfax.

He gestured for me to come. Time seemed to take forever as I wondered what I would see when I got over there. I hoped and prayed that Haldrek would be okay. That he would recover. I didn't want to lose him. I didn't want to be High Queen if that meant he was dead.

When I reached his side, I gasped and knelt on the stone floor. His face was puffy and bruised, blood covering whatever wasn't injured. His armor had been pulled off and replaced with tight bandages across his entire torso. I didn't know how long they had been on him. I assumed not long, but some were already turning red. He stared up at the ceiling, his breathing shallow and slow.

"Haldrek?"

His eyes turned to me and his mouth quirked up. He made a sound, then grimaced.

"Don't talk. Just rest. I'm fine. Physically at least." I didn't know how to explain how I was feeling. Everything was still surreal, like this was a game or movie and not real. Either way, Haldrek didn't need to deal with that. If he was worried about me, I wanted to ease that worry, not increase it.

"Haldrek has been calling for you, much to the frustration of the healers. I think, in part, because you aren't a haldraga yet." Hrimfax said, his voice barely audible.

"Why? Does that matter?"

Haldrek made another sound and I squeezed his hand to comfort him.

"Being bound to a dragon gives a warrior extra strength and durability, so to speak. If you aren't a haldraga, it's easier for you to die in battle."

"Well, I'm not dead yet." I returned my focus to Haldrek. "And you're not allowed to die. I'll have my dad kick you back to the realm of the living, zombie or no zombie." Haldrek said nothing, but his mouth quirked up again.

Footsteps hurried into the room behind us and I looked up to see one of my warriors push in between people and stand next to me. I didn't remember his name, but I remembered him from Svangendom and knew he was a Hethurin.

"My thegn, I was told to come to your aid."

"Is there anything you can do for Thegn Andrattür?"

He looked over Haldrek and then raised his hands over Haldrek's torso. After a moment, he nodded. "I won't be able to completely heal him, but I can heal some of the internal bleeding."

"There's internal bleeding?" My eyes widened. "Yes. Do what you can to help him."

He nodded and placed his hands on Haldrek's torso. A golden glow emanated from the Hethurin's hands and Haldrek grimaced, squeezing my hand.

After a moment, he relaxed and his breathing grew more relaxed. Deeper.

"That's all I trust myself to do right now. I've stopped the bleeding on the inside." The Hethurin looked around at a few people around us. "The other healers can probably take over now. But Thegn Andrattür will need lots of rest to be fully healed."

"Thank you."

He slipped away and through the crowd as I focused on Haldrek. "You heard him. Rest. I'm not going anywhere." Giving him a kiss on the forehead, I stood up and tried not to wobble.

"Thank you, Ina." Both Hrimfax and Aallotar spoke at the same time.

Aallotar gestured for me to follow her. "If you are feeling better, I wanted to speak to you about something."

I nodded, and with one last glance at Haldrek, I followed her.

Chapter Thirteen

I walked with Aallotar along a long path that paralleled the rear part of the main hall. On either side, open rooms were filled with cots. They had once held Blodnar soldiers and now held injured Lohikärrans. We passed them and into another hallway that curled around and then straightened out. On our left was door after door leading to various rooms, some of them already in use and others still closed off.

"I know this place like the back of my hand. Growing up, it was my refuge. As much as I loved my grandparents and the palace at Drattüjert, there was still too much scandal over my heritage to truly feel comfortable there. My uncle and his partner, Saami, were my safe place. I knew I could roam this thegn hall without servants looking at me reproachfully or people whispering behind my back."

I nodded but said nothing. Aallotar's backstory...I remembered hearing something about it, but I couldn't remember specifics. Anything from before this morning felt hazy now in my mind.

Aallotar turned to me and smiled. "That's neither here nor there now, I suppose. I have a question for you. Before we realized the Blodnar were preparing for battle, Haldrek mentioned something." She opened one of the closed doors. I followed her in and saw a room filled with maps, papers, and a large open barrel full of something that smelled worse than the metallic stench downstairs.

"Whoever put this in here was either an idiot or planning to blow this whole place to Lyrroth. Haldrek said you called this stuff gunpowder?"

I nodded. "Yeah, it's an explosive used a lot where I'm from." The bolt launcher came back to mind. There had been so much chaos on the battle field. Had they used the gunpowder for that, or were they planning something else?

Aallotar looked at the papers on the table, talking more to herself than to me. "They've been using this to power some kind of weapon to take down dragons. Did they use this stuff in the battle of Drattüjert?" Her eyes widened for a minute before looking at me.

I stared at the papers on the table. The words were gibberish to me, some language other than English or Lohikärran runes. But the rudimentary drawings were perfectly clear. Whatever machine they were using the gunpowder for, hadn't been on the field today, but the Blodnar had been tinkering with it.

"They might have the machines fully or partially completed. We can see how the Blodnar plan to use them."

"I had the same idea. Some of my warriors are looking for the machines within the hall and the village as we speak. But in the meantime, tell me what you know about this gunpowder. And if you need to rest, let me know. Today was difficult for all of us, but I know this is difficult. You weren't raised to fight like the rest of us were."

I nodded and my head swam. Looking around, I sat on a stool next to the table. "This isn't as refined as the gunpowder we had in Fargo. You know it makes things explode. Keep it away from heat and fire. It also needs to stay dry if you want to use it."

Aallotar's head popped up. "How do we use it?"

I inhaled. Some of the kids from the outlying farms knew how to make their own ammunition, but I didn't know any specifics.

"In Fargo, they'd take a piece of ammo. A metal bullet. Put gunpowder behind it and put that all in a metal case. Then the gun would light the gunpowder and that would shoot the bullet. I don't know the specifics, but that's the gist of it."

Aallotar nodded. "Not a quick fix, but something to explore in the future. Good to know." She hesitated, then said, "I'm glad you and Haldrek's half-sister are on our side. If our neighbors are using new magic or technology, we need to learn how to use it. At the very least to defend ourselves. But I'd rather use it for offensive measures."

"Offensive measures?"

Aallotar nodded. "The Blodnar and their empire have beaten and bruised Lohikärra for far too long. I'd love to take the battle to them. But..." She returned her focus to the papers on the table. "That will be up to Haldrek, and possibly you, in the future." Turning to me, she smiled. "Either way, I consider you an asset to our side, even if Raynord is being a bastard. Idiot could have lost us both the battle and the war."

"Did we lose a lot of men in this battle?" The thought of Modolf pushing me out of the way of that bolt made me shudder.

Aallotar shook her head. "I don't know yet. We had fifteen hundred, give or take, to the Blodnar's five hundred. When their commander brought his forces to us, he did us a favor." She laughed. "Probably didn't realize until the last moment just how many people we had."

"I'm surprised he didn't send spies."

"He did. They didn't make it far." Aallotar's smile hinted at something unspoken. It made my head spin. I tried not to worry about it for now. Everything was already so spacey and dreamlike—any new information poured through my thoughts like sand.

Our conversation lulled for a bit as I listened to moans and groans, as well as some crying, in the rooms around us. I hoped my warriors were doing okay. I knew I should check on them once I didn't feel so removed from everything.

"I will never forgive the Blodnar for what they've done to my people. My family," Aallotar whispered, anger filling every word. My attention reverted to her. "As soon as we take Drattüjert back, as soon as this war is over, every man, woman, and child with a drop of Blodnar blood will be removed from Heidrunefoss. And if I were in charge, all of Lohikärra."

My skin prickled and my head swam as I tried to think of something to say. A voice inside my head told me I should question that. Another voice told me not to rock the boat.

"Even those who never held a blade?"

Aallotar frowned. "No one of Blodnar ancestry can be trusted, Ina. They've been trying to destroy us since I was a small child. They killed my grandparents, my beloved uncles, my cousins, with no mercy. Why in Lyrroth should I show them mercy?"

"Because people don't necessarily get to choose who they are born to." I hesitated, not wanting to get into a fight with Aallotar. "The Hethurin—"

She bobbed her head in annoyance. "Yes, yes, the Hethurin. Half elf, half human. I know of their loyalty and skill. I saw it under your father and now under you. But the Blodnar and *their* half-breeds—they have neither loyalty nor skill."

I sighed, my head still spinning and my exhaustion growing. Changing minds would have to wait for another day. If it came at all.

"What would people in your world do in a situation like this?"

I looked up. Aallotar still stood staring at the papers on the table.

"It would depend." Honestly, I didn't think people back home would have a much different reaction. Though they wouldn't call for killing or eliminating people just because of their ancestry. Hopefully we'd gotten past that. "But major governments wouldn't be calling on the execution of children because of who their parents were. At least not now."

Aallotar popped her head up. "Did they do it in the past?"

I nodded. "It's considered a shameful part of history. For any country that did it."

"I wouldn't call for murdering *babies*. That's what the Blodnar do."

"Then don't be like the Blodnar," I snapped, my patience growing thin. Immediately, I regretted it. "Show all of Sethys how civilized Lohikärra is. How we can defend ourselves, but also have mercy."

Aallotar nodded. "Lohikärra is civilized. When we want to be." She stared at the barrel of gunpowder. "I'm going to have some of my people secure this gunpowder mixture. See what we could do with it. No fire, no liquid." Turning to me, she said, "Why don't you go rest? There should be an empty bed in the room where they have Haldrek. He'll probably fret if he doesn't see you again, and that's the last thing we need right now."

I slowly made my way back to the room where Haldrek was recovering. As soon as I entered, a sharp voiced barked out:

"What are you doing in here? You're not even that injured! Let Haldrek rest!"

Raynord made a beeline for me, but I refused to move. I was getting sick and tired of his bullshit.

"Aallotar told me to come in here and rest. I'm tired." I tried to duck around him, but he moved to block me again.

"You can rest elsewhere. There's plenty of space in this thegn hall. You don't need to be in this room."

"But I would rather be in this room. This is Aallotar's thegn hall, not yours, so just let me rest." I ducked the other way, and he blocked me again.

"I can't allow it."

"Why?" I stared him straight in eyes. "Because you're going to do anything you can to get Haldrek with one of your granddaughters, even if it means sowing division? You are being petty. And a shitty thegn. The last thing Lohikärra needs is an inbred ruling family." I ducked under his arm and the next thing I knew, I was on my back outside the door, gasping. The muscles in my back spasmed with pain as anger and embarrassment flooded my body. I tried to get up, but only managed to roll on my side and blink away tears.

"You don't know the first thing about being High Queen. You're not even a haldraga! You barely know how to be a thegn. How could you *think* you could aid Haldrek in ruling Lohikärra? That's what *I* care about. My loyalty is to Lohikärra. If ensuring its survival means locking horns with the green, inept, newly named Thegn of Svartån, so be it."

I glanced around to see people staring at us. Being the center of attention once again, and not in a good way, made me want to hide. There were whispers behind me as soon as Raynord mentioned I wasn't a haldraga, and I wondered how much people were questioning me already. But I wasn't about to let Raynord push me around. Scrambling to my feet, I got back in his face.

"Let me in that room."

"No. If you insist on masquerading as a competent thegn, then go check on your men. If you have the energy to argue with me, then you have the energy to make sure your men aren't all dead from your suicidal tactics."

He stepped back and before I could step forward, he slammed the door in my face. My anger boiled over into rage against the man. I wanted to pound on the door and cuss him out. If it wasn't for the fact that Haldrek was sleeping and people were still watching me, I would have made a bigger fuss. Instead, I spun around and made my way downstairs, my fury fueling me.

For what it was worth, I knew I needed to check on my men, at least to see how many were still alive. Not that I was going to admit that to Raynord. As tired as I was a few moments ago, I was too angry to rest now.

Bursting out of the thegn hall, I looked around. People were staring at me here in the courtyard as well. No one who wore the insignia of Svartån was anywhere to be found. Continuing into the village, I saw fewer people and my anger began to slide into anxiety. Where were my men? My warriors? Some of them had survived, right? Otherwise, who had brought me up to the thegn hall? I had had near five hundred warriors. There was no way the Blodnar had obliterated one third of our forces in that battle.

"Thegn Svartån!"

I spun around after I passed through the village gates. The sun had reached its zenith and, despite our more northern latitude, it still beat down on me. The warrior who stood at what was left of the gates wore the Svartån insignia and I relaxed.

"Where are you going?" He jogged up to me, his attention darting between me, the battlefield, and the sky. Above us, dragons both large and small circled liked vultures.

"I was going to check on the warriors of Svartån. I didn't see anyone in the village or at the estate. So I was going to..." I stopped and stared at the battlefield. My stomach twisted as I looked over the corpses. In the distance, a few smaller dragons feasted on the dead, batting away at the blue haze that were the spirits. I shuddered. "The dead need their rites done. Especially those from Svartån."

"Will you wait a moment then, my thegn? It's not safe to be out here, even with the dragons. I'll go find a few more warriors and we'll keep watch as you do the rites."

I nodded, vaguely aware of his words and his footsteps returning to the village. A few of the ghostly warriors were still fighting. Others were walking around aimlessly. Even with the attack on Svangendom around the time of my arrival, this was the most dead I'd seen. Ever.

A few of the spirits noticed I was watching them and waved me over. It surprised me, but seeing no threats, I began walking toward them. As I reached the edge of the battlefield, I began stepping over bodies, trying not to look too closely, but also making sure I could find those who were of Svartån and in need of rites.

The spirits kept walking forward until I was well into the middle of the battlefield.

"Where are you going? Where are your bodies?" I looked around, confused, as they shook their heads.

To my left, a bolt was embedded in the ground. Modolf's limp body covered it and his spirit stood nearby, examining the whole scene. When he looked at me, my throat tightened and I fought in vain to keep my tears from blurring my vision. It wasn't fair. Modolf shouldn't be dead. The memories of him in Eldingheimr and cheering me on when I felt like a weak thegn ached in my heart. If not for him, I would be in the Realm of Ghosts right now. I whispered, "You of all people should definitely go to Mirroth." Raising my hands, I began the rites to send him to Mirroth. He smiled calmly as I spoke and a wave of pride rushed over me. In my mind's eye, as soon as I finished, he bowed and his bluish ghostly form faded away.

My voice was hoarse as I whispered, "Thank you. For everything." I took a deep breath and added, "May we meet again one day, friend."

Opening my eyes, I let the exhaustion from the ritual sink into my bones. My body and soul wanted to rest, but I knew there would be little time for that in the near future.

A shadow passed over me and I gasped. A familiar dragon came from behind and spun around elegantly on a wing tip. Rhaegos's voice flooded my mind.

Calm, little one. Hold tight to your pendant or Lohikärra won't have the leader it needs.

I scrambled to pull out my pendant, wondering what that had to do with anything.

"Thegn Svartån!"

I spun around to see some of my warriors running full speed at me, wide-eyed with terror.

Tell them to wait. Your pendant and I will ensure your safety.

"Stop! I'm okay!"

They paused, then began running toward the village. Before I could do or say anything, a massive weight hit me and I was facedown in the mud. The immense weight crushed me, forcing the air from my lungs. My pendant clicked and darkness consumed me.

Chapter Fourteen

Darkness encased me, squeezing like a vice and though I couldn't see anything, I sensed I wasn't alone.

"Thegn Svartån…" I opened my eyes only to see my father, or what was left of him, staring at me. I gasped, wanting to scream, but my lungs were void of air. The part of his face, where the flesh remained, smiled at me. It was a terrifying contrast.

"I'm proud of you, Inka. But I need to tell you something before you see Rhaegos." His voice was raspy as reddish liquid oozed from his neck and soaked his beard.

"What?" My voice was so quiet, I could barely hear it.

"Rorik. Rorik Niemi. Necromancer. Save Drattüjert. Save us." He gasped the last words and looked up as something darkened the air above us. Air whipped past me as my father fell to his knees.

"Protect her, Rhaegos."

I wanted ask more questions, but nothing came out. Instead, everything plunged further into darkness and my father disappeared. An intense weight fell over me, forcing air from my lungs and consciousness from my mind.

It was still dark when I returned to my senses. But in a strange way, it was a *lighter* darkness. I got the impression the darkness wasn't because of nighttime or being in a room. If it hadn't been for the runes lit up in front of me, I would have thought I was dead. Instead, just like in the Lohikärran video games, the runes for stamina, magic, and fortitude flashed in and out of existence. My exhaustion had disappeared, but I still had no idea what was going on. The runes finally disappeared, leaving me in the dark.

"It would have been wiser for you to release your pendant every time it filled up, but this works too."

I twisted around as the space lightened up. Behind me was a familiar, smiling face. Rhaegos. She was mostly in human form, but her hair, as soon as it hit the ground, shifted into what looked more like a dragon's tail. Her nails were also long, looking more like talons than actual nails. While most of her attire was in muted earthy colors and looked similar to the dresses Lohikärran women wore, there seemed to be something woven into it. As she moved, the fabric shimmered with shades of metallic green and purple.

"Am I...? No. I'm not dead. Where am I?" I surveyed the space as my thoughts returned to my father. What had that been? Another realm? The Realm of Ghosts or something else? Had that been another aspect like I'd seen in the dungeon before fighting Seirye? As for this place, nothing stood out to clue me into where I was. I sensed that I was no longer in the same realm as my father, but no color or substance oriented me to anything here except for Rhaegos and I. Just a plain white space with enough light to see each other.

"Do you think I would kill you, little one?" A hint of mirth in her tone made me relax. She wasn't mad at my questions. More amused. Still, I shook my head to dissuade any thoughts she might have of me being rude.

"You are in the Realm of Dragons. Which is probably why this place seems so strange to you. It isn't a place like your Earth or even Sethys. It's made for dragons. The sensations here are beyond what most mortals can comprehend."

"Is that why it's mostly blank? Empty?"

Rhaegos nodded. "What you can see here and what I can see are very different. I've dulled what you are able to sense, so you can focus on what I need to tell you."

"What you need to tell me?" I wrapped my arms around myself in an attempt to gain some comfort. As I did, I realized my armor was gone. I was in a smooth, creamy white dress, decorated not unlike the one I wore at my coronation, with hemming on the collar and cuffs that I knew were symbols of *something*. Rune-like shapes denoting something beyond what I understood currently. Despite not being as fine as what Rhaegos wore, or even what I'd worn when I became thegn, it was both plain and regal at the same time.

"It is your time to become a haldraga. I will be your dragon." She cocked her head. "Do you understand?"

I shook my head. "Is this the haldraga ceremony? Like what Haldrek and Mattie went through?"

She nodded. "My kin Teminth and Sivath chose each of them respectively. Each helps the individual they bind with increase their power and potential. You are needed here in Lohikärra at this time. There is darkness coming that you and Haldrek will need to face together in order to ensure Lohikärra's safety and survival."

I shuddered. Did Rhaegos know anything about the other thegns who thought me incompetent? Raynord's desperate attempts to make his granddaughter the High Queen? I was glad that she thought so highly of me, but at the same time, I had no idea how I'd handle everything.

"I will be with you."

"Huh?" I focused on Rhaegos, suddenly embarrassed I'd zoned off into my own thoughts.

She smiled. "I can sense your thoughts. Not quite read them, but you are concerned. About your abilities. About your experiences since arriving here in Lohikärra."

"Yeah, I guess. There are a few people who question my abilities. I haven't exactly been in Lohikärra for that long. And I'm still only, like, eighteen."

"I'm aware. The dragon stone that brought you here was one of my scales. I knew the moment you arrived. Which was exactly *when* you needed to arrive."

I cocked my head in confusion. "I wasn't meant to come to Lohikärra before I did?"

Rhaegos shook her head. "Your life, your experiences, are what Lohikärra needs now. Not someone who grew up here being groomed for the courts of Drattüjert." Her mouth quirked upward at the edges. "My kin who are already with the other thegns, well, we dragons talk, so to speak. I know the Thegn of Drattrede speaks poorly of you. His dragon kin is softening him, but you humans are stubborn sometimes. As one who is half of this world and half of another, you have abilities others here do not have. It is your destiny to use those abilities for the good of Lohikärra and its people."

A thought popped into my head. "What about those who are only half-Lohikärran?"

Rhaegos smiled. "We dragons do not care about the heritage of those who serve us and seek our aid. There are some powerful beings who do, but we are not among them. If a person were half Blodnar and Ixafean, but they sought the dragons' aid or to serve us, they would not be rejected."

"I'm glad to hear that. It seems like there are too many people who want Lohikärra to be only for Lohikärrans, that 'half-breeds' like myself aren't welcome."

"Those people will have to learn. It is no longer possible for Lohikärra to stay isolated. Nor is that a good thing. That is why you and Mathilde—Mattie—were brought here. Not only do you have abilities others don't, you are here to show Lohikärra that 'half-breeds,' as you call them, are necessary and good for this land. Bjornulf was a half breed, after all."

"Ottkatla's descendants, too?"

Rhaegos flashed a broad smile. "They were. The Hethurin are just as much heirs to this land as full blooded Lohikärrans."

I nodded, letting the knowledge fill me up. It felt like I was learning more than was possible in the time we were talking. Another question popped into my head.

"Does this have anything to do with aspects? Like what I saw in the dungeon that one time? I know that doesn't have anything to do with me becoming a haldraga, but—"

Rhaegos laughed. "What you are experiencing right now is very different than what you did with the aspect you saw, though there are some similarities. Mattie is very intuitive to dragon magic. She was right to guess that what you saw was an aspect, a part of you that can sometimes emerge during times of great duress."

"But why did it look like my father?"

"He was the only Thegn of Svartån you truly knew at that point, so when you questioned your ability to be the Thegn of Svartån, it appeared."

I nodded, taking in the knowledge as much as I could. My thoughts returned to the present situation.

"Am I unconscious like Mattie right now? And she has Sivath as a dragon guide, like you and I will be?"

Rhaegos nodded. "Time passes differently in the Realm of Dragons than it does in either Lohikärra or Fargo. As for Sivath and Mattie, as you call her—Sivath has almost always been tied to the House of Andrattür. He knows he needed to bestow his power on Wiglaf's other descendant at this time. Even as the Blodnar took his strength in battle, I asked him to go on one final mission, so his strength would not be wasted by the Blodnar, as many of our kin's have."

"That makes sense. The same as what you're doing with me now."

She nodded again. "It is your turn to become a *haldraga*. To use your unique powers and align with that of Haldrek. Lohikärra needs you and you will need me. You know this. I will give you my power to push out the Blodnar and silence your critics, just as I will give you guidance in the future." The sides of her mouth flicked upwards in a sly grin. "It is your destiny to aid the one we dragons call the Restorer. Your Haldrek. Regardless of what others may do or try."

I smiled as well. "I will do whatever I can to help Haldrek restore Lohikärra."

"And remind him that he must do whatever he can to help you *reform* Lohikärra."

Before I could say anything more, a brightness emanated from behind Rhaegos and I flinched, closing my eyes with a gasp.

Chapter Fifteen

When I returned to consciousness, I could hear people shouting a few feet from where I lay. Staying still, I listened, waiting to see how much of a danger the people might be to me.

"You're being ridiculous, Haldrek. She's been unconscious for over a week now. I have never seen or heard of a haldraga ceremony going that long. Even if her body is still alive, her mind will not be."

Opening one eye, I saw Haldrek's broad shoulders blocking my view of who spoke. He wore a loose tunic and pants. There was no sign of bandages or other injuries either. He looked normal again. At least from this angle. The urge to go up and embrace him overwhelmed me.

"Thegn Andrattür... if I may speak..."

"No, you may not, Hardbein. There's no reason for you to be a part of this discussion. You're lucky I don't cut you down here and now, seeing as you tried to kill the current Thegn of Svartån only a few months ago."

"Late thegn, Haldrek. She is dead. For all intents and purposes."

"Shut up, Raynord."

"Excuse me?"

I bit my bottom lip to keep from laughing. Haldrek had no tolerance for either Raynord or Hardbein right now and I was happy for his defense.

"Sorry. Shut up, *Uncle* Raynord."

"You may be the heir to the title of High King, but you don't get to start acting like it yet."

"I'm not. I'm acting as a man who is still peevish that you nearly got him killed in battle."

"Thegn Andrattür, I must agree with Thegn Drattrede here. It has been far too long that she has been this way. As she has no heirs, I am next in line for the title of Thegn of Svartån. I've already begun issuing orders to the Svartån warriors."

Haldrek said nothing, but I caught a glimpse of him grabbing Hardbein—now sporting a garish leather eye patch—by the shoulders and throwing him across the room. I shut my eyes as Hardbein landed with a thud on the floor.

"Haldrek, what in Sethys are you doing?"

"Get out, Uncle Raynord. You and Hardbein are not aiding the situation." The conversation paused for several long moments and then Haldrek said, "Ina still wears the thegn armor. If she was dead, it would return to Ottkatla's Barrow. Until then, or until she wakes up, I don't want to see either of you."

There was more silence, then the thudding of feet across the floor. A few moments more and the door slammed shut. Haldrek sighed loudly and his footsteps came closer to where I lay.

He knelt next to me and his beard hairs prickled my forehead as he kissed me. His hand enveloped around mine, a steady warmth sinking into my flesh. "Please wake up soon, Ina. I know Rhaegos must have a lot to tell you, but..." A drop of something wet, a tear, hit the bridge of my nose and I twitched.

"Ina?" Haldrek pulled his face away and I opened my eyes as I squeezed his hand.

"I'm here. How'd you know that I bonded with Rhaegos?"

"You heard that?"

I nodded. My body didn't feel sore or achy at all, but I didn't know whether to attribute that to Rhaegos or my pendant. "I also heard Hardbein trying to take my title again. When did he arrive?" I tried to remember if he'd been here before I became a haldraga.

"Bjorn brought his forces to aid Aallotar the day after the battle and the morning after Rhaegos and you joined together. As soon as I was awake and healed, Hardbein began pestering me about taking your spot. I have a feeling Bjorn may have held his forces in reserve until after the battle."

"How would he have known? And how long did it take for you to heal?" I sat up slowly, taking in Haldrek's face. No longer was it bloody, puffy, or bruised. It was as if he'd never been injured in the first place.

"When your warriors brought you up here, they mentioned your pendant. Aallotar got the bright idea to check mine and press it to my chest. It was full and healed me in an instant. As for Bjorn, I don't know how he could have known, unless he was in contact with the Blodnar or someone connected to them, like Gustav. But I find it convenient that he arrives the day *after* a major battle."

The conversation lulled and Haldrek grabbed me tight, pulling me into a hug. "You don't know how much I missed you. How worried I was."

"I thought becoming a haldraga was a relatively safe thing? You said that when Mattie became a haldraga." My stomach growled loudly and I stared at it in surprise.

Haldrek pulled back and gestured for me to wait. He hurried to a part of the room that was out of view and returned a few moments later with a large platter of half-eaten food, as well as a large pitcher of something that sloshed as he walked.

"It's not the fanciest meal for a new haldraga, but here's some meat bread and sweetened *kavasir*. Aallotar refuses to let me drink mead until she is certain I've returned to full health. It was beginning to affect my mood." He laughed, setting the platter on the stool he had been sitting on and gestured for me to start eating.

"Is this your food?"

He nodded. "Aallotar has had her servants bring me up far too much food to eat these past few days. Every haldraga I've known has been ravenous when they wake up."

Sure enough, my mouth began watering as soon as I reached for the food. Once it was inside my mouth, I chewed as fast as I could, taking a desperate sip of the *kavasir* to aid with swallowing. Once my hunger was satiated enough for me to take a break, I paused.

"I promise I'm not normally this gluttonous." I took another gulp of the *kavasir* as Haldrek laughed again.

"You should have seen me after I woke up from bonding with Teminth. I ate like I'd been starving my entire life. I'm sure Mattie had a hearty appetite as well. It's a good sign to be this hungry after bonding with your dragon."

"That reminds me..." I patted my chest for my pendant. It was still there, but Haldrek shook his head as he pulled his from his tunic. It was then that I noticed he wore only his tunic and pants, no armor or foot gear whatsoever.

"I already let Mattie know as soon as I was aware of what was going on. She'll want to hear from you." He pulled his pendant from under his shirt, popped it open and pressed his thumb to the glass.

"Mathilde Gunvald. Svangendom." He turned the pendant to me as the glass shimmered with an inky blackness. After a second, Mattie's face appeared. As soon as she saw me, a large smile crossed her face.

"I was hoping this was the reason Haldrek was calling. How are you feeling?"

I raised the meat bread so that she could see it. "Hungry."

"I bet. You were unconscious for a while. It's been..." Mattie glanced up as if trying to count something in her head. "Tomorrow would be a week and a half."

I shook my head. "It doesn't feel like it's been a week and a half. All I remember is having a short conversation with Rhaegos and..."

"And then waking up? That's how it was with Sivath. He told me stuff, like what to expect as a haldraga, and then next thing I knew, I was waking up and it had been over a week. Part of me is curious as to how that all works, but the other part feels like it'd be too abstract a concept to wrap my head around."

I nodded and took another bite of my meat bread. "Raynord still isn't too happy with me being alive. And Hardbein is here. I woke up to Haldrek tossing him from the room."

Haldrek laughed, then grimaced. "The day after Bjorn arrived, I overheard him and Raynord casually talking about what they'd do once Ina was dead. I haven't spoken to Bjorn since then and Ina saw how I tolerated Hardbein."

"What?" Mattie and I both went wide eyed, her at me and me at Haldrek. I was surprised by this, despite knowing Raynord's animosity.

"They weren't plotting your death, just talking about how they were sure you'd get killed in future battles and how Hardbein would be a much better thegn. Bjorn said that Hardbein being in charge of Svartån would mean a closer relationship between Lansiranikä and Svartån. Raynord didn't seem too happy about that idea though." Haldrek sighed, as if unconvinced by the last statement.

I blinked. "The fact that they were anticipating my death is almost as bad as planning it."

"Do they know you've already signed a document declaring who would be your successor should you die without an heir?" Mattie asked.

I shook my head. "Nor that my heir is currently Modolf's widow." The thought hit me in the gut. Did she even know that he was dead yet?

Mattie's pendant fell and I watched as she moved toward a bookcase.

"Skuti already has a copy of the declaration in this library of yours, Ina. I think there is a magical element, though. It's something I want to investigate more." We heard the sound of her pushing books around until she said, "Aha!"

Mattie's face popped up again. "Astrid Koridottir. She's the one you chose as your successor should you die."

"What are the chances Hardbein will try to bully her if I die?" *Or disappear*. Honestly, given what had happened over the past few months, I wouldn't be surprised if they'd just make me disappear in order to get what they wanted.

"It's almost certain he would. Though, if the woman was married to Modolf, I assume she's a tough person. Either way, we don't want it to get that far."

I nodded, worry making my stomach churn now that it was now pleasantly full.

"Well, if you're feeling anything like how I was, I'll let you rest." She laughed a little, her mouth quirking upwards. "Sivath says hello to Rhaegos and to tell her to be easy on you."

The sensation of laughter vibrated through my head. *You'll be fine.*

"She heard that."

Mattie smiled as the pendant went dark. Haldrek closed it, returning it to beneath his tunic.

I looked at him and asked, "Now what? Being a haldraga should open a lot of things to me now. I was hoping for a little more respect, but I feel like Raynord is going to hate me no matter what. Especially with both he and Bjorn chomping at the bit for my death." I laughed bitterly. "Mainly because they want better access to you."

Haldrek leaned his forehead forward and I met it, resting against him gently.

"We could fix that," he whispered softly.

"Fix your uncle hating me? I doubt it."

Haldrek laughed. "No. I think Raynord will always be, well, perhaps he'll be more respectful in the future. But I think we could fix the fact that you're competition." He tilted his head so we were cheek to cheek. The softness of his beard was pleasurable as it grazed my jaw when he planted a kiss on my neck. A pleasant thrill engulfed my body. Up and down my spine, the sensation from where he kissed me made me shiver and I gasped. I stiffened a little from the physical affection, a physical reaction to the last time we'd gotten close. But I pushed that aside as the urge to embrace Haldrek took over. The image of me pushing him over and getting on top of him flashed through my mind. I paused at the audacity of the thought.

I heard Rhaegos laugh inside my mind. *Relax. He's fine. You can trust him.*

Haldrek continued to kiss my neck and made his way to my collarbone. Another burst of excitement and pleasure radiated through my body, the desire to be as close to him as possible increasing. I leaned over and stabilized my hands on his legs just above his knees. A thought floated through my head of him kissing many more places on my body. I had one question before I let myself fully relax.

"If I asked you to stop, would you?"

Haldrek stopped. My stomach tightened up as I wondered if I'd killed the mood. Again.

"Do you want me to stop?"

I hesitated for a moment. "No. But if I asked, would you?"

"Of course." He didn't move as I exhaled, fully relaxing into him. I shifted so I was sitting on his leg, straddling it. Only then did I realized where his hands were, wrapped around the small of my waist, encompassing me in his embrace. I turned, finding my lips at the top of his jawbone and right behind his ear.

I slowly kissed him there and whispered, "I love you, Haldrek."

"And I love you, Ina. With every fiber of my being." He kissed me on the collarbone again, sending electricity down my spine again. "Will you marry me then? Be *mine drawing*?"

I pulled my head away from his for a moment in surprise. Both to register what he said and to not blast him in the ear when I spoke. "Your what?"

He laughed softly. "Sorry. *Mine drawing* means 'my queen' in Lohikärran. Will you be my queen, Ina?"

My heart squeezed tight in my chest. The first thought that came to mind was 'yes'. But my mouth went numb as I tried to speak. A dozen different thoughts flooded my head as I tried to move my lips. I knew in my head why Haldrek was proposing, but the voices told me I was too young, too different, that I didn't belong here, and worst, that I didn't deserve this. I didn't deserve to feel happy.

This is your fate. You and Haldrek will do many great things together. Trust him. Trust yourself.

"Ina?"

"Yes." The word finally popped out of my mouth. I loved him more than I could say and he loved me. He wanted to marry me, and it seemed we were destined to do something important together here in Lohikärra. "Yes, I will marry you. Absolutely."

He pulled me toward him and we kissed again. I let myself relax. I let him pull me over his other leg so I was straddling his waist. As we kept kissing, I curled my arms around his neck. The electricity coursing through my body changed into something heavier, more intense. I couldn't describe it, but I enjoyed the feeling and didn't want it to stop.

A few moments later, we heard someone tap softly on the wooden door. Both Haldrek and I looked up as Aallotar called out, "Haldrek?" and the door creaked open.

As soon as she saw us, her eyebrows shot up and she stepped back, closing the door. "I heard that Ina had recovered and I wanted to see how she—you two—how everything was going. I didn't mean to bother you. Um...if you need me for anything, I'll be in my quarters."

I slipped onto my cot as Haldrek stood up.

"You can come in. If you... I was actually just thinking, cousin... How is morale?"

Aallotar opened the door again and stepped inside. "Not good, but not bad. Many of our warriors are in the Realm of Ghosts and the rest are far from home. There's been some tension between the Svartån troops and the Lansiranikä troops, but otherwise, nothing surprising."

"Do you think the men could stand to have some kind of celebration?"

Aallotar nodded. "Of course. I think a night of beer and mead and good food would do much to lift the men's spirits. What do you have in mind?" A small, impish grin crept to her face as she looked from me to Haldrek.

"I was thinking a wedding celebration. I asked Ina to be my queen and she accepted."

Aallotar's grin turned into a full-fledged smile. "Congratulations, you two." She laughed. "Haldrek, you certainly aren't leaving anything to the last moment."

"Both the High King and High Queen are required to be *haldragas*. Now that Ina is a *haldraga*, what is there to stop us?"

"Absolutely nothing, cousin. I believe this will do more for the morale of the men than you can possibly imagine. I'll get people started on preparations, if you'd like."

Haldrek's smile grew wider as he glanced from Aallotar to me and back. "That would wonderful, cousin. Thank you."

Chapter Sixteen

I ended up sleeping in another room that night, one that had been remade after the Blodnar had been kicked out. Haldrek had offered to let me sleep in the room he had been given, but I had a feeling it would be hard to focus on anything else during the next few days if we were in the same room. We had been passionately kissing both before and after Aallotar's arrival, so I figured spending a few more nights in my own room would keep me—us—out of trouble. Now that we were all but married, not much kept us from going beyond kissing. Despite the fact that I enjoyed the idea of sex with Haldrek, a sense of trepidation still loomed over the actual act.

As soon as I fell asleep, however, I found myself in a hazy dream. Haldrek and I were together somewhere, though I couldn't see him. I was in a large, soft bed covered in furs, much like my bed at Svangendom. Haldrek's presence was next to me. Though I couldn't see him, it comforted me. He was warm and safe. As I cuddled next to him, enveloped in the sensation, another presence came over me and I froze. It was familiar, but darker, more ominous. I felt naked and vulnerable, as much as I pulled away, it got closer. The presence curled up behind me, sticking to me as I tried to escape. Haldrek's presence was now gone. I crossed my legs and arms, trying to make myself as small as possible. Laughter echoed around me as the presence seeped in and around me like some kind of liquid or gas. I tried to wake up, telling myself this was a dream.

Then the laughter stopped. It was replaced by a whisper. "You're mine. Not even Haldrek can save you."

I willed myself to wake up as the presence squeezed me tight, smothering me.

I woke up.

It was dim outside, as dark as it got now that we were in August. Most of thegn hall was quiet, telling me it was still early. I sat up and cloaked myself with my wolfskin blanket, trying to push the fear and shame weighing heavily on my mind. The voice had been Robert's. I hadn't had a dream like that in months, not since the first few weeks after my arrival in Lohikärra. Robert wasn't here. He couldn't be here, right? I was safe from him as long as I was in Lohikärra, right?

Rhaegos? I thought out loud, wondering if she had any insight into what I'd experienced. Yet there was no response.

Brushing the sweat from my brow and the tears from my cheeks, I wondered what I would do after Haldrek and I got married. Was the nightmare an omen of something to come? Would I have these dreams after Haldrek and I got married? This wasn't the first time I'd had these nightmares, and I didn't want them to ruin my romantic times with Haldrek in the future. Honestly, I wished they would disappear altogether. I wished Robert would disappear altogether.

Resting my head on my knees, I tried to think of other things. Happy memories that were few and far between, the goals that lay ahead of me. Slowly my tears dried and my body relaxed as I dozed off.

The next few days went by quickly. My nightmares continued to plague me, but I tried to brush them off during the day, training with my men in the morning and strategizing with the other thegns in the afternoon. The thegn hall was abuzz with excitement over the upcoming 'warrior's wedding' between Haldrek and I, and the excitement only made me more nervous.

The morning of the ceremony, not even a week after having become a *haldraga*, I found myself in a large room filled with what I imagined were various toiletries. A large metal tub, ornately designed and made specifically for bathing, sat on the far edge against the wall. Tables full of bottles stood on either side of the tub. Aallotar, her partner Vilde, and a variety of female servants who had been recruited to help me prepare for the ceremony were in the room. Mattie had arrived the day before with Llamryl, much to my surprise and pleasure.

Despite the fact that the idea of being naked in front of a bunch of people made me uncomfortable, no one else seemed fazed by the idea. I was quickly stripped of my clothes and led to the warm bath.

As the women helped to scrub me clean, Aallotar and Mattie helped me memorize the ceremonial vows Haldrek and I were supposed to both speak. While it didn't surprise me that Mattie knew the vows—given how much she had studied the video game lore and then the books at Svangendom—Aallotar's knowledge surprised me. She had grown up here, but she didn't strike me as the type to care about weddings and all the other frilly stuff we were currently dealing with.

"How come you know so much about all of this? You…" I twisted around to look at her while a servant yanked at my hair scrubbing it with some kind of floral soap. The servant jerked my head back.

"Don't come off as the type to be into marital rituals?" She laughed and glanced over at Vilde. "I can enjoy some of the more traditionally feminine things in life. Even if I may be required to take on—and enjoy—some of the more masculine things such as fighting. Plus, many of the abthanry were required to get married before my grandfather. Given my peculiar status as the bastard grandchild of the High King, I was often assigned to assist my grandfather in the parts of the ceremony that required a second or third witness. Especially when my cousins refused to do it."

I nodded and dunked my head under the water, washing away whatever concoction had been put in my hair to clean. Popping my head out of the water, the women continued to fuss over me as I saw Mattie's mouth quirk up. It was evident she was trying not to laugh.

"You'll be next, Mattie, you know that, right? I see how you and Llamryl look at each other."

Mattie's eyes went wide and she looked away for a moment, but she failed to suppress her smile. Aallotar turned her attention to Mattie.

"Who's Llamryl?"

Mattie stared daggers at me as I giggled and turned around.

"He's my friend. A very good friend."

"A friend with benefits." I blurted out. Something soft but solid hit my head and I laughed again. After the stress of the last few weeks, it felt good to silly for a few moments.

"You two are affectionate? Do I need to let Haldrek know?"

"My *half* brother doesn't need to know anything about my personal life. Nor do I think he's interested. He's more interested in what's going to happen in his bed tonight than mine."

Aallotar howled with laughter and my cheeks heated up as a few of the other women laughed with her.

"That's true. But seeing as you'll be the Thegn of Andrattür after Haldrek becomes High King, you'll have to let him know if and when you make things official with this Llamryl person. Once he's High King, one of his duties will be to legitimize the marriages of any thegns who come before him. Otherwise, while you may have the rights and privileges of a thegn and the abthanry, your partner will not."

Mattie said nothing, but she made a humming sound like she always did when she was processing new information that didn't exactly make her happy.

"Aallotar?" I twisted my head to see her and got it yanked back by the women who were combing my hair. Despite being tied up for battle and everything, it had still gotten horribly tangled and knotted.

"Hmm?"

"Would me marrying Haldrek affect my title in anyway? As Thegn of Svartån?" I grimaced as one of the women began working on a more painful tangle.

Aallotar sat next to Mattie and shook her head. "No. You will still be the Thegn of Svartån, as you are becoming High Queen by marriage, not in your own right. Not that Hardbein probably won't try something. Or Bjorn. But Haldrek will nip that in the bud. Especially after the stunt that Bjorn and Hardbein pulled while you were becoming a haldraga."

"So the only reason he's here is because Bjorn and Raynord thought I was dead?"

Aallotar nodded. "There's no reason for him to be here otherwise. I haven't seen any of his men training. Neither have my informants."

"And if I'm still alive? Why is he still here?"

"Because if they think you're going down in battle real soon, having him on hand to 'lead the troops' will be convenient to their plans," Mattie added. "They may think you were just lucky in not dying last time."

I groaned. Another thing to worry about in the future.

Aallotar shook her head. "Don't worry about Hardbein. I doubt he or anyone else would do anything tonight. Not only would that cause irreparable rifts in camp, but given that Bjorn and Hardbein have already made a play for your title, I doubt they'd do anything to actively take it from you."

I raised an eyebrow at her.

"No one's going to try and shank you at your wedding," Mattie clarified. "Even if someone was stupid enough to do that, how many people do you think would be on top of them, ready to kill them? Above all, Haldrek."

I laughed, remembering how he had tossed Hardbein from the room when I'd awoken as a haldraga. Still, a weight laid on my chest. Whether it was from worry about tonight or the future in general, I didn't know.

It was nearly time for the evening meal when I left the room with Mattie, Aallotar, and the rest of the women who had been tending to me. The halls around us bustled with noise, a mixture of people singing, talking, and general merrymaking. The delicious smells that wafted through the entire thegn hall would have made me hungry, but my nervousness took precedence as I walked down the stairs, still hidden from most of the crowd. Though I still wore my armor and had Freya's Menace by my hip, I felt far too dressed up, compared to what I usually wore. Mattie had somehow found a fancy cape with the insignia of Svartån on it and brought it with her from Svangendom. Aallotar had also presented me with a wreath of flowers for my hair.

Before we entered the main hall, she stopped me, fussing with the wreath again. "Typically, weddings are held in the month just before the winter solstice for good luck. And brides wear a wreath of dried flowers to be crushed after they are wed. Symbolizing how something else will be crushed..."

I stared at her in horror. "What?"

She ignored my expression as she continued to make sure my wreath was solidly in place. "Thankfully, we only had fresh flowers around here, which symbolize durability—as in a long-lasting union." She smiled broadly at me as I began my walk to the main room. The noise had settled and everyone stared at me as I walked in, nudged along by Aallotar and Mattie.

When we made it to the central dais, I found it decorated with a variety of flowers, greenery, and weapons. The hall had been reconfigured, with the tables and stools placed in a 'U' shape where there had once been rows and rows of cots. The other thegns and their gesiths sat along the edges, standing up as I arrived. I saw my remaining gesiths among them as well.

I looked over to where Haldrek was standing and gasped. He looked *regal*. Even more than when I had first seen him in his thegn armor. He was in his thegn armor now, but it looked different, grander, more clean? I smiled. He wore a cape as well, with what I assumed was the insignia of Andrattür on it. The cape was made of a rich red and hemmed with some kind of silky fur. He also wore a wreath of greenery around his head as he beamed at me. I continued to gape as either Aallotar or Mattie nudged me forward until I was just in front of him.

"It only took you two six months to finally get together."

I was surprised to see Keldan standing alongside us on the dais, an amused smile on his face. There was a bit of hearty laughter from the thegns and gesiths behind us. Turning to Haldrek, I asked, "When?"

"This morning." Haldrek smiled broadly.

"Normally, the High King would preside over an auspicious ceremony such as this." Keldan glanced at Haldrek before turning to me. "However, in the absence of a High King, it is the duty of the current first priest to Tenelth to do so."

I nodded as Keldan opened up his scroll. He tightened one end and loosened the other before gesturing to us. "Take each other's left hand as though shaking it, then put your first two fingers on each other's wrists. Cross your right hands over and, Ina, you put your hand on top of your grasped hands, and Haldrek, you put your right hand over hers. Good."

He began chanting in Lohikärra and I felt a comforting tingle go up my spine. Looking at Haldrek, I saw that he was grinning like a fool at me. When Keldan finished, he looked at both of us and said, "Now it is time for each of you to say your parts. I will guide you. Ina, you will begin."

I took a deep breath as he continued, "*You cannot possess me, for I belong to myself. But I give you that which is mine to give.*"

"You cannot possess me, for I belong to myself. But I give you that which is mine to give."

"You cannot command me, for I am a free person. But I shall serve you in those ways you require." Haldrek continued, warranting a raised eyebrow from Keldan before he continued.

"*And the mead will taste sweeter coming from my hand.*"

In unison, Haldrek and I repeated the phrase. Keldan nodded to me and continued,

"*I pledge that yours will be the name I cry aloud at night.*"

"I pledge that yours will be the name I cry aloud at night."

"*And the eyes into which I smile in the morning.*"

"And the eyes into which I smile into the morning." I blinked, trying to keep my tears at bay. Haldrek wasn't weepy, was he?

Keldan looked over at Haldrek. "*I pledge to you the first bite from my meat, and the first drink from my cup.*"

"I pledge to you the first bite from my meat, and the first drink from my cup."

Keldan turned to me. "*I pledge to be a shield for your back as you are for mine. And to tell no strangers our grievances.*"

"I pledge to be a shield for your back as you are for mine. And to tell no strangers our grievances."

As Keldan focused on Haldrek, Haldrek shook his head and tried to blink his own tears away, making me smile. So he was getting weepy, too.

"*I pledge to not seek to change thee in anyway...*"

"I pledge to not seek to change thee in anyway..."

"*I shall respect thee, thy beliefs, thy people, and thy ways as I respect myself.*"

"I shall respect thee, thy beliefs, thy people, and thy ways as I respect myself."

Keldan opened the scroll a little bit more and said, "This is the last part. You two say it together, all right?"

Haldrek and I both nodded before turning our attention to each other.

"I pledge to be loyal to you for as long as Tenelth and his descent protect Lohikärra."

"I pledge to be loyal to you for as long as Tenelth and his descent protect Lohikärra."

"This is my vow to you. This is a marriage of equals."

"This is my vow to you. This is a marriage of equals."

Keldan cleared his throat and closed the book.

"As the first priest of Tenelth, I proclaim you two married and bonded before the people of Lohikärra and before the dragon descendants of Tenelth."

The crowd began to cheer as Haldrek released my hands. He wrapped his arms around me, pulling me in for a passionate kiss. I flung my arms around his neck and held him in that kiss for several seconds, much to the enjoyment of the crowd.

Chapter Seventeen

After the ceremony, we enjoyed a hearty feast that had been in the making since Haldrek's proposal. Merriment abounded around us, as did music and laughter. Those who were not eating or drinking were dancing as several warriors played instruments boisterously. One musician nearby played a familiar song about Bjornulf and Freya, making me think of other couples in Lohikärran history. Would Haldrek and I end up like those couples? Haldrek would certainly be remembered, but it was hard to fathom myself as anything more than a footnote. Mattie and Llamryl slipped off from the group around us after eating. Dancing and bonfires were outside and, knowing them, they were going to dance out there.

Even Raynord and Bjorn were begrudgingly cheerful as they had their fill of meat, mead, and other treats spread all over the tables. Haldrek and I were toasted numerous times throughout the evening, and after a few, Aallotar stood up to make her own toast.

Raising her mead cup above her head, she proclaimed, "To our future High King and High Queen of Lohikärra! May you feel no rain, for each of you will be a shelter to the other. May you feel no cold, for each of you will be warmth for the other. May there be no loneliness for, though you are two persons, but there is one life before you. May you go to your dwelling place *in Drattüjert* to enter into the days of your togetherness. And may your days be good and long together!"

We cheered to the toast and kissed, as we had with all the others. After our kiss, Haldrek leaned over and whispered, "This celebration will go on all night, with or without us. Let me know when you're ready to go."

I inhaled, partially ready to go, but also terrified of what might happen tonight. Would I freeze or panic? Would my nightmare return as it had for the last week? Would I ruin the night for Haldrek? I'd pushed those worries away for the last few days, but now I couldn't.

"Would you hate me if I said I was nervous?"

Haldrek laughed and kissed me on the neck. "People are watching us, so they can think we are eager, but I'll admit to being nervous tonight as well."

I sat up in surprise as Haldrek grinned.

"Perhaps it's time for the couple to take their farewell?" Keldan shouted, raising his voice above the din of the hall.

Haldrek turned to him and nodded as I ducked my head in embarrassment. "I think it *is* time for us to take our leave." He helped me up as the people around us raised their cups to us and I heard a few more cheers, some of which were more colorful.

Haldrek led me upstairs and up to the third floor where we were alone.

"Aallotar showed me the room she had made up for us. I think she's having more fun with this than she's letting on."

"I didn't figure her for being into celebrations like this."

"Neither did I. However, she's a shrewd leader, with her finger always on the pulse of what's going on, both with her peers and her warriors. She knows that these warriors—hers, ours, and the rest—need a celebration before going after Drattüjert. Morale and such."

"I'm glad we could help."

Haldrek laughed as he opened the one door with light glowing around the edges. Inside was a lavishly decorated room, with a large four poster bed on the far wall, covered in furs and other thick, rich fabrics. Closing the door, Haldrek gently kissed me on the lips and made his way to my neck before whispering, "Tell me, what are you nervous about?"

"Everything." I leaned against his shoulder, embarrassed to not be more in the mood. "I've been having nightmares ever since I woke up from the ritual."

He looked up at me in surprise. "Nightmares about what? Us?"

I shook my head. "About Robert. I think. Every time the nightmare is the same. I hear his voice taunting me and I get so scared. I feel naked and vulnerable. Then I wake up, sweating and terrified. About being touched. About the future. About everything. In my dreams, when I feel like you're there, I'm happy. But then the nightmare creeps in and I wake up feeling sick and I can't sleep and..."

Tears started rolling down my cheeks as Haldrek held me tightly in his arms. I pressed my cheek against the rough parts of his armor, as if in penance for my worries.

"I'm sorry. Tonight should be us enjoying each other, not me freaking out about my dreams."

"Don't worry. Let's go sit. On the bed. We..." He sighed. "We don't have to do anything too quickly. We have all night and I want *both* of us to enjoy it."

I nodded and let him guide me to bed. Taking off my cloak, wreath, and armor because they felt too constricting all of a sudden, I stared at him and then the massive bed, covered in an ocean of fabric and fur.

"You... you can sit if you want." He took off his cloak, wreath, and weapons as well, placing them next to mine on a nearby chair as I sat down.

When he sat, he curled his arm around me and pulled me into his chest. It was comforting, not threatening, so I relaxed, wrapping my arms around him.

"Tell me more about your dream. If you want to or if you can. I don't know how detailed it was or..."

"It felt like my nightmares before. They were also about Robert." I paused to think. "You remember that morning in February or March, when I scratched you?"

Haldrek nodded. "You thought I was Robert. Your nightmares have been like that?"

"Kinda. I feel like he's behind me in the dream. No matter how much I hide or pull away or do anything, it doesn't stop. The presence just...keeps forcing itself on me." Tears started coming down my cheeks again as Haldrek squeezed me tight.

He kissed me on the top of my head. "Like you're not in control."

I nodded, embarrassed to still be crying. I was sure this was *not* what Haldrek was expecting to do on our wedding night. I cringed inside as we sat there, curled up next to each other but not saying anything. Was I already disappointing him? Was he was questioning himself about his decision to marry me? Maybe one of his cousins would have been a better choice, as gross as that was. At least they wouldn't have the baggage I had.

"How would you feel if you were in control?"

I sat back and looked at him in confusion. "What? What do you mean?"

"In your dream, Robert—or his presence—kept forcing himself on you. You felt out of control, like nothing you did could stop him. Would it help you if *you* took control of us being intimate?"

I stared at him, searching for any hint of his true emotions. He was being serious as far as I could tell. But as far as I knew, guys didn't want girls to be the one in control. Not in the bedroom and certainly not here in Lohikärra, right?

"Would that make you feel weird if I was?"

Haldrek shook his head and showed me one of the draw strings on his pants. "This is the easiest one to loosen. If you want to. You're in control tonight."

I smiled and after a moment, gingerly pulled the draw strings loose. Leaning in for a kiss, I searched for draw strings on the other side as he guided my hand toward it. He did the same with my pants, taking his time to loosen them. I focused more on his soft kisses to keep my panic from rising. To focus on the pleasure of his touch and let myself relax. Enjoy the moment. I was safe with Haldrek and I *wanted* to be with him. Pulling myself onto his leg, I moved on to his tunic and began loosening the strings at his neck. His kisses made their way to my jaw and neck as I felt his strong arms and the dense curves of his chest. There was something surprisingly pleasing about feeling his body through his tunic. He leaned back and pulled my leg over him so I was straddling his waist. I paused.

He stopped stroking my leg. "Too fast?"

I shook my head. "I'm not too heavy, am I?"

A belly laugh from him made me bounce a little. "You're the opposite of heavy. My armor feels heavier than you do right now."

I laughed before leaning forward and kissing him again. We were nose to nose. Just being this close to him got me excited. The warmth from his skin was intoxicating, as was whatever scent was coming from him. A mixture of sweetness from the mead and something woodsy from whatever he had bathed with. I nestled my face into his neck, kissing it as he caressed my back and thighs.

"Tell me if I need to slow down." He moaned a little and continued caressing my thighs, pressing his fingers against the inside of them. It felt good to have Haldrek touch me. Unlike my dream, I wanted more. I laid on his chest for a few moments, brushing my fingers through his hair before he whispered, "Pants?"

I laughed again and rolled off of him, letting him tug my pants to my ankles before I kicked them off. I did the same with his. Sitting up, I saw something sticking straight up against the fabric of his tunic. I stopped, looking wide eyed at Haldrek.

He smiled and raised an eyebrow. "I'm a little excited down there. I can't help it. I had a beautiful woman on top of me and, well, that's what happens."

I blushed and gently poked it. Haldrek snorted. "You think it'll fit?"

"Maybe? It's bigger than I expected."

That sent Haldrek into another fit of laughter.

Except for a few anatomical pictures Mattie and I had found online and minimal instruction in sex ed about the male anatomy in school, I'd never actually seen a penis before. Left in only our undershirts and underwear, he pulled himself next to me again and began kissing me on the neck. Heat from inside my body, and an intense awareness of where our bodies touched, washed over me as he pulled the collar of my shift over my shoulder and continued kissing there. As he got to my bra strap, he stopped and looked at me in confusion.

"What else do you have on?"

It was my turn to laugh as I fiddled with my bra hooks. "That would be my bra. It's not hard to take off."

"Do you have any other clothing under your shift?"

I nodded, pulling my arms in and my bra off quickly. "Actual underwear."

He slowly felt around my waist and pulled at the waistband in confusion. "Huh."

"I should probably take those off as well. If...you know..."

"You're in charge tonight, *mine drawing*."

I was. Taking a deep breath, I took my underwear off and dropped it on the ground. I was naked now, more vulnerable than ever before, but excitement replaced anxiety. Laying on my back, I looked at Haldrek as he leaned on his side next to me, his tunic now gone. I didn't dare look down, knowing he had *nothing* on now. He caressed my side and my stomach, making his way up to my chest and playing with my breasts as if exploring them for the first time.

The first line from our vows popped into my head again. "You cannot possess me, for I belong to myself." I whispered, "But I can give you that which is mine to give." With that, I pulled Haldrek in for another kiss and on top of me.

Like it had for the last few nights, my nightmare came calling soon after I'd fallen asleep. Once again, the dream presence hovered over me, too close for comfort, seeping in and around me like a toxic gas. It whispered, "You're mine. Not even Haldrek can save you."

I lunged away from the dream presence and much to my surprise, I was able to move. I fell forward onto a hard stone floor and there I froze, listening to voices above me.

"I want her dead. She is of no use to me alive." The voice sounded familiar, but younger. Like someone my age. As I tried to pinpoint the voice, I realized it sounded similar to Gustav's voice from the cart, only now it was less raggedy and worn. But it carried the same haughty, demanding tone. Was this a dream? Or a memory? A strange mixture of both? Or something different?

"But...I was told..." Robert's voice stumbled over his words in a way that I'd never heard before. Even with my mother. He sounded terrified. But there was no mistaking Robert's voice.

"I don't care what you were told and I don't care about the cost. In a few short months, *I* will be charge. Not just here, but over all of Lohikärra."

I pulled my head up to see Robert bowing on one knee in front of a young man who reminded me of Gustav.

"As you command, Thegn-heir Rorik."

Rorik? Was that Gustav's son? If it was, when had he spoken to Robert? Robert wasn't from Lohikärra, was he? He couldn't be. How had he gotten to Fargo, if he was?

The people disappeared and I began falling. I hit something hard with my knees and forearms. Darkness surrounded me, but I could sense Robert's presence nearby as I scrambled to my knees, feeling around for a more defensive position.

Something hard hit my backside and I went flying forward. I spun around, expecting my back to start hurting. No pain, just fear as I tried to make out something, anything, in the darkness. Whatever had hit me stepped closer. Though I was still blinded by the darkness, I heard the soft, purposeful thud of footsteps.

"You're mine. Not even Haldrek can save you. I have a mission and I'll complete it."

"Stop saying that. What do you want?" I felt naked and vulnerable again, afraid of where the next blow would come from. Raising my arms in defense, I listened for something, anything, to tell me where Robert was.

"My thegn wanted you out of the picture until he could figure what to do with you. I failed at that. So now his son wants you dead. I won't fail at that. Killing is easy."

A blow came full force at my face and I stumbled backwards, reeling. Another punch hit my side and I collapsed to the ground. Before he could attack again, I righted myself, rolling into a standing position. Still, I could see nothing in the darkness.

"I'll enjoy this. Just like in that dragons-forsaken town of Fargo." A hand thrust out from the darkness and pulled me into the air. Though I could still breathe, I felt Robert's hand squeezing my throat tight. He was trying to kill me.

"Help!" I gasped. Not that I knew of anything that could help me.

The hand began shaking me. "No one will save you. No one's here to hear you cry. Not Mattie, not anyone."

I tried swinging my legs in a futile attempt to kick Robert, only ever hitting air, as tears formed in my eyes.

Then the hand dropped me and I laid motionless on the ground, staring up at Robert, just like the many times he'd hit me growing up, knocking me to the ground. This time he dropped on top of me, his arms caging me in on both sides. I flinched, curling up as tight as I could. His immense weight on top of me pushed me flat on the ground. I whimpered. Robert's face reappeared from the darkness, a terrifying smirk on his face.

"I will kill you. But not before I have my fun with you."

I woke up with a scream. Bolting from wherever I'd been laying, I tumbled to the hard stone floor, my feet and legs tangled up in something.

"Ina?" Haldrek's voice, though panicked, brought me back to reality. I was no longer in the dream. Burying my head into the fur blanket still tightly gripped in my hand, I began sobbing. Relief over the dream being gone and anger and despair that it had ruined another night's sleep washed over me.

Haldrek's hand touched my shoulder blades and I felt his body heat warm me up. Was he still naked? Was I? And why was he a freaking furnace? I shuddered from the cold.

"Stupid nightmare. I'm sorry," I choked out, smothering myself in the furry blanket again. Haldrek picked me up as he sat on the floor with his legs crossed. Despite the pile of blankets that surrounded us, I still felt the brush of naked skin a couple of times as we shifted to get comfortable. The light in the room was dim with pre-dawn light. I curled up on Haldrek's chest, listening to his heartbeat and letting mine sync up with it.

His forearm moved against my stomach and his hand rested in the space between my breasts, my heartbeat thumping against it.

"Did you have that nightmare again?" His voice was groggy. I felt the stickiness and heat from his chest on my arm and side. Just his touch calmed me, and the fear from the dream began to fade.

"Yes. And no. It was the same presence. Trying to overwhelm me. But then it changed. Robert was bowing before someone. A young... that thegn you don't like." My brain couldn't grasp the name, but I could still see the faces.

"Gustav?"

I nodded. "Robert called him Thegn-heir Rorik. Why does that name sound familiar?"

"Because Rorik is Gustav's son. You may have heard it mentioned in passing. What did Rorik do?"

"He told Robert to kill me. There was something about Robert getting orders from Gustav. But now Rorik was ordering him around."

"Huh." Haldrek squeezed me tight. I snuggled tighter into his embrace. His body warmth was more than enough to keep the chill away.

"Then they disappeared and I started getting attacked in the darkness. Robert said he was going to kill me, but he was going to have his fun with me first." Tears bubbled up from my eyes as the helplessness and terror hit me again.

"I'm sorry, Ina. I will never let anyone hurt you." He squeezed me again.

I still felt awful. After everything, last night had been enjoyable and I had hoped—even a tiny bit—that my nightmare would go away.

Haldrek leaned over, squishing me into his chest, and stood up, carrying me in his arms back to the bed. It creaked as he placed the combined weight of us on the bed. Wrapping me in layers of thick wool and fur, he began kissing the side of my neck and shoulder while stroking my stomach with the tips of his fingers. I shuddered as goosebumps covered my exposed skin. Not that the sensation was unpleasant.

"If I ever meet this Robert, he will feel my ire for tormenting you so all of these years. You shouldn't have to fear your dreams."

He continued to trace shapes between my breasts and belly button, which I had to admit felt good. Slowly, I began to relax again. Propping his head on one hand, Haldrek opened an eye and looked at me with a grin.

"But if you're awake now, we could…"

He leaned into kiss me again, letting his hand wander past my belly button and onto my thighs. I relaxed, enjoying the quiet time with him. The intense emotions from my dreams faded away as the room slowly lightened up. We'd have to return to real life soon enough. I'd have to confront my nightmares once again. But for now, I could relax and enjoy myself.

In between lingering kisses on my neck, he asked, "Other than your nightmare, did you enjoy last night?"

I nodded. "Barring the dream, I wouldn't have changed anything."

As he continued playing gently between my thighs, tickling me and rubbing me in ways that made my soreness down there feel better, he whispered, "If I could change one thing about last night , it would be that I could have entertained you longer. I'm afraid our time together was too short for either of our liking."

I laughed before gasping as he hit a spot that felt *really* good. "You're making up for it now."

"Oh really?" His eyes were both open as he stroked whatever spot that was again and a pleasurable, tingly feeling washed over me again.

"Yes. You can keep doing that for as long as you want." I wrapped my arms around his neck and pulled him toward me for a kiss until he was on top of me. I felt his hand slip from between my thighs as another part slipped in. I gasped and smiled, more than happy to continue like this with Haldrek.

"Practice makes perfect, I guess," I whispered as I pulled him in for another kiss.

Chapter Eighteen

The only reason Haldrek and I left our bed later that morning was because our stomachs grumbled too much. Thankfully, someone had put a tray of food outside our door. We ate leisurely as people outside the thegn hall began to stir. It seemed most everyone had enjoyed the previous night's celebration and were only now rising from their beds.

After our meal, I began to get dressed in my armor. Haldrek walked over to where I stood and slipped his hands around my waist.

"You don't have to get dressed if you don't want to. We can take our time this morning. No one is going to blame us." He began kissing my neck and I shivered with enjoyment. A little moan escaped my lips. He knew exactly how to tempt me.

As much as I wanted to have more alone time with Haldrek, I knew I needed to train with my men and continue acting as their thegn. I also wanted to talk to Mattie and Llamryl and see what was going on in Svangendom, to make sure all was still well there.

"Later. Tonight. I want more." Haldrek kept kissing me and playing with my hands to keep me from tying my pants up. I giggled at the distraction, enjoying it. "But right now—"

A pounding at the door made Haldrek and I both jump. A familiar voice spoke, and as it did, my skin began to crawl.

"Haldrek! Open up! You don't know how hard you are to get a hold of. I sent messengers, but it seems none of them have reached you."

The noise of armor clanking and Aallotar's voice joined Gustav in the hallway.

"What in the name of the dragons are you doing here? I abided by the rule of hospitality and allowed you entrance here. That doesn't give you the right to harass people in my thegn hall."

The sound of scuffling added to the noise outside. Haldrek quickly got dressed in his tunic and pants. I slipped my own clothes on and moved to the other side of the room where I couldn't be seen from the door.

"Thegn Etelaranikä." Haldrek's voice was reserved as he opened the door, just wide enough for his body. Still, a hint of anger colored his tone. I froze, my instincts taking over. While I trusted Haldrek to keep me safe, and had only met Gustav once, everything I knew about him so far made me doubt he would be very friendly toward me if he saw me right now. The image of his son, Rorik, shoved its way into my mind and I flinched.

Footsteps echoed in the hall. "Gustav, you will have time to speak with Haldrek once he has eaten and gotten ready for the day. As you can see, he had a late evening." Raynord panted as though out of breath.

"Did you tell him where Haldrek was sleeping?" Aallotar snapped.

"I did not. One of your servants told him. I meant to chase Gustav down and stop him. We may have our disagreements, Aallotar, but I would never encourage a fellow thegn to harass my nephew. Especially after all of the celebrations last night."

"Umm-hmm." Disbelief dripped from Aallotar's tone, but she said nothing more.

"I can see that you all were enjoying yourselves." Gustav's tone lowered as though he were thinking about something. "I noticed that many of the soldiers here were a bit unprepared and groggy when I arrived. Almost as if they had been up all night as well."

"As I said before, it was an evening of celebration, Thegn Etelaranikä." Haldrek said, "Which I think even Raynord would agree was good for morale."

The conversation paused for a moment and then Gustav's tone pivoted again, hinting at a slight accusation. "Why so formal when you address me, Haldrek? Are we not peers? Did we not fight the Blodnar together not too distantly?"

"We did, but you know as well as I do that once the Blodnar are dispatched, that we will no longer be peers. Along with fighting, I have been preparing for that role."

"By receiving me so formally? And not the other thegns?"

I cringed at Gustav's tone and slightly prayed that Haldrek would tread carefully with him. I sensed Thegn Etelaranikä laying a trap. How well did Haldrek sense it?

After a tense moment, Haldrek spoke. "Thegn Drattrede is my uncle, whom I have known since my youth, and so in my preparations, I misspoke due to familiarity. It is too early for this."

Gustav laughed shortly. "I forget you weren't raised up to be the High King. Your learning curve must be steep indeed." Haldrek was silent, pausing the conversation. After a few moments, Gustave continued, "I come with a possible bit of good news, something that might turn the tide against the Blodnar. At Drattüjert."

"And?" Haldrek sounded tired. Like he had heard this proposal before.

"And with it some negotiations to strengthen our great Lohikärra."

Raynord sighed and I heard a shoe squeak as someone shifted their foot in the hall.

"*Not again.*" Haldrek's tone was low and tired. "What negotiations do you speak of, Thegn Etelaranikä?"

"Despite your attempts to avoid me," Gustav hesitated, "my future High King, I believe it is in your best interest to at least listen to me."

"Oh?"

"Yes. As you already know, once we are rid of the Blodnar, you will be High King. Every High King needs a Queen. To which I offer you my daughter, Sibila."

Raynord scoffed and Haldrek groaned. Gustav snapped at Raynord. "At least my Sibila isn't already related to our future High King."

"Isn't your daughter elf touched, Gustav?" Raynord retorted.

"It is true that she is of a strange nature. However, she is a docile creature and obedient. And even those elf touched may bear normal offspring."

My stomach twisted in pity for the poor girl as I heard Haldrek grunt in disgust and Raynord sigh. Gustav seemed oblivious to the reactions as he continued.

"If you will agree to marry my daughter, then perhaps we together, my forces and the ones you and your related thegns have amassed, will be able to destroy the Blodnar once and for all."

Haldrek was silent. A worry began to worm its way into my head, that he was actually considering it for the good of Lohikärra. Not that I believed Gustav for a minute and Haldrek knew what I knew. Logically, I knew Haldrek would say no, but the worry refused to leave. With everything that had happened to me growing up, I still feared any sort of betrayal or rejection. Especially with all that had happened over the last twenty-four hours, I now feared betrayal. If it were from Haldrek, it would devastate me. As farfetched as the logical side of me knew that would be.

"Thegn Etelaranikä..." Haldrek sighed. "Did anyone mention *why* the warriors were all celebrating late into the night?"

"I did not ask. I am here for one reason only. To speak with you. I have no time for idle chatter."

"Ina..." Haldrek turned and gestured for me to join him.

I looked myself over. I was fairly decent with my pants on and undershift tucked into it. Taking a deep breath, I walked over, knowing something was going to happen, but trusting that I'd be okay with Haldrek by my side.

I smiled as Haldrek gave me a big, gentle kiss on the lips. We looked at Gustav—Thegn Etelaranikä—and I could already see the anger brewing in his face.

Haldrek's arm wrapped around me, holding me firm. "Last night, the camp celebrated the union between myself and Ina, who you may know as —"

"Thegn Svartån." Gustav growled, not taking his eyes off me. My insides churned as memories of my dream flooded my mind. I gripped the back of Haldrek's tunic to steady myself. When Gustav looked at Haldrek, he said, "You have made a very unwise decision. Both for yourselves and for Lohikärra." He stormed down the hall and out of sight. Even Raynord looked surprised at his reaction.

I stood there for a moment until Haldrek squeezed me into his side, comforting me. "We'll be fine. Thegn Etelaranikä was never a man I trusted or wished to be aligned with." He sighed. "He would never have been my ally, even if I did agree to his proposal."

Raynord turned to us and opened his mouth, but before he could say anything, Haldrek stopped him.

"And if I had agreed to marry one of your granddaughters, uncle, Thegn Etelaranikä would have done the same thing. At least with Ina, I know I have someone who can fight by my side."

Raynord shook his head. "I know. Not that I was going to mention that." He sighed and turned to me, resignation deepening his wrinkles. "I would have preferred Haldrek marry one of my granddaughters, that is correct, but what is done is done and I am not be the viper Gustav is." Raynord looked at Haldrek and grimaced. "You will have to deal with him one way or another and I fear you are right. Gustav would have never been your ally. He is too consumed with want of power." He rubbed the bridge of his nose. "Even more than I am."

We were silent for a long time, mulling over what had just happened and what to do next, until a warrior rushed up to Aallotar, eyes wide with panic. The warrior leaned in, whispering something that put a scowl on her face. Her expression darkened as she turned to Raynord.

"Bjorn Susi just ordered his men to pack up and return to Lansiranikä. Do you know—?"

Raynord looked up at her in surprise. "No. I would never." He exhaled. "Though he did try to convince me to ready my men, telling me he heard rumors of Blodnar heading up the coast to Drattrede. I told him I had not heard those rumors and dismissed them out of hand."

Aallotar's eyes widened as she turned to us. "Bjorn was never here to help us, was he?"

Haldrek shook his head. "I'm beginning to believe he was always here on Thegn Etelaranikä's behalf."

Raynord turned to Haldrek and hung his head. "Please accept my apologies. I have played the fool, it seems."

Haldrek scowled. "You were trying to ally yourself with Bjorn in order to manipulate me. Now we are all paying the price."

"Just like you did on the battlefield, nearly getting Haldrek killed. Now I wonder who is going to repair your blunder this time, uncle?" Aallotar snapped.

Raynord looked at ground as he clenched his fists together. "Watch your tongue, Aallotar. I am fully aware of my misdeeds and their implications. I intend to repair them, even if it means..." He took a deep breath. "I allow you all to take charge."

"Like you should have from the beginning?" Aallotar snapped. "Don't tell me what to do. Not when you're a guest in my thegn hall."

Raynord's expression darkened at her and I cleared my throat.

"We'll be able to fix this. We just can't be passive and let Gustav throw a tantrum because he didn't get his way."

"What are we going to do?" Aallotar crossed her arms, but wasn't confrontational about it.

Haldrek looked down at me for a moment, then at his cousin. "We know a few things. One, Gustav is going to do something to make things difficult in this war with the Blodnar. In fact, I wouldn't be surprised if he sided with them now. I'm almost certain he betrayed us in the last battle at Drattüjert. Bjorn, it seems, has sided with him." Haldrek returned his focus to me. "Which means there might be raids into Svartån from Lansiranikä."

I nodded grimly. I needed to find Mattie and Llamryl and have them send word to the towns and villages along the border.

"We know that Gustav's son is a necromancer, too," Haldrek continued.

"Rorik's what?" Aallotar stared at Haldrek.

Haldrek nodded his head. "I believe Rorik to be a necromancer. Ina's father told her about there being a necromancer, remember? You remember how he used to always be doing those strange things with the wildlife when we were younger? I wouldn't be surprised if he was a necromancer. And I wouldn't be surprised if he used those skills to assist the Blodnar—or at least his father." Haldrek continued. "Eliminating *that* threat would help us greatly."

I grimaced, the memory of my father coming to mind. I'd forgotten it in the hubbub of becoming a haldraga and getting married. "Haldrek's right. Rorik is a necromancer. My dad..." I looked over at Haldrek. "Right before I saw Rhaegos and became a haldraga, I saw my dad again. It was brief and with everything that happened afterwards..."

"It slipped your mind?"

I nodded. "Sorry."

"Don't need to be sorry." Haldrek squeezed me tight. "Just confirms what I thought."

"What do we do now?" Aallotar's expression softened to one of concern. "We can't fight a necromancer. I mean we can, but we'd need to prepare." She focused on Haldrek.

"I'll contact my *husceorl* and have him look up what my ancestors did in situations like this. In the meantime, we continue to keep an eye on Drattüjert. And Gustav."

"If Rorik is using necromantic magic, we need to figure what kind of spells he's using. We'll be in a world of hurt if he's using dragon magic."

My stomach churned. "The use of dragon magic could cause people in the Realm of Ghosts to start decomposing, couldn't it?"

Aallotar nodded. "Possibly. Either way, if Rorik is using necromancy, he needs to be eliminated. He's not going to be stopped unless he's dead and plunged to the depths of Lyrroth."

"He'll likely use his spells to reanimate any dead Blodnar soldiers." Raynord began pacing, scratching his beard. He looked around, as if realizing that we were still in the hallway, then he began walking away from our door and toward the stairs.

"Where are you going?" Haldrek frowned as his uncle turned to him.

"I may be a fool, but I can do at least one thing right, and that's send the dead off to Mirroth *or* Lyrroth."

I frowned at him. "How many soldiers are still on the battlefield? In what state?" Lohikärra was a colder climate, but it was still summer.

Raynord laughed. "Only the Blodnar. I've dealt with worse battle aftermaths. Rotting corpses don't bother me." He disappeared from the hallway and into the thegn hall's staircase, leaving the three of us.

I straightened up from where I had been leaning on Haldrek. "I should go find Mattie and Llamryl. If we're lucky, they'll be in Svartån by tomorrow."

He nodded and turned to Aallotar. "If you could get your informants or warriors or whoever to destroy the black powder, I think that may hinder the Blodnar as well. The less of them we have to fight while dealing with a necromancer, the better."

Aallotar gave him a knowing smile. "I'm already one step ahead of you, cousin. I sent my people out this morning."

Chapter Nineteen

After getting fully dressed in our armor, Haldrek left for one of the lower rooms to talk to some of his warriors. I put together a bowl of leftover breakfast items to give to Mattie and Llamryl, in case they or anyone else in camp had slept in. The idea of food going to waste still made me uncomfortable, and Aallotar's servants had made far more than either Haldrek or I could ever eat in one sitting.

Footsteps hurried toward the door and I stopped as a man in a Svartån tabard fell to his knee at the door, not quite crossing the threshold.

"My thegn! Mursi of the Hethurin asked me to find you. Something happened last night."

"What happened?"

"I don't know. He just told me to go fetch you. The servants downstairs said you might still be here."

Without another word, I dropped the bowl of food and hurried to where the Svartån warriors had camped with the Svarhestån warriors. The tents were set up on the edge of the estate's wall, and I hoped against hope that I would find either Mattie or Llamryl in my old tent. Pausing for a moment, I ducked my head inside. However, it was empty.

"My thegn!"

I looked up to see Mursi, one of the Hethurin from Svangendom, jogging over to me. The other warrior stood nearby, waiting and watching. Whatever had happened last night, I was sure gossip about it was spreading like wildfire throughout the camp as we stood there.

"What's going on? Where's Mattie? Or Llamryl?"

"Armod is tending to Llamryl as we speak. And Mattie —" His face fell and he averted his gaze. "I'm sorry, my thegn."

"Where's Mattie?" My eyes widened and my voice trembled, a laundry list of worst-case scenarios rolling through my mind. Panic hit me like a flood. Where was Mattie? What had happened to her? Llamryl wouldn't have let anyone hurt her without a fight. So if he was injured...

Mursi pulled me over across the camp to where a small group of Hethurin were gathered outside a tent. When we got there, the crowd dispersed for me and I ducked in to see Llamryl, bloodied and bruised. His eyes were swelled shut and his clothing ripped, revealing fresh cuts to his torso.

"Llamryl! What happened?" I knelt across from the man I assumed was Armod and looked for some sign of life from Llamryl. His chest rose slightly and I exhaled with relief.

Armod looked up at me from where he was tending to Llamryl, a golden light emanating from his hands. "My men and I found Llamryl early this morning just outside the western village gate. He was in this condition and mumbling about something."

Llamryl writhed around on the bedroll and pulled something out of his pocket. I gaped as I took it, a sick feeling filling my stomach and squeezing the air out of my chest.

"Mattie's pendant."

"Rorik," Llamryl gasped. "He took her." He moved to get up, but both Armod and I pushed him down again.

Shit. I looked at him and took a deep breath, shaking off the worry in my body. Or at least appear to be less worried. "I'll take care of this, Llamryl. You keep resting. Let Armod heal you."

Llamryl nodded and tried to open one eye. His eyelid snapped shut. "We were... umm... and we got attacked. I'm sorry, my thegn. I should have... I thought I could protect Mattie."

"It's fine. I'll take care of this. I promise. Did the men say anything while attacking you two?"

Llamryl groaned. "They talked in a tongue I've never heard, but I heard the names Rorik and Mattie over and over." He took a deep breath and I squeezed his hand.

"I'm going to find Mattie. If Rorik has done anything to her, I will kill him myself."

Llamryl smiled. "Thank you, my thegn. Please don't tell Haldrek about..."

"Mattie's love life doesn't concern Haldrek one way or another. So don't worry about it. Worry about healing." I forced my way out of the tent and began walking to the thegn hall.

"Where are you going?" Mursi asked, hurrying alongside me.

"I'm going to let Thegn Andrattür know what just happened. Nothing about her and Llamryl. That's her business. But I'm assuming Rorik kidnapped Mattie for a reason and Haldrek needs to know. I have a feeling he and I are going to be leaving soon as well." I palmed the pendant in my hand, brushing my thumb over the insignia of Andrattür on the back of it, before looking at Mursi. "Rorik isn't the only trouble we have on the horizon. Send a patrol of your fastest and have the other gesiths do the same. There is a small chance we'll be getting raids on the border with Lansiranikä soon. I want the people of Svartån prepared and able to protect themselves."

Mursi nodded and as soon as he disappeared into the Svartån camp, I picked up my speed, now running into the thegn hall as fast as I could.

I burst through the doors of the thegn hall, expecting to find Haldrek somewhere on the first floor. Warriors and servants alike milled about. For a moment, nothing felt real. I wasn't me, just a player in the games. The people here were NPCs, not real and the news about Mattie, a surreal quest. I shook my head and blinked a few times to clear my mind. A few people started staring at me—normal people behavior, not NPC behavior—and many of them wore Andrattür's insignia on their tabards. But Haldrek was nowhere in sight.

"Haldrek?" My voice squeaked as my senses returned and I tried to keep it sounding calm.

I ducked into one room with plenty of people making a semi-circle around a table. Haldrek popped his head out of the crowd and slipped out, other people taking his place. Aallotar's voice lifted above the general noise coming from the main hall.

Haldrek pulled me aside, to a corner of the room where fewer people stood. "Are you all right? What's going on?"

"Mattie's gone." I took a deep breath to collect myself. "Rorik. Apparently he kidnapped her some time last night."

"Wait. What? Who told you this?"

"Llamryl. He's in poor condition in the Svartån camp. He said some men attacked him and Mattie, just outside the village gates last night. He didn't understand much of what they were saying, but he understood 'Rorik' and 'Mattie.' Then Llamryl pulled this out of his pocket." I showed Haldrek the pendant. He took it, touching the ripped edges of the leather strip the pendant hung on.

"Why Mattie? Why would Rorik go after her before his father had approached me?"

I bit my lip as I tried to figure out what was going on. It didn't make sense. At least...

"We're assuming that Rorik and his father are working together. What if they're not? I mean..." I lowered my voice. "Rorik is a necromancer. Necromancers aren't known for being team players. Maybe they're going for the same goal, but differently?"

Haldrek grimaced. "Either way, we need to get to Rorik and figure out what he is doing. Gustav is dangerous, but I'm afraid Rorik might be more dangerous."

I nodded. Haldrek looked around, both at me and at the room. No one was paying attention to us, all eyes focused on Aallotar. "We're ready, for the most part, but I think there are a few things we need to do before we go after Rorik and Mattie. Have you sent any of your men back to Svartån?

"I'm sending three patrols as we speak. Where are we headed, anyway?"

Haldrek walked away as if he was ignoring me, but instead he stopped in front of a map of Lohikärra.

"Why would Rorik need Mattie?"

I shrugged. "Do necromancers need blood sacrifices?" It was a stupid question, but the only thing I could think of.

"They do. But Rorik could use any person for that, unfortunately. He wouldn't go out of his way to kidnap Mattie, just to kill her. He needs Mattie for something specifically. Something that's unique to her."

I tried to think of reasons why Mattie would be special. Why she was unique to Lohikärra. Then it hit me.

"Haldrek..."

"What?" He looked away from the map, focusing on me.

"Dragons. Who in Lohikärra can talk to dragons?"

He frowned. "More than just me and Mattie. My two aunts who are still living can talk to dragons."

"But how easily could Rorik get to them?"

"Not very. What would he want from the dragons? Both he and his father know the dragons would never work for or with those who would betray them. Dragons have better sense about dishonest people." He tapped the map with his finger. "There are only a couple places Gustav or Rorik might go. If they are aligned with the Blodnar, they'll either go to—"

"Drattüjert!" Aallotar interjected behind, making me jump. I turned around to see her warriors leave the room and her standing behind us. As she put her hand up in apology, she looked up at Haldrek and said, "A couple of my scouts just returned. They said they saw the Thegn of Etelaranikä riding to Drattüjert." She sighed in frustration. "I was hoping we could gather our forces and make an attack on the Blodnar at Drattüjert, but if Gustav and Rorik are aiding them..." She shook her head. "A direct attack with a full army won't do anything. We need something more nuanced."

"Agreed." Haldrek looked at me. "That makes our decision. I'm guessing Drattüjert is where Rorik is taking Mattie, even if he's not in league with his father."

Aallotar stared at both of us in surprise. "Mattie's gone?"

I nodded, trying to ignore the anxious churning in my stomach. The words coming out of my mouth sounded numb and robotic. "Rorik had some Etelaranikä warriors kidnap Mattie late last night. For some reason. We don't know yet."

"What about that man she was with last night?"

"My healers are trying to help him as we speak. Rorik's men injured Llamryl pretty badly." I blinked a few times to clear my head again. I didn't like how strange I felt.

Aallotar nodded. Looking at Haldrek, she asked, "Do you need scouts or any warriors to go with you?"

He shook his head. "I was planning on just Ina and I going after Rorik. Less people, less likely that we'll be noticed coming after them."

"Then I'll have my servants get some provisions for you two to take. I'll talk to Hrimfax and let him know what you two are doing."

Haldrek smiled. "Thank you, cousin." He looked at me and grinned. "Let's head to Drattüjert."

Chapter Twenty

We rode hard that day and by the time we made it to a resting place, my entire body was sore. My hips and thighs were especially in a world of hurt. Yet the pain and stiff cold breezes kept me my mind focused on this reality. Haldrek helped me off my horse and into the old abandoned tower we had decided to spend the night in. It reminded me in some ways of Osvif's Refuge and the other guard towers we'd taken shelter over the past few months.

After eating a cold meal of meat bread and kavasir, Haldrek led me up some crumbling, yet stable stairs to the top of the tower. I gasped as soon as we got to the top. I could see why he'd made the effort. The 360-degree view, during twilight, was stunning. Around us was mostly flat grasslands with a few small hills. To the east stood Aallotar's thegn hall, though it was beyond the horizon now. In the west, along the edge of sky and land, the sun dipped behind a ridge of rocky cliffs with a large walled fortress-looking place on top. It looked small now, but I knew its true size was much more formidable.

"This wasn't exactly how I imagined spending our mead month, but that is our destination tomorrow." Haldrek wrapped his arms around my waist, protecting me from the chill night breezes blowing across the grasslands behind us.

I smiled at the thought. Chasing after necromancers or rouge thegns wasn't what I thought I'd be doing once I got married. Not that I ever thought about being married until recently. Focusing on Drattüjert in the distance, I said, "It looks imposing."

Haldrek laughed. "That's the point. Drattüjert was built on a high ridge, looking over the plains of Heidrunefoss and Nerthusån. It's said that's where Tenelth is buried and where all the High Kings and Queens are buried. It's the jewel of Lohikärra." He rested his chin between my neck and shoulder and his beard tickled my exposed skin. "At least, it *was*. But we'll restore it."

"That's what Rhaegos called you during my ritual, you know. The Restorer."

"Huh. I was told to find the Reformer at my ritual." He squeezed me tight. "And to never let go."

I laughed as he nuzzled my neck, kissing it. "Are you being serious?"

He nodded. "Interestingly enough, Teminth said that I needed to protect the Reformer, because while my destiny is to restore Lohikärra, all of my work would be for nothing without the Reformer. I had no idea what he meant until after you arrived."

I was quiet as I mulled over what he had said, what it meant for our future. *Our future.* I smiled to myself, hoping that was a true statement. I still didn't know if I fully belonged in Lohikärra, but I wanted to. Especially now.

I gazed into the grasslands below us, valleys really, as the plains weren't actually flat, but looked rippled like cloth from where we stood. About halfway between us and Drattüjert, just below one of the ripples, I saw smoke wafting up.

"Haldrek..."

"I see it too. It looks like we're not too far behind Rorik's men and whoever else took Mattie. If we ride early and hard tomorrow, we might just catch up to them."

The idea that we could take them tonight danced in my mind. But I brushed it off, knowing even if we did sneak up on them, we'd be too exhausted to fight. Aallotar's words came back to mind. "You think it's Rorik? Or do you think it's his father? Because wasn't Thegn Etelaranikä the one Aallotar's scouts said was riding this way?"

"Possibly. I still think the two of them are working together, even if Rorik kidnapped Mattie before his father did anything. And even if Rorik thinks he's acting alone." Haldrek relaxed his arms and stood up straighter. "I think we'll find all of our answers once we catch up to them." He began walking down from the tower, holding his hand out for me. "If we mean to catch them before they make it to Drattüjert, we should probably head to bed, my love. That way we'll be up before them."

I took his hand and followed him to the middle floor, where we had set up our sparse but warm bedding. It was both weird and comforting to be sleeping by his side, body to body, this time around. Kept warm by his body heat as we cuddled, I only realized how tired I was when I fell asleep almost instantly.

While I was grateful that my regular nightmare hadn't made another appearance, when I returned to consciousness, I found myself in a dark but familiar place. I could only see the dim outline of pillars and a massive dais, but the overbearing feeling of despair smothered me as I looked around, searching for someone or something to focus on. I was in the Realm of Ghosts again, but something was deeply wrong. I could feel it in my bones. This wasn't the way I'd ever remembered it. The last time I had been here, the darkest part of the realm still had at least *some* ambient light in it. But now? Complete and utter darkness.

Not just a lack of light, but a physical darkness, similar to the presence that had crept into my dreams just before our wedding.

"Ina…" My father gasped next to me and I jumped, my heart racing and senses hyper alert to whatever was coming next. His voice was nothing like I'd ever heard before. It was rough and broken, like last time, but now a sense of fear and resignation filled it as well.

"Dad? I can't see you. What's going on?"

"Kill my body. Let me go." Something cold and slimy slumped against my leg and I screamed.

"Dad…" Panic welled up in my throat as I stumbled to my feet. He moaned and a bluish light popped up behind me. It lit up the room, revealing many bodies in various states of decomposition. They all writhed around like my father, body parts only being held together by half rotted sinews and the clothes they wore. I turned to the bluish light. A few of the bodies dragging themselves toward it, grasping at it in vain. The light pulled at me as well and, against my better judgement, I walked over to its source. The closer I got, the more I realized it was a large gem. The bluish light resembled some kind of fire swirling and crackling inside of the gem. Much to my surprise, Rhaegos's breathing echoed at the edge of my mind. It was labored and when she shuddered, my body shook as well.

Oh wicked, wicked child. You play with power you cannot control.

Rhaegos's voice gasped as badly as my father's had and I stepped away from the gem. Was this what was causing all the distress?

Protect us, little one. Keep the gem from his reach.

My stomach dropped and I reached for the gem, but just like the others grasping for it, my hand went through it.

Was this something in the Realm of the Living causing chaos in the Realm of Ghosts? As I went to touch the gem again, I felt a solid force push itself through my body like a wave. I recoiled from the gem and stumbled over something. A spirit? Or the body of someone else who had been reanimated and was decomposing here? The person groaned as I tried to pull myself off of them. I had to get closer to the presence that had pushed through me.

As I got up, I felt a strong pressure pushing me down and away from the person. Resisting it, I walked forward, one step at a time, until I was within touching distance. With his back to me, all I could see was a man in what looked to be finely woven mage robes. He reached for the gem. I felt a sick foreboding as he touched it, as if the fire burning within the gem now burned inside of me, torching and gutting every fiber and cell of my being. I gasped, trying to ignore the pain. How was I going to get the gem if I couldn't physically grab it?

The spirits around me began to moan as hooded figure ignored them. He laughed as he fingered the facets of the long gem. The urge to vomit came hard and fast as the man squeezed the gem and put it to his chest. A dragon screeched as if it was just above us. Dropping to my knees, I dry heaved and the man turned around. Even with my eyes locked on the floor, I sensed his stare boring into my back. He looked away and the spirits around me began to moan. I pulled my head up, desperate to see who or what was causing this. The blue gem cast an eerie light on his face, revealing a gaunt yet young-looking face with a pallor that rivaled the Isillas. A name came to mind—I knew exactly who he was.

Rorik.

"Finally." He stared at me with jet black eyes and vile smirk. My stomach lurched and I fell to my side, curling up in the fetal position and getting a full view of the person as he faced me. The light from the crystal brightened. Dark hair and sickly skin lit up ominously in the light of the gem he held. Or was somehow attached to him. He raised his arms and an overwhelm scent of body funk and decay hit me. I gagged. A ripping, tearing sensation coursed through me as I watched him. Rhaegos began to make a gnashing, guttural sound in my head, then pulled away. Her presence was replaced by emptiness and an anger toward this person began to fill it.

"Rorik." I whispered, gritting my teeth just before I blacked out once again.

"Ina! Wake up! Please."

I was surprised to hear Haldrek's panicked sob as I opened my eyes. The room we were in was still dark, except for a smoldering fire in a nearby brazier. Light began to creep in through the window above us, but just barely. One of Haldrek's hands was on my cheek, stroking it furiously in an attempt to wake me up, the other firmly gripping my shoulder. I stared at him and wondered for a moment if we were back in that inn on the edge of Svartån. Haldrek's eyes were wide with fear, but I felt a surreal calming sensation come over me. Not that I felt calm. My heart raced and my hands were damp with sweat, but I felt detached from the moment. Like I was just playing a character in the video games and this was a cut scene.

I blinked, trying to ground myself. "Haldrek? Where are we? What's going on?"

He shook his head. "I don't know what's going on. Something. Something bad." He sat me up and I flopped against him, my muscles refusing to hold me up. Now I was beginning to panic. "You went into the Realm of Ghosts again." His voice was calmer, but still fearful. "What happened there?"

I thought back to my time in the Realm of Ghosts. Everything was still vivid, as if it had just happened. "My dad and the others...He begged me to kill his body and then..." I blinked again as I stared at Haldrek, trying to focus on his features, on something real, to make sure I wasn't still in some kind of dream realm or game reality. I felt it again, the hollowness from the Realm of Ghosts, lingering at the edge of my mind where Rhaegos had been for the last week or so. "Something's wrong. Where—?"

I was interrupted by the anguished screech of a dragon. Several more followed and Haldrek rummaged in the bag behind my head. He pulled out a bottle and uncorked it by my mouth.

"Drink this. You'll need your strength."

The tonic was vile but I forced it down my throat, trying not to gag.

"What happened in the Realm of Ghosts? The only time you go there is if you've been pulled there by your father."

I slowly sat up as Haldrek helped me up against a wall and began packing our belongings.

"There was a gem. A bluish gem. It had a fire in it. And Rhaegos... the gem is connected to the dragons somehow. The spirits kept trying to grab it, but they couldn't because it wasn't in the Realm of Ghosts. I went to grab it, but a force pushed through me. A person. Like they were both in the Realm of Ghosts and not in it at the same time. Rorik..."

"What about Rorik? Was he in the Realm of Ghosts?" Haldrek stopped, furrowing his brow.

"Yes. And no. It was like he was both in the Realm of Ghosts and the Realm of the Living. The blue gem. I couldn't grab it. My hand kept going through it, but he grabbed the gem, which made the spirits, including my father, start to moan in pain and then a dragon screeched..." I stopped as the tonic tried to push itself up my throat. My memories began to fade as I tried to remember everything. Rhaegos had begun acting strangely as well.

"Like the one we just heard?"

I nodded, returning my focus to Haldrek. "But Rorik's not in Drattüjert. He can't be. Can he?"

Haldrek stopped his fiddling and sighed. "Anything's possible now. I heard that first dragon screech. That's what woke me up. It feels like Teminth is being pulled from me. He's not completely gone, but I can't talk to him anymore."

"Same. I felt like my insides, my spirit, was being ripped in half as Rorik grabbed the gem. What is that gem anyway? It had a connection to the dragons."

Haldrek shook his head. "I don't know for sure, but from how you described it, I wouldn't be surprised if it was part of Tenelth's Staff. I hope it isn't though."

My stomach sank like it had rocks in it. "If that gem is part of Tenelth's Staff? How screwed are we?"

"Pretty screwed, as you say. Tenelth's Staff is a powerful magical object given to Bjornulf when he joined all the peoples of Lohikärra. The gem is a vessel for dragon magic and dragon souls, if you will. While it is in the staff, it is mostly symbolic of the wielder's right to rule over Lohikärra." He exhaled, as if struggling with some kind of injury. "But once pulled from the staff, it can become a dangerous weapon. If Rorik has it, he could lead an army of dragons against whatever foe he desired. Instead of being the guardians of Lohikärra, the dragons could become the destroyers of Lohikärra."

"Would Rorik having the gem cause the feeling of something being wrong with the dragons? Or them being stripped from haldragas?"

Haldrek nodded, his expression grim. "I hope not, but if that's the case, I need to check something." He got up and headed to where the horses were. I curled up, trying to remember anything more from the Realm of Ghosts. It felt like I had wrung everything from my memory that I could.

When Haldrek returned, he knelt next to me and asked, "Can you stand?"

I pulled myself up against the wall and nodded. Whatever he had given me had refilled the physical energy Rorik had drained from me in the Realm of Ghosts. Haldrek helped me downstairs and on to my horse before getting on to his. He still looked a little shaken as he turned his horse to me. Even his voice hinted at it.

"We need to fly to Drattüjert as fast as we can. I'm guessing the camp from last night is already packed up, so I doubt anyone will still be there." He turned his horse toward the city and said, "Let's go get Rorik."

I nodded grimly and set off after him as quickly as my horse could take me.

Chapter Twenty-One

The sun was just reaching the horizon, dipping below the mountains, when we reached the gate of Drattüjert. We'd ridden all day as quickly as we could without exhausting our mounts, yet it felt as if we were going too slow. Now in front of the city, I surveyed the area in the fading light. The gate, despite its size, was ripped loose from the arch that would have held it otherwise. The metal chains splayed out from it like snakes, and rock pieces from the broken walls studded the grass around us. Rotting bits of corpses still littered the ground, though most of the bodies had been picked clean of their flesh. A clear path of horse hooves had led us to this point, but we and our horses were the only living creatures around.

"Where...?" Haldrek got off his horse, letting it amble over to some grass. "Where are the dragons?"

I got off my horse as well. "Maybe they're off fighting?" The words rang hollow as I spoke them, but it was the only explanation I could give. Or rather the only explanation I wanted to give. If the dragons weren't here, where were they? Was Rorik already using them to terrorize some part of Lohikärra? Svartån? Andrattür?

"No." Haldrek's voice brought me out of my thoughts. "There's always at least one or two dragons flying around Drattüjert. Even when they're fighting."

"What about when the Blodnar overran Drattüjert the first time?"

"They didn't kill the dragons. We were betrayed from within, and once our warriors were weakened, the Blodnar stormed the gate. Just as many of their soldiers were killed by the dragons as we killed." He gestured to the debris around us. "It's too quiet right now. Something's wrong."

"What do we do? Try and find the dragons? Or try and find Mattie?"

His mouth hung open for a moment as he looked around. "I think we need to go into the city. Especially..."

"Especially what?"

"When you went to the Realm of Ghosts, where did you go? Was it some place familiar?"

"It was dark, but the little I could see made me think of a palace or hall. It was the same place I first saw my dad when I came here to Lohikärra—a throne room or something. And the gem Rorik grabbed was on a throne-looking chair."

Haldrek nodded grimly, gesturing for me to follow him as he pulled out his sword. "I think I know where you went. The actual throne room in the palace. That's where Kalle fell, as well as your father and the few others who fought alongside my uncle."

I nodded and followed suit as we walked up a set of stairs and across the fallen bridge gate. "You think Rorik, and whoever else is with him, are in the palace?"

"I'd bet Mirratoft on it." Haldrek kept himself slightly in front of me as we stepped into the city proper. I gasped as I looked at the bodies that lay in the streets. Only a few people were sprawled out on the ground, and while they looked dead, the number of ghosts were far fewer than the number of bodies. All the ghosts were of warriors, soldiers and guards, though the bodies included civilians.

"They massacred the people here." Haldrek's voice was hard with anger and I looked at him.

"No. They're not all dead. There's not that many ghosts." I trailed off as I looked at the bodies. Most of them looked like they were sleeping, or in a trance. The civilian bodies bore no sign of decomposition, only in the soldiers whose ghosts still roamed around.

"What?" Haldrek turned to me as I continued to observe the scene. The bodies that weren't decomposing—that looked like they were just sleeping—seemed to be pushed aside, as if they had fallen where they stood and someone had moved them out of the way. I looked up the street and saw the same thing. A path had been cleared as far as I could see.

"I think most of the people here were put under some kind of sleeping spell? At least those who didn't die fighting. I mean, there are the soldiers and guards." I covered my mouth and nose as we passed a pile of dead and decayed bodies. "It looks like the ones still here have been rotting since the Blodnar overtook this place. They haven't had their rites done—they're looking at me."

"Are they pestering you?"

I shook my head. "It's almost as if they're still on patrol. Guarding the city."

Haldrek nodded. "You think Rorik did this?"

I shrugged. "I can't see why he wouldn't. If he's..." I stopped, remembering the dream from two nights ago. I'd been so focused on the fact that Robert was taking orders from someone here in Lohikärra that I'd ignored what Rorik had said. He intended to rule over not just the thegn lands he was entitled to, but all of Lohikärra.

"If he what, Ina?" He nudged me with his sword hand, bringing me back to this reality.

"Rorik is a thegn-heir, isn't he? He'll take his father's spot once Gustav is dead."

"Yes, but what does that have to do with Drattüjert and putting people under a sleeping spell?"

I turned to Haldrek. "The people of Drattüjert serve Rorik better alive than dead. It's hard to be a ruler of a place if all its occupants are dead. Even if you are a necromancer." I continued walking down the path, sword at the ready. In the games, whenever things were this deathly quiet, it meant something big was coming up. I wanted to be prepared, especially if it was something like zombies.

Haldrek followed beside me, his footsteps being one of the few things I heard. That made me stop.

"What?"

"Where are the animals?"

"What?" He turned to me in confusion.

"Are there no animals in Drattüjert normally? Dogs, cats, birds, mice? The only thing I hear when we're walking is you and me. No animal sounds, no nothing. Would a sleeping spell work on them too?" I looked at the various buildings around us. In the dusky light, one eave had a small bee or hornet's nest underneath it, but nothing in or around it. "Haldrek, I think whatever happened to the dragons affected all the rest of the animals too."

He sheathed his sword for a moment and put his free hand on my shoulder and said, "We should probably go then. Try to figure what in Lyrroth is going on."

I nodded and kept my eye on the main road as the sun light got dimmer behind us. Once we got to the main square in front of the fortress-turned-palace, it was dark, but the bluish glow of the spirits led the way. I felt Haldrek bump into me a few times as I guided us into the palace.

As we made our way through the broken doors, I heard moaning and grunts coming from somewhere in the interior. I froze and Haldrek brushed past me as he pushed forward into the long hallway.

"Zombies?" I whispered, the air disappearing from my lungs.

"If zombies are re-animated corpses, then yes. Remember how we fought those *ru-umii*?"

"Back to back?"

Haldrek nodded. "If you could cast some fire balls or light or something, now that it's getting dark, that would help."

I nodded and cast a fireball down the hall, much as I had in Ottkatla's Barrow. No zombies were illuminated, but I saw where some torches still hung. Casting a fire ball at a few of them, I lit our way into the palace. While it was easier to see what lay ahead, the hallway was no less ominous.

It was here I began to see the ghosts and decayed bodies of those who worked in the palace. I grimaced and tried to ignore the spirits who begged at my feet. In my mind, I promised to return and do their rites once Rorik and the Blodnar had been dealt with. The smell of rotted flesh permeated the hall as I hid my nose and mouth with my hand. Some of the spirits rushed toward me, ignoring my attempts to avoid them. As they pleaded with me, I noticed their spirits seemed to rot now as well. My heart ached for them as I whispered, "I'll come back, I promise."

"More ghosts?" Haldrek asked as he kept his back to mine, watching for any undead that might pop up.

I nodded. "Yes. When we are done with Rorik and his father, we'll need to return here and give these people their rites so they can pass on to Mirroth."

"Agreed. I never thought I'd say this, but the ghosts don't scare me so much anymore."

I laughed softly, then stopped before a set of doors. I could hear noises on the other side.

"I think they're in there." My chest tightened and I closed my eyes, trying not to panic. If my dreams were correct, this was where my dad had been killed and where the zombie version of him now roamed. If Haldrek didn't kill him, I would have to. How would that affect him in the Realm of Ghosts? Would he have a spirit to send to Mirroth in the end?

Haldrek turned around. "That's awfully convenient. All in one spot."

"Unless it's meant to slow us down and keep us from where we're supposed to go."

He turned to me in surprise as I shrugged. "Just like the *ruumii* in Ottkatla's Barrow and just like the monsters in the video games. You hit a group of creatures right before you find the ultimate bad guy. They're there to wear you out or make you retreat."

"We can't, though."

"I know." I nodded, trying to prepare myself for what was beyond those doors. "This is the throne room, right?"

"Correct." Haldrek and I looked behind us once more, at the hallway. About a dozen other hallways sprouted off from it at regular intervals where the torches were. I shuddered as I looked at the dead bodies we had just passed, wondering what was different between them and the zombies in the next room.

Focusing on the door, which wore a scorch mark from my initial fireball, I asked, "Are we ready?"

Haldrek nodded. He took a deep breath and pushed open the door.

Chapter Twenty-Two

Inside stood—or rather slouched—a room full of mobile corpses. The smell hit me hard and I doubled over, gagging as a nearby zombie warrior charged us. Haldrek spun around, nearly cleaving the zombie's head off and sending him into a wall.

"Ina!"

I looked up to see we had all of the zombies' attentions on us. Haldrek backed up to me.

"Sorry," I mumbled as I saw a few of the zombies start to amble my way. Despite the decay, I thought one of them looked like my father.

"Just try to fight them off the best you can. Breath through your mouth."

One of the zombies lunged for me. I slammed my shield across his chest before stabbing him and swiveling around to hit another one.

One by one, Haldrek and I cut down the zombies until their grunting and moaning ceased. In the darkness of the room, I saw bluish people start to reappear as I leaned up against Haldrek's back. That was one small mercy. At least, I hoped it was.

"Did we get all of them?" I whispered, trying to find familiar faces from the Realm of the Dead among the ghosts. I had yet to see my father, even though a few of the people were recognizable. An older man with a crown stood by where Haldrek had destroyed his zombie. I guessed he was High King Kalle.

"I think—" Haldrek's answer was cut off by an angry, agonized roar. A familiar but twisted, rotting face stared at me. My heart sank and my mind went blank.

"Dad?" I gasped as the zombie ran at me, sword lifted. In a split second, Haldrek's sword made contact with my dad. His zombie's sword was above my head and I stepped away in shock. The other zombies had been easy to defeat.

"Ina! Help me!" Haldrek used his sword as a lever and kicked the zombie away, sending him staggering.

I stared wide-eyed at my dad as he regained his balance and Haldrek took a defensive stance. Yet the zombie seemed to have no interest in him, only me. I tightened my grip on my sword and shield, but hesitated to attack.

"Ina. You need to kill him."

I gulped, raising my sword as he charged at me once again with a roar. Shaking, I met the blow with my shield, but it made me stagger. The zombie groaned, as if in pain, before raising his sword and swinging at me again. I stumbled away, out of the sword's reach, and looked for another approach, in order to attack him.

"Ina! He's *not* your father!" Haldrek came running over to me.

The zombie swung around and charged at Haldrek, who met the blow and glanced his sword toward the zombie's arm. It shrieked, dropping its weapon before turning around, searching for me as I ducked around the dim room.

Haldrek was right. Though the creature looked like my father, it acted as if possessed by something. I gasped—and then gagged— as the thought hit me. *Of course.* This is what my father's voice had meant when he told me to kill his body. This rotting meat sack wasn't my father. It was merely his body reanimated.

I found my footing against a pillar and, just as the zombie caught sight of me, I cut it across the chest, knocking the creature to the ground and stabbing it in the heart. An agonizing cry came from my throat. One I didn't know I could make.

The zombie looked up at me wide eyed for a second before its eyes rolled back. The decayed muscles and sinews relaxed and the bluish hue of my father materialized in front of me, smiling.

I smiled in relief as his mouth moved to say something. He pointed in the direction his zombie had come from, then gestured for me to go. I hesitated for a moment before I heard all of the spirits whisper as one:

"*Go!*"

I nodded and turned to Haldrek. "Let's find Rorik and Mattie. I think we're finished in here."

Haldrek and I ran through the door my dad had pointed at. It led into a massive open air courtyard garden, the likes of which I had never seen. A wide paved path framed the courtyard and I saw someone to our left, on the opposite corner of the path, casting some kind of spell into the center of the courtyard—or rather fiddling with something that was supposed to be casting a spell. The hooded figure was almost identical to the person from my most recent dream.

A bluish light flickered from inside of a cup next to him. Above it was a disc that reflected and focused the light, sending a ray toward the middle.

"What in Tenelth's name...?" I turned to see Haldrek staring at the courtyard too. A buzzing sound emanated from the center, which grew more steady as the mage—Rorik—manipulated the crystal and the device it was in.

Once he had stopped fiddling with it, he turned to us and stopped.

"Finally." He took a step toward us and the urge to run overwhelmed me. The same pressure and sick foreboding threatened to crush me as my knees began to buckle. Before I had a chance to move, however, I was jerked toward him.

"Ina!"

I hit the ground near a pathway into the middle of the garden, immobilized. There the whooshing sound became deafening as a tornado-shaped vortex formed, taking over most of the garden. A few vines from the closest columns were pulled toward the tornado, ripping away and disappearing into the vortex with a handful of sparks.

"Finally you're here, *Thegn of Svartån*." Rorik walked over, unaffected by the pull of the vortex, and lifted my face up. He spat in it as I heard a dull thunk behind me.

"Thegn of Andrattür. Don't think you can save your..." Rorik paused with a smirk. "Wife, now is it? Don't think you can save her that easily. I have plans for her. Just like her friend who also doesn't belong here."

"Where's Mattie?" I snapped, twisting my head away and letting the pull of the vortex wipe the spit from my eye.

"I threw her in the vortex. I have no idea where it goes, but she went there. Along with my father."

Haldrek coughed. "You threw your father into the vortex?"

"Me? No. That half-breed dragged him in. After the dragons got sucked in, she and he and any living, waking thing in Drattüjert as well."

"What about you?" I turned to face him and guessed he had manipulated his spirit to move outside of his body last night—he no longer had blackened eyes—but he was a solid figure right now.

"I have the power to rip open vortexes between worlds, reanimate the dead, and so much more. You think I don't know how to keep myself from being sucked into my own creation?" He cradled my cheek while pulling my helmet off. I knew he was going to do something, but he had somehow frozen me. I fought the stiffness covering every inch of my body. In a flash, he dropped my helmet and slapped me across the face. Whatever had been holding me in place released, and I was pulled toward the vortex. My muscles became limp and I rolled close enough to the vortex to feel it start to pull me in.

I tried to roll away as Haldrek stumbled over to me, ignoring Rorik. In that moment, I knew he'd made a mistake. As soon as Haldrek's hand grabbed mine, a blast of black vapor shot from Rorik's hand, lifting us both in the air. Haldrek was yanked up by his feet, pulling me up along with him. Before I had a chance to think or scream, Haldrek and I were sucked into the vortex.

Chapter Twenty-Three

The first thing I saw as Haldrek and I were thrust from the vortex were gray clouds. I shut my eyes and braced for impact as I began tumbling again, my stomach lurching. My shoulders hit something hard and metallic and I went bouncing off the side of a slanted roof before I hit the ground. Something fleshy broke my fall and I slumped on the ground next to it, aching and sore.

Haldrek grunted, then groaned. "Ugh. Where are we?" He shook himself off and sat up. I opened my eyes in surprise. Above us, dragons, both physical and not, swarmed. Their screeching amplified the shrillness of the tornado sirens wailing around us. Sitting up, I realized the area we were in was void of people.

Honestly, that was what surprised me the most. Of course people took cover when tornadoes broke out, but usually it was somewhere where they could watch the excitement without actually being in the storm. But now I wondered where everyone was. We had landed in the mall parking lot. Could everyone else see the dragons like I did? Or was there another reason? If they could, why wasn't the mall swarming with police and military people?

I watched as a smaller dragon plunged at a couple of cars and tossed them like they were toys. Standing up on wobbly legs with Haldrek's help, I whispered, "We've got to get out of here."

"Where are we, Ina? What is this place?"

"Fargo."

"Ina! Haldrek! Run!"

I turned around to see Mattie running full speed at us with a handful of Blodnar behind her. She shed a couple of ropes from around her arms as she shoved Haldrek and me into moving.

As we ran across the parking lot, we dodged a few more flying cars and chunks of debris, making our way to one of the outlying buildings. I glanced behind me to see the Blodnar attackers retreating from the dragons and the cars they were tossing around. Pulling the doors open, we stumbled into the cafe restaurant. Looking up, I saw a few people who had sheltered in the building staring at us.

Mattie guided us toward an empty table behind a half wall and away from the small group of people. Their attention was locked on us. She met their stares and they looked away.

As soon as we were slumped on the floor, Haldrek made a barrier with a couple of freestanding tables between us and the other group. I leaned over to Mattie. "What are we doing back in Fargo?"

"That son of bitch, Rorik, sent us here, along with the dragons, a whole lotta Blodnar, his father, and anything else he wanted out of the way. He's a psychopath. Just like your mother. He plans on becoming the High King as soon as he can."

"Who stands between him and the throne?"

"Us, his father—who is a nut job himself—and Modolf's wife if the people of Svartån believe you dead. Etelaranikä comes in line for the throne after Andrattür and Svartån, so if we're out of the picture..."

"Rorik can claim the throne." I groaned. "That's why he didn't kill most of the people in the city."

"He didn't kill anyone in the city. That was the Blodnar from the initial attack. He just put anyone still living into a sleeping trance until he could claim the throne."

"What's keeping him from doing that now?"

"Almost nothing. As soon as people believe we're dead..."

"Lohikärra is under his control." I groaned again. Turning to Haldrek, I saw he was on his back, sweating like he was in pain.

"Haldrek?" I knelt next to him and brushed the sweat off his forehead. "What's wrong?" I began to panic, thinking he had injured himself in the fall.

"Teminth is going crazy inside my head. Just like his kin outside. I don't know why though. It feels like I'm being ripped apart."

"Haldrek." I held his hand as he grimaced again, his body going stiff. Mattie reached over and put a small vial near his mouth.

"Drink this. I swiped one from Gustav. It's a concoction to put Teminth to sleep for a little bit."

Haldrek opened his mouth, allowing Mattie to pour the tonic in. As he swallowed, his body relaxed and he looked up at us with a smile.

"I'm glad you're alive, Ina." He turned to Mattie. "You too, Mattie."

She raised an eyebrow at him. "I'm only your sister." Putting the vial away, she helped him up against a bench.

"Why aren't you two in pain? You have the dragons within you?"

Mattie shook her head and nodded toward the windows. "Sivath and Rhaegos are out there with their kin." She looked at Haldrek. "Rorik did something to pull the dragon spirits from the haldragas—or at least as many as he could. I think Gustav's dragon is still with him, but it's been asleep for a while now. Yours was trying to get out." She stood up and started dusting herself off. "I'm sorry, I'm still trying to wrap my head around all of this. We need to figure a way to return to Lohikärra or, at the very least, send the Blodnar and the dragons back. The longer the dragons are here, the worse it's going to get. They don't belong in this world and it's affecting them."

Haldrek nodded. "I can hear them. They're speaking nonsense, and it feels like they're in the middle of a battle."

"So how do we return everything to normal?" My body still ached from the fall and the thought of staying in Fargo didn't help. Though everything here was familiar—I had lived in Fargo my entire life—I had come to feel more at home in Lohikärra in the last few months. Looking over at Haldrek, the thought occurred to me: once the dragons returned to Lohikärra, he would too. I didn't want to lose him. Not now.

"Are you all right, Ina?" Haldrek and Mattie both stared at me as he brushed his hand against my cheek, wiping a few tears away.

"I... I'm just..." I shook my head. "We need to figure out how to return to Lohikärra. All of us, the dragons, and even the Blodnar and Thegn Etelaranikä."

Mattie nodded and leaned against the half wall. She glanced at the people still staring at us and lowered her voice. "I overheard how Rorik created the vortex. He used dragon souls to open it. Like the dragon scale you had, Ina. That's why..." She looked at Haldrek. "Gustav has been in league with the Blodnar for ages, it seems. It was him who gave the Blodnar the information on the launchers and gun powder they've been using. Rorik's been harvesting the dragon souls to create some of the crystals. Not just the one around his neck."

"So..." I had so many questions. Haldrek looked a bit overwhelmed as well. "Is that why Rorik used his necromancy powers to make zombies out of the people in the palace?"

Mattie nodded. We all flinched as one of the dragons flew particularly close to where we were hiding and shrieked. She looked out the window again before continuing. "Once the dragons knew how to avoid the launchers—for the most part—and were able to drive the Blodnar from the city, Rorik was getting less and less dragon souls, so he used his necromancy to bring the dead abthanry back to life and harvest their dragon souls. But he could only do that to those who hadn't made it to Mirroth."

"Which is why only some of the dead in the palace were made into zombies."

Mattie nodded again as a deafening roar boomed over us and the building shook. Haldrek curled his body around me as people screamed and debris began to litter the floor around us. He kicked the tables that created our barricade, sending them flying, and gave an order to everyone in the building:

"Run!"

Mattie, Haldrek, and I ran through the debris along with the other people. A particularly large dragon had landed on the roof and was stomping around on it, waving its wings around and throwing chunks of destroyed building materials into the air. As we crossed the parking lot, heading toward the closest undamaged building, a familiar car screeched in front of us and I froze. My eyes widened, as did my mother's, her mouth slightly ajar. She was still in her scrubs, but that was the least confusing part of this whole situation. What was she even doing here at the mall? If she was in her scrubs, she was either on her way to a shift or getting off of one. But above all, an overwhelming sense of being trapped fell over me.

My mother lowered her head to look at me through the passenger side window. An ugly scowl crossed her face as she pointed to the passenger seat between the two of us.

"In here. Now."

I shook my head and pushed Haldrek toward the mall entrance we were headed to. My mother blocked us by moving the car forward.

"I say *now*. Don't disobey me."

"No. I don't…I'm eighteen now." My tongue seemed to go limp and the words fell flat. I had a hard time saying what I wanted to. That I was an adult and she couldn't tell me what do anymore. But the thought of saying that terrified me. There was too much fear and not enough anger for me to confront her like I had in the past.

"What did you say?"

"She said no." Haldrek's voice was deep and ominous, despite the hint of physical pain lingering in it. "Who are you to speak to a thegn of Lohikärra like that?"

My mother turned her focus to Haldrek and panic rose up inside me on his behalf. But he stared just as hard as she did.

"I'm her mother, you drugged out idiot. What the hell are talking about her being a thegn of Lohikärra? That's a game. This is real life." She switched to me. "You. Get in the car. I don't care if you're eighteen. You're still coming with me."

"Why are you here, Mrs. Svanunge?" Mattie snapped, standing on the other side of the car. "You always told Ina how she was no longer your problem or responsibility once she's eighteen. What do you want with her now?"

My mother spun her attention to Mattie. "Because she's my daughter. And I want answers. I got into a lot of hot water because you two disappeared on me like that."

With her focus diverted, I pushed Haldrek in front of me and tried to slip behind the car before my mother could reverse it. As we ran, the car accelerated backwards, hitting Haldrek in the knees and knocking him on top of me.

"Argh!" He crumpled to the ground and winced.

"Haldrek!" Mattie and I went to help him up as my mother leaned her head out the window.

"Get. In. The. Car. Now," she shouted. "Or. Else."

Mattie spun around. "You're effing crazy! Why the hell would we do something like that? I hope a dragon eats you." She returned her focus to Haldrek as we helped him out of way of my mother's car.

"A dragon?" My mother howled with laughter. "Are you drugged out too? Is that what happened? You two ran away to join some other drugged out nutters and spend all of your inheritance? Did Ina convince you to do this? Because I ain't paying for—"

Another dragon flew dangerously close to us, whipping nearby trees and bushes around. The tornado sirens went off again. My mother began looking around for wherever the chaos was coming from. Mattie ducked down and whispered, "Go. She's in a clean uniform, which means she was probably headed to work. There will be people around to keep her in line there. I'll get Haldrek out of her way and into the mall. When you have a chance, get back here."

"What? What about the dragons? The Blodnar?" I glanced around at them as the dragons prowled the skies, looking for things to attack.

"Ina! Get. In. The. Car!" My mother revved the engine, making me jump.

"Go. I have a plan. The dragons won't touch us. I think. Who knows? They might even keep you safe in their rage. Just go." Mattie glanced in my mother's direction. My stomach churned and my own fury welled up inside me at the idea of returning to her. Letting her take me away from Mattie and Haldrek. But I wanted them to be safe. Haldrek squeezed my hand and struggled to sit up.

"I'm not going to let her take you, Ina. That woman…" He grimaced as Mattie tried to help him.

"You are in no shape to fight right now, Haldrek. Ina can handle her mother." Mattie turned to me as I reluctantly nodded. I hoped I could handle my mother. If I wanted to return to Lohikärra, I needed to find a way to escape without her chasing me.

"Fine. Get him bandaged up. Just don't leave Fargo until I return."

Mattie grinned. "Don't worry. We won't."

Chapter Twenty-Four

I stood up, hands in the air, and walked over to the passenger side of the car. My mother unlocked the door and I waited until Mattie and Haldrek had scooted further away before getting in.

"Put your seat belt on."

"No." I folded my arms. "I'll be fine."

"Excuse me? I told you to put your seatbelt on. Do it."

"And if I don't?" I stared at her, anger welling up inside of me. The only reason I was in this car was because I wanted to keep Haldrek and Mattie safe. Maybe if we got in a car wreck, I'd be transported to Lohikärra again. Stranger things had happened, and just the reminder there was another world out there put some fire back in me.

"Then I'll put it on you." She grabbed the seatbelt and jerked it across my chest and lap. "There are who knows how many tornadoes or whatever these storms are swarming around here. I had to haul my butt over here to save you because Robert said he saw you at the mall and you don't even have the decency to put your seatbelt on for me. You *want* me to get a ticket when a cop sees me drive by without you buckled in?" The buckle clicked and she returned to her position gripping the steering wheel.

"Given the storms, I doubt they're going to care." I was slammed into the seat as she stepped on the gas pedal. So that was why my mother was here. But if Robert told her I was here, how did he know?

"Don't you dare sass me like that. I came over here to save you from these storms and what do I find? You and Mattie and some Viking wannabe jock drug addict frolicking around the mall parking lot like idiots. You really are mental, aren't you? Delusional? Or you're on drugs? I bet you're on drugs. That would explain the stupid getup you have on." She shook her head. "You are a waste of time and an embarrassment to me. I wish you'd never been born."

"Then why the hell do you want me in your car? I'm eighteen. You're no longer responsible for me. Leave me alone and pretend like I don't exist."

"I want answers. You *humiliated* me when you disappeared. Child Protective Services came banging on my door, asking why I wasn't sending you to school and where were you? Started investigating *me*! I lost my old job because of you!"

"Then what's with the scrubs? You just like driving around in them?"

She smacked my mouth with the back of her hand. The small band with fake gems on her middle finger cut my lip. "Don't you dare sass me like that. I got a new job. I'm not a worthless leech like you. Doesn't pay as well though. Actually have to rely on Robert for part of the rent. Disgusting slob. I'm a better human than him. I'm a better human than *you*. What do I get for that, though? Nothing. No good deed goes unpunished."

I refused to respond and instead looked out the window, focusing on the stormy 'clouds' in the sky. The dragons weren't physical entities like they were in Lohikärra. Instead they were cloudy, opaque shapes that roiled and thundered like actual storms. But they weren't entirely like normal tornadoes or thunderstorms. They shifted between black, gray, and a variety of other muted, earth-toned colors. Flashes of dark purple, green, and sickly yellow interspersed with the gray and black. The dragons, and the clouds that formed them, looked sick and ominous. The lack of rain also added to the sense of danger, and the *feeling* of the atmosphere was different than when tornadoes were about to roll through. The dragons were screeching and tumbling all over the place, sometimes twisting around like the beginning of a tornado, then dissipating. This looked nothing like the normal storms that came through every summer, yet the few people on the road or sidewalks treated them as they would normal summer storms.

"What are you looking at?" my mother snapped. I ignored her until she swerved the car, running over a curb and making my head hit the roof of the car. I turned to see a malicious smirk on her face.

"Answer me. What are you looking at?"

I turned away from her, not wanting to talk anymore than I had to. "Dragons," I muttered.

She let out a shrill laugh. "Oh my god. You *are* on drugs. There are no dragons anywhere in Fargo. That's what a druggie would say. So that's what you've been doing the last six months? You ran away with Mattie, met up with that nut job, and fucked any dude who'd pay for your next hit or give you a meal?"

"I am not on drugs. You wouldn't understand what I've been doing for the last six months if you tried," I whispered, trying to ignore her. The less I reacted, the better. I knew that at my core, but it hurt not to react.

"We'll see. I'll take you up to get your labs done. Find your needle marks. When the results come back, we'll see just how whacked out you are. If you're pregnant, woo hoo! Just wait until I send the CPS after you! Don't expect to be keeping that kid."

I had to restrain myself from glancing at her, despite the anger growing and tightening inside my chest. If anyone was acting crazy, it was her. If there was anything I had learned from fighting, it was when to act and when not to act. I was not on drugs and not pregnant, no matter what crazy ideas my mother spouted off.

It was only a few minutes later that we arrived at the hospital. That surprised me. Instead of the old hospital where my mother had worked for years, we were in front of the new one that had still been under construction when I had last been in Fargo. For all her bitter complaining about losing her old job and having to get a new one, she hadn't exactly hit rock bottom.

"Why are we at this hospital?"

My mother coughed in derision. "Because I work here now. This is the new job I got. It doesn't pay as well and my co-workers are idiots, but it's better than nothing. I guess. C'mon, get your butt out of the car. I don't have time to waste." My mother parked in the parking lot near the emergency door exit and undid my seatbelt without another word.

I looked around at the new campus. Dragons swirled around the buildings and across the highway, but did little to damage anything. Mattie had been right in that regard. The dragons seemed to be avoiding me, even as they caused chaos almost everywhere else. I felt bad for the people in the hospital. It wasn't tornados, but if the weather was this chaotic and I was stuck in a hospital, I'd be terrified.

As she left the car, she walked around and waved someone over. *Robert.* I cringed inside as I saw him in his security guard getup. Either he had been at the mall when the dragons arrived, or he had gotten a side job as a security guard at my mom's work while I had been away. He glanced at me with a creepy smile, then walked over to the car door and opened it.

"C'mon, get out. You've caused your mom a lot of worry. Good thing I saw you and your little dress-up buddies at the mall earlier."

I refused to budge. "Unless you were at the mall a half hour ago, you didn't see me."

His eyes widened and his jaw clenched for a split second before he laughed nervously. "No, I saw you earlier. You've been scrounging around the mall food court the last few days. I... I just wanted your mother to come pick you up instead of picking you up myself." He paused, staring into my eyes uncomfortably. "I'm your friend right now. Remember?"

I stared at him in disbelief. "No. You're lying. And I'm not leaving this car."

A long angry whistle, like the wind picking up speed, came from behind me and Robert's eyes widened again, his jaw slackening. He grabbed my arm and yanked me from the car. Much to my surprise, he spun me around, pinning me to the ground in a defensive stance as the wind intensified. The rush of wind pulled at my clothing and armor as much as it did his security uniform. The dragon roared as it pulled up into the air a few feet from us and just above the cars in the parking lot, not doing much damage except for setting off a few car alarms.

Ina...Save us...

I looked up in surprised at the dragon as it circled around and back down, as if coming in for the attack again. In an instant, I realized it looked almost identical to the 'ice dragons' of Aldinnvollr. The guardians of Rhaegos's shrine. The realization hit me that the two situations were similar.

"By the dragons..." Robert whispered and I twisted to face him. He was still on top of me and his breath was rancid, but... *He could see the dragons?*

"For heavens' sake, you two. Get up! I don't have all day." My mother's expression turned into a dark sneer as she patted her uniform. Her hair was windblown, but otherwise she acted as if nothing had happened. "Damn it. I forgot my badge and key card."

She walked over to the driver's side of the car, ignoring the gusts of wind as the dragon zoomed above her head. Robert pulled me up and slammed the passenger side door closed, still eyeing the creature. Its speed increased every time it circled. He slowly walked backwards, holding me in front of him as if I were a shield.

"Where is that stupid thing!" My mother was fully in her car as I watched the dragon zoom up across the parking lot and widen its jaws. My chest and neck froze in terror. As much as I wanted to look away, I couldn't.

In a flash, the dragon picked up the car with my mother inside it. I screamed and Robert clamped his disgusting hand over my mouth as the dragon tossed the car into its maw, shaking it like a dog toy. It zoomed off, dropping the crinkled car in the middle of Highway 94.

"What in the name of Tenelth?" Robert hissed in disbelief. I continued to stare at the freeway even though I couldn't see the carnage. Was she really...dead? Sirens started blaring around me again, both tornado and police sirens this time, as Robert dragged me into the hospital. Despite the emergency room waiting area being packed with people, most were watching various televisions or the carnage going on outside. Only a few people looked up as Robert hauled me down one of the halls.

I continued to stare in the direction of the highway as Robert hauled me along the near empty hallway. A few people looked at me curiously, but no one said anything to either of us. When I stumbled on a tile and nearly tripped, I turned to Robert and tried to pull out of his grip. Unfortunately, he held on tight and squeezed my wrist until my hand began to hurt.

"Where are you taking me?" I stopped, wondering if being a dead weight would slow him.

"Since your mother is gone now, it's *my* job to take care of you." He opened the door to a storage room and shoved me in before closing the door behind him. "Finally do the job I was sent here to do."

I turned around and stared at him for a moment, seeing only the man from my nightmare. We were in a supply closet now, with only one door, and he stood between me and it. "I'm eighteen. I can take care of myself now, Robert," I said quickly, just as a far more ominous idea engrained itself into my head. He wasn't referring to taking care of me as a child. He would never do that. He was talking about something else. I felt around for a weapon on my body. Of course none of my weapons had come through the vortex.

He gave a short laugh. "I'm not talking about *that*. And for the love of Freya and Bjornulf, don't call me Robert. It's Hrothbere. You should know that by now." He took a step toward me and I stepped back to keep my distance. "I've played stupid all these years. Been treated like dirt by your mother when, in Lohikärra, a whore like her would have been beaten to death for the way she's acted. We can forget all of that now. All of these stupid acts. You've been to Lohikärra. You know it's real. And guess what? You're eighteen now. An adult. I can do whatever I want to you now."

Hrothbere was Robert. It made sense and I felt like an idiot for not realizing it earlier. The names even sounded familiar. The emotions from my dreams returned with a fury and the room squeezed close around me. I knew exactly what Robert want to do with me now. Have his way with me and then kill me, at least if he was working for Rorik.

"I'm married now." The words fell flat. As soon as I said them, I knew they would have no effect.

He took another step toward me and a lecherous smirk lit up his face. "Doesn't matter."

I backed into the shelving unit full of medical odds and ends. Boxes of stuff. Possibly sharp stuff. As I felt around behind me, my heart started racing and I tried to think of a way to stall him.

"Wait! Who do you work for?"

He stopped and frowned at me, his eyes narrowing in confusion. "What? You've been to Lohikärra and you don't know who sent me? Are you really that stupid?"

"No. I mean is it Gustav or Rorik? Who's your boss?"

"Both of them. What does it matter?" He took another step toward me.

"One of them wants me alive and the other wants me dead. Who do you work for? Gustav or Rorik?"

Robert hesitated, then smirked. "Whoever pays better." He took another step toward me and I stepped back.

"How much are they paying you?"

A dragon screeched angrily outside. A few people down the hall screamed. Robert paused and I took the opportunity to ask, "You can see them too, can't you?"

He scowled, but didn't move forward. "No shit. Why do you want to know what they're paying me? You offering me a better deal?"

"Maybe." If I could get Robert to work for me instead of Rorik or Gustav, that could make my life easier in the short term, even if I didn't trust him. "You want to return to Lohikärra? Make plenty of gold? Have women throwing themselves at you?"

He growled at me and said, "Of course. I've been waiting twelve long years for this. You think you can get me back there?"

"Of course. Mattie and I went there before. Why couldn't we do it again?"

Robert scowled. "That was an accident. You can't go back the same way again."

I kept my focus on him as I felt for what was in the boxes behind me. "Rorik created a vortex—a portal—with dragon souls. There are dragons here right now. It wouldn't be hard to change it."

"You're willing to sacrifice dragons to return to Lohikärra?" His shoulders relaxed ever so slightly.

"Maybe. But if you don't let me out, I can't do anything."

He stared at me for what seemed like an eternity. I inhaled as fear slowly filled my body like flood waters. The box behind me had needles in it, but they were all wrapped in plastic. While Robert only had his baton as a weapon, he also had a pair of handcuffs he could use to disable me if I wasn't careful. I hoped I didn't have to resort to violence, but if I had to...

"No deal. I don't trust you. I have a mission to fulfill."

"You trust Gustav and Rorik more than me?" The words tumbled from my mouth before I could think. "What mission is so important that you're not willing to get something better?" I raised my voice and rushed to tear open one of the needles. If he wasn't buying my idea now, I'd have to resort to some kind of violence.

"Gustav saved me and my brother from death. I owe him more than you could ever imagine. Now that Rorik will be in charge, I need to kill you and destroy the house of Svanunge. You belong in Lohikärra as much as I belong here." He pulled his baton out of its holster. Just as he swung at my head, I grabbed his wrist with one hand and lunged at his face with the needle. I doubted it would do much damage, but all I wanted was enough time to run away.

The needle sank into his forehead and I dragged it across his face, just missing his eye, but enough to make the blood flow freely. He started screaming as he dropped his baton and held the injury with one hand. I spun around so I was between him and the exit. Kicking him into the shelves, I turned to the door and flung it open.

I made my way to the nearest way out and began running as fast as I could across the parking lot. The dragons continued to scream as I dodged past a few cars and crossed a few streets. I knew I looked like a crazy person, but the only things I care about right now were getting away from Robert and returning to Mattie and Haldrek.

Chapter Twenty-Five

What had been a quick drive across the highway for my mother turned into a much longer path for me. I stayed away from pedestrians and cars with people in them. I knew I stuck out like a sore thumb in my armor, and I was certain Robert would report me to law enforcement. It wasn't until I crossed over the 94 that I stopped running. A group of large trees beside a hotel and a corporate park stood nearby. A small refuge, far enough from either that anyone taking refuge in those buildings wouldn't be able to see me. At least not well enough to identify me. Shaking as I collapsed under the nearest tree, I looked around to see if anyone was chasing me. Sirens continued to go off, but the police sirens were soft and in the distance. If Robert had called the cops on me, they were nowhere in sight. The only sirens I could hear were the tornado warnings, still wailing as the dragons swarmed around buildings and over cars nearby.

My heart sank as I thought of my options here in Fargo. Six months ago, before I'd even known Lohikärra was real, they had been limited. That's why the idea of leaving as soon as I was done with high school had been so tantalizing. But now I was eighteen, a 'high school dropout,' a supposed drug addict, and broke. At least in this world. The only people I trusted were Mattie and Haldrek, and all three of us were in big trouble if we stayed in Fargo. I didn't belong here. Not anymore. Not that I ever had. I had only been in Lohikärra for five months and it felt more like home than Fargo ever did.

But plenty of people in Lohikärra didn't believe I belonged. People from Svartån, other thegns... I curled up in a ball with my head on my knees and began bawling. I belonged nowhere. No matter how hard I tried.

The wind began to pick up around me, whipping my hair hard enough that it hurt when the strands hit my face. A few more car alarms went off at the hotel and I began to be lifted off the ground. I panicked, grabbing the tree next to me for support, latching on with both arms and legs as dead leaves and wood chips from the ground began to fly around me and hit me in the head.

Ina... Save me...again...

I looked up and saw one ghostly dragon twisting in the air. The sight of the dragon in pain made my heart ache.

"Rhaegos?" I whispered.

The dragon arced backwards and let out a wrenching scream that made me cover my ears. The wind pulled me away from the tree, and I hit the ground with a resounding thud.

Save me... home...

My heart beat began racing with the wind from the dragon as it intensified in its spinning, then zoomed off into the sky.

The silence—or rather lack of rushing air—afterward was almost as deafening as Rhaegos's storm. I looked up at the darkening sky and could only see glimmers of the dragons. They howled and I knew in my gut it was just like at Rhaegos's shrine. I couldn't talk to the dragons, but I could hear and feel their emotions. They needed to go home as much as I needed to find mine. The only problem was that I couldn't find what needed to be fixed. I had a sinking feeling I'd need to make my way back to the mall for that. Under the swiftly darkening sky, I felt more like I was in a video game than I ever did in Lohikärra, even with its magic, dragons, and my ability to see ghosts.

Looking around, it hit me exactly why Fargo wasn't my home. Fargo never had my heart. As cheesy as it was, home was where your loved ones were and Fargo wasn't where my loved ones were. My loved ones were all in Lohikärra or belonged in Lohikärra. Mattie, Haldrek, Thandes, Llamryl, and their families. Even people who were now in the Realm of Ghosts were once in Lohikärra. Lohikärra wasn't perfect, far from it, but it was the closest place I had to a home.

Getting up, I tried to orient myself to the mall. That's where the vortex sent Haldrek and I and that's where he and Mattie would be—trying to get home.

It was dark by the time I got to the mall. Between the storms and the broken lights, the vast, almost empty parking lot was downright creepy. Debris from the broken building where Haldrek, Mattie, and I had taken refuge earlier littered the ground. I gingerly made my way between the large chunks of broken wood and cinder block. Pausing, I squatted behind a pile of rubble and listened for any noises above the shrill cries of the dragons and tornado sirens. Nothing.

As I moved from the shadow of the ruined restaurant, movement caught my eye. I turned to the left and ducked behind a scraggly bush. A couple of men walked along the edge of the parking lot, looking between the sky and the insides of the cars. Not that anything in the cars would be of value to them. They were talking, but their mutterings were indiscernible. Still, I got the impression they were not happy to be out right now. They continued moving and I squatted lower to the ground, hoping the bush was big enough to hide me.

"Stupid patrol. It's not like Gustav knows what to do here anyway."

"Of course he knows. He needs both the Thegns of Andrattür and Svartån captured in order to become the High King once they're dead."

"Then what in Lyrroth is he doing? He had us chase after that dark-skinned girl, only to have her escape us. He says the Thegns of Svartån and Andrattür are here too. But no one has seen them. Why would they come to this dragon-forsaken place?" The first man shuddered. "This place gives me the creeps. Not just because of the dragons acting the way they are."

"Idiot. This is the homeland of the Thegn of Svartån and her dark-skinned ally. If we conquer this land, they'll have nowhere to turn to for aid."

Silence. "You really were knocked on the head as a child, weren't you? You think the thegn or thegn-heir would have tossed us *and* the dragons here to conquer this place? We could easily take it without the dragons." More silence. "Or the dragons without *us*." The voice rose. "No matter. I still don't get why we're here or how we'll conquer this land with the dragons as crazed as they are."

"No..." A hint of irritation colored the other man's voice. "You heard the stories too. Where did the Blodnar get their dragon-slaying weapons? This place. Thegn Etelaranikä said others have traveled between here and Sethys. Not just Lohikärrans. Blodnar too."

"Pff. You take everything at face value. We're here for something. But not even the thegn or his son know what that something is."

A dragon sailed above us, shrieking, and the two men flattened to the ground. Several car alarms went off, followed by a litany of obscenities from the warriors. When the wind died down, the two men popped up and ran past me without another glance.

I shook my head in disbelief. These warriors were just as much in the dark as I was. It sounded as if whatever plan Gustav or Rorik had wasn't being explained to the warriors under them. And possibly the Blodnar fighters who were fighting with them. If I could find Mattie and Haldrek, we could use that to our advantage. I didn't know how, but we could figure it out later.

As soon as I was sure no other patrols were coming along, I snuck through the rows of cars. After having worked here for almost two years, I knew roughly where all the entrances were. As long as I could get in, I might be able to find Mattie and Haldrek. I had a few ideas about where they may be hiding. The dragons continued to swirl above me, but the darkness felt like a cloak as I hurried across the parking lot. If Robert had sent police after me, they hadn't arrived yet. Maybe they had found some of the Blodnar or Etelaranikän patrol groups and were dealing with them. As entertaining as that would be to watch, it meant less focus on me. And the longer I was 'invisible' to the police, the better. As far as they were concerned, I was a crazy, strung-out druggie.

I found a side door unlocked near a couple of the department stores and the game store Mattie and I had been to before all of this started and slipped in. Stopping for a moment, I listened for any nearby movement. Around the corner and in the direction of the food court, I could hear something. But the immediate corridor blanketed me in darkness, covering me as I snuck past closed up shops. I knew the layout like the back of my hand, so I continued as my eyes adjusted to the dark. Nearing the food court, I heard voices and saw a dim light, like a fire, around the corner.

Did they seriously create a fire inside the mall? Or were they using something else? I cringed at the thought of how much damage they and the dragons were causing. Hiding behind the mall's large decorative buffalo statue, I watched as two men in Blodnar armor walked by. My stomach roiled with anger. It was more than evident now that Gustav had betrayed his fellow thegns—including my father—and aligned himself with the Blodnar.

Shit. Had Mattie and Haldrek even made it into the mall? If they had, had they been captured by the Blodnar? The food court had plenty of places where people could hide. Both Haldrek's and my weapons had been dragged from us by the force of the vortex, so I assumed they were still in Lohikärra. Unfortunately, that meant they were likely in Rorik's hands.

The Blodnar soldiers and Etelaranikän warriors still had their weapons though. How was that possible? It baffled me, but I pushed the thought aside for the time being. Before I could do anything, I needed to find a way to defend myself. Or else.

I watched the soldiers and warriors pass me several times, observing their interactions as they walked between the food court and the entrance I had come in. The sounds from outside were muted, giving me some much-needed time to think. It seemed as if I'd had luck on my side when I snuck in. The Blodnar and Etelaranikän warriors patrolled regularly, so if I'd been a few minutes earlier or later, I would have gotten caught.

They also didn't seem to be on the best of terms. They tolerated each other, but they weren't friendly. Even the 'war camp' I could see from the decorative buffalo was split into two different sections: one with Blodnar soldiers and another with Etelaranikän warriors.

If I found Mattie and Haldrek, that was something else to tell them. A house divided and all that.

As the next pair of guards passed me, I decided to move, staying in the shadows. There was a large potted plant with a bench next to it, not more than a few feet from me. If I could get to that spot and stay in the shadows, I could hear more of what was going on. Perhaps even see if Gustav was with this group or not.

Sneaking forward, a loud voice pulled any possible attention from me.

"Are you kidding me?"

Gustav stepped into the makeshift center of the camp of men and directly in front of me, no more than a dozen feet away. I shrank into the shadows, feeling a little too close for comfort.

"We've looked everywhere. This place is as large as the High King's palace and there are metal grates in front of many of the rooms. I've had my men try to dismember them, but even that is taking time."

Gustav growled and then said, "Of course Rorik's vortex had to send us to a place where the two half-breeds would be familiar."

The man in front of him—an Etelaranikän—frowned. "Wasn't that your plan, my thegn? To come to the place where Thegn Svartån and the other woman were from?"

"It was. But this indoor marketplace, whatever it is, it's not unfamiliar to them. The fact that the dark-skinned half-breed disappeared so quickly means she, at least, knows this place as if she grew up in this building." Gustav grumbled again. "Keep searching! Don't come back until you find them!"

The man hurried off and I glanced around to make sure no one saw me. As much as I hated being in Fargo, at least it was a miserable place for Gustav as well. If Mattie could keep herself and Haldrek safe, all the better.

I continued to watch Gustav as he began pacing. He was angry—his body language made that loud and clear. But he was also close enough I could see how tense he was, how he held himself. He kept rubbing the nape of his neck and pulling at his hair.

He knew something he wasn't telling any of his men, and it was irritating him to no end.

A thought hit me as I watched him. Why was *he* here? Rorik had mentioned Gustav's arrival had been an accident, but Gustav made it sound like he had intended to be here. At least initially. Their conflicting stories made me wonder how much they were actually working together. How sure was Gustav that Rorik was working for him? If the nightmare from my wedding night was any indication, Rorik had greater plans for himself than to just take orders from his father. If his father stood in the way of his plans...I shuddered. My body drooped under the weight of foreboding. Gustav was a nuisance, but he wasn't the person we had to worry about. It was Rorik.

Gustav moved away from where he'd been pacing, a groan on his lips as he walked from my sight. I exhaled and looked around to see what my next move would be. The food court was in the middle of everything, so it would take a great deal of sneaking in order to stay hidden.

Just as I mulled over the possibilities, my stomach grumbled and I froze. The few fighters within my view were too far away or otherwise didn't react. I sighed with relief.

Someone's hand clamped over my mouth and I jumped, biting and clawing at the person's hand. A pointy dagger pressed into my spine and I stopped.

"Gotcha, bitch."

Chapter Twenty-Six

Robert's voice made me want to vomit. How he'd gotten here so fast, I didn't know. He slowly lifted me up until I was standing and whispered, "If Thegn Etelaranikä hadn't demanded you alive, I would kill you right now." He shoved his face into my neck, making me cringe as I felt the blood from his injuries on my neck.

Marching me forward, he cleared his throat. "Thegn Etelaranikä. I bring you something you've requested."

Gustav returned from wherever he had been mingling and looked at me triumphantly.

"You finally did something right for once, Hrothbere." He looked past me and grimaced. "What in Lyrroth happened to your face?"

"She put up a fight. But I still won."

I kept my expression bland. Of course Robert would ignore the fact that I'd escaped him at least once. But I'd been an idiot to not keep an eye on anyone behind me. Given that Robert and Gustav had every reason to kill me now, maybe I'd been the bigger idiot not to kill Robert when I'd had the chance.

Gustav focused his attention on me. "I have plenty of questions for you. But I'm sure you're wondering how this man knows me?"

I stared at him until he stiffened up. "Robert told me you sent him to keep me from Lohikärra. He works for you. That's not that surprising."

"I knew you would return to Lohikärra at some point. But I wanted to bring you there on *my* terms, once I figured how to create these dragon portals at will. Your father was a pain in my side from the time we were youths. Always succeeding where I had failed. When I heard him spouting off about an heir in a distant land he planned to bring back to Lohikärra, I decided to foil that plan. Use you to my advantage."

"So you believed my father when other thegns didn't?"

Gustav laughed. "Of course I did. I may have loathed him, but I never thought him a liar." He looked around for a moment. His men watched our interaction with eagerness and I felt a heavy weight in my gut. I hoped Mattie kept Haldrek hidden. We'd be screwed if Gustav had all of us together.

Returning his focus to me, Gustav stepped forward and I stiffened up, mentally preparing myself for whatever he was about to do.

"You don't belong in Lohikärra. You never will. This place, this barren wasteland, this is your home. It is nothing like what Lohikärra should become. Will become."

"A land devoid of dragons and ruled by a necromancer?" The words popped out of my mouth before I could calculate Gustav's reaction.

His face pinched inward, turning red with anger. His hand came in from the side and my cheek stung as he slapped me. My ears popped as I opened my mouth, my vision still spinning.

"I should have just had Robert kill you as soon as he arrived here."

"I can kill her now." Robert's dagger pushed forward into my spine and I gasped.

"No." Gustav looked away from me. "The person I truly want now is Haldrek. He and she are the only people standing in my way of becoming High King. If we have her here, alive, we can pull him and his half-breed half-sister out of hiding."

"They won't do that. They won't fall for it," I whispered.

"Oh really? You're telling me Haldrek won't try to rescue his *wife*?"

I smiled as a thought popped into my head. "I'm just a bed warmer. I thought... I thought I was more, but..."

"Oh please. I'm not that dumb." Gustav took my chin in his hand and stared at me until I blinked. "I know very well Thegn Andrattür is smitten with you. He is much too honorable to not come find you." Gustav paused. "That's why he can't become the High King. He's too honorable. He can't stomach doing the hard tasks required of a High King. The dirty work."

He dropped my head and I let it flop. "I think you're underestimating Haldrek. But that's fine. That makes my life easier."

He yanked my head up once more and slapped me across the other cheek.

"Go put her in the cage. She can sit there and wait until we grab Thegn Andrattür."

Robert went to move me, but I let myself become deadweight and he stumbled. Knowing I was going to be stuck for the time being, I turned my attention to Gustav.

"What are you going to do when Rorik decides to keep you here in Fargo?"

Gustav scowled. "He won't do that. As soon as the three of you are captured, he'll reverse the portal and I'll return as High King, leaving you to live and die with the dragons. Here. In this wretched place."

Robert dragged me to my feet and increased the pressure of his knife against my spine. I stumbled forward, hoping I'd done enough to help Mattie and Haldrek.

Robert shoved me behind the counter of one of the fast-food places. Ironically, it was the Mexican joint Mattie and I had worked at prior to arriving in Lohikärra. He grunted in pain as he sat me on ground and started tying my wrists and ankles together. Much to my surprise, he was quiet, with no surly insults or creepy overtures. Instead he focused on binding me as tight as he could, while blood from his injury still dripped from time to time onto my hands and clothing.

Once I was bound, he left, grumbling. Two Etelaranikän warriors were guarding the swinging half door, as if it were the only entrance to the food place. I glanced over at the kitchen door – it was ajar. That door had a penchant for jamming, making it a pain in the butt to open and close unless it was propped open. But as it was now, I could slip into the kitchen unnoticed. I pulled at the ropes at my hands and feet. Robert had tied them securely, but not secure enough. I had some wiggle room. Part of me wished I'd had learned how to tie and untie knots in Lohikärra. I had more use for that knowledge there than I did here, but it would have been handy either way.

Glancing up at the guards, I noticed that they weren't paying attention to me. The one closer to where I sat was slouched on the counter. Tied up, I obviously wasn't considered a threat. I focused on the ropes binding my feet. The knot Robert had tied was big, but not complicated. The guards were still ignoring me, so I began to fiddle with the knot, trying to find the ends of it. When one of them popped out, I smiled. I tugged on it, but it didn't have much give.

"What you doing over there?"

I froze and waited to see if the question had been directed at me. There was a clatter at another food booth nearby.

"I'm looking for food. What do you think I'm doing? Your thegn dragged us here and did nothing about feeding us. I'm finding food." More noise around the corner.

"You're supposed to be looking for the other two. The thegn and his half-breed sister."

I bristled at the way they talked about Mattie, but I was glad to hear they were distracted. Toying with the rope even more, I loosened the knot and started wiggling my ankles back and forth. The knot undid itself and the ropes fell loose. I began to fiddle with the ropes tying my hands together. They were a little tougher because I couldn't use my fingers, but I still feel them loosening.

A crash nearby stopped me. My guards' attention was directed at the noise.

"Get out of my way! I'm hungry."

"You're supposed to be looking for the two we still ain't got. Gimme that plate!"

"If your stupid thegn had fed us..."

Other voices entered the fray and I took the distraction to push myself toward the kitchen door. The rope around my hands wasn't coming off as easily as I had planned, but I knew the kitchen would have two things I needed: sharp objects and an exit into the rest of the building.

Shifting toward the door, I kept watching the guards. The one who had been relaxing was now standing straight up, hand on his spear. If I could get into the kitchen without them seeing me...

The warrior with spear turned around and we locked eyes. Before he could open his mouth, I pushed myself up the door, swinging it open and rolling into the kitchen. It was a tiny kitchen, made for little more than prepping food and grilling some meat, but there were knife blocks. I grabbed two of the sharpest ones as the door burst open behind me. Running through the emergency door that led outside, the alarm started to wail. Not that it mattered. They knew I was trying to escape anyway.

I tried to think where Haldrek and Mattie might be and how I could find them if I was back outside now. A handful of warriors chased after me, and I clenched the two knives in my bound hands. Above us, dragons continued to circle, screeching and dive bombing the mall parking lot erratically.

Looking behind me, I dove to the side as a dragon dive-bombed the warriors still chasing me. It shrieked loud enough to make my ears ring and my head spin. The knives went flying from my hands and into the bushes.

Shit.

"INA!"

Mattie and Haldrek stood inside a door that went back into the mall. Haldrek looked less weary and in better health. I grinned and started crawling toward them as Haldrek ran to me and hefted me over his shoulder. I grunted as the air got knocked out of my lungs.

"We need to hurry. The dragons are slowly sinking into madness."

Mattie kept the door open just long enough for us to get in. As soon as she shut the door, the wall shuddered from a wind gust.

"I'm so glad you're alive." Haldrek sat me next to a potted plant as Mattie kept a lookout. He untied my hands quicker than I'd been able to untie my legs.

As soon as I relaxed, he asked, "How did you escape? Your mother is as mad as the dragons outside."

I laughed sharply. My emotions tumbled all over the place as I ducked my head and tears flowed down my cheeks. Why was I crying? And why now? I wasn't *sad* about her death. I didn't know how to feel right now. Angry? Depressed? Scared? I just felt numb. Looking up at him, I whispered, "Dragon killed her. She had Robert—Hrothbere—drag me from the car and then a dragon snapped it up with her inside." The image popped into my mind and I pushed it away. How was I even supposed to feel about her death? Right now, I felt equal parts horror, numbness, and relief.

"I'd say I was sorry if she hadn't tried to kill me."

I laughed and wrapped my arms around his shoulders. "One day I might be able to explain how I feel, but right now, I just want to go home."

"Lohikärra?"

I nodded, taking comfort in his presence. "Lohikärra."

"We should hurry." Mattie's voice interrupted us and we looked up. She glanced behind her. "Gustav's men are still patrolling, but we might have a few minutes because of the scuffle going on in the food court." She smirked. "Gustav shouldn't have run his men on empty bellies."

Haldrek pulled me up, and as soon as I was standing, we were off.

Chapter Twenty-Seven

We had to slip outside again to reach the part of the mall where Mattie and Haldrek had found refuge. Slipping inside, we made our way through the department store entrance farthest away from where it connected with the main mall.

Mattie gestured for me to squeeze through the half-open door with her. Much to my surprise, Haldrek was able to fit through the small opening as well. After we slipped in, she guided us to the farthest part of the store. Haldrek picked something up and fiddled with it until a light came on. A flashlight. He held it, examining it every few seconds.

"This is fascinating magic. Or technology. Heatless torches."

I grinned, glad to see him in better spirits. Leaning in, I gave him the biggest hug I could. After everything I had gone through today, I just wanted to feel safe in his embrace.

"I'm sorry. For not protecting you," he whispered, focusing the flashlight on the ground. In the dimness, I could see a few camping chairs had been dragged into a circle, as well as some glassware and snacks usually advertised by a checkout counter.

I laughed, my voice still soft. "My mother hit you with a car. I'm just glad you are alive. Especially with the Blodnar crawling around here."

"The Blodnar, I can handle." Haldrek grumbled, still holding me tight.

"We're going to have to figure how to either fight or avoid them and get up to the roof," Mattie commented, returning from the front of the store. "Seeing as we need to get the dragons back where they belong and we don't have the weapons that we had in Lohikärra."

Staying in the circle of Haldrek's arms, I faced Mattie. "Have you figured out a way to reverse the vortex?"

Mattie nodded. "I think. Rorik used crystals and magic in order to create the vortex. If I can use glassware or something else as crystals, I think I can reverse his portal magic to pull all the dragons and people from Lohikärra back to Lohikärra."

"What about pulling animals from our world into Lohikärra?" I took a step away from Haldrek in concern. We didn't want to create more chaos.

"I don't know. If I reverse the portal magic, I think it will just return the Lohikärra creatures, but we'll see." Mattie glanced away, and I could tell that she wasn't telling us everything.

"Do you want me to help you find what you need to reverse the vortex?"

Mattie returned her focus to us and shook her head. "I'm sure I can find what I'm looking for." She wiggled the flashlight she had grabbed, turning it on. "They should have more glass or crystal glasses over in the dining area."

As she walked away, I returned to hugging Haldrek. He sat on the ground and held me for a few minutes before asking, "So this is your home? Fargo? It's an interesting place. Though I'll admit it's not exactly what I was expecting after I heard your father's stories."

"I bet. Fargo isn't that big or fancy of a city, but I don't think there's anything in Lohikärra like it." I laughed shortly. "That said, this isn't my home. It is where I was born and grew up, yes, but that's it."

He was quiet again for a little bit. I wondered what was going through his head. Was my response not what he expected?

"Are you glad to be back?" he asked slowly.

I shook my head, burying it in his chest armor. "No. Lohikärra is more home than this place ever was."

"So you'll want to return when Mattie figures out how to reverse everything?"

I nodded and, after another moment, looked up at him. "Did Mattie say anything about whether she wants to return?" I knew Lohikärra hadn't been ideal for her, even with Llamryl and the others we'd gotten to know over the past few months. If she returned to Fargo, or Earth in general, she'd have plenty of money to survive and do whatever she wanted to do. College had never been an option for me, but I knew she had been interested in a few places.

"I didn't ask her. Would you stay here if she did?"

I shook my head. What did I have left here? Mattie had her inheritance, but I only had her friendship. Even if Mattie stayed here and was willing to use her money to keep us off the streets, I still wouldn't have much. I'd be leaving everything I truly cared about behind in Lohikärra. Despite the short time that I'd been there, there was too much that made me want to return.

"I... No... I would have more to lose staying here than staying in Lohikärra." I smiled at him. "I don't want to lose you. Not yet."

He smiled and leaned over to kiss me. I savored it, wondering if Mattie's hesitance had anything to do with our ability to return. If that was the case, well, I tried not to think about it. Lohikärra was home now. I wanted to go home.

As he relaxed out of the kiss, Haldrek asked, "You mentioned the dragons helped you escape your mother, but you were also dealing with Robert—Hrothbere? I'm assuming he didn't release you because of them?"

I shook my head, not really wanting to remember everything that had happened in the last few hours. Now that we had a moment of peace, a moment of safety, all of my uncomfortable feelings bubbled up, threatening to overwhelm me.

The image of my mother's car being crushed and tossed etched itself into my mind. I tried not to imagine what her last moments were like. Was she scared? Angry? Or had the attack killed her instantly? Even though I hated my mother and loathed everything she had done to me, I still felt tears well up in my eyes. I knew the terrible feeling of being helpless. Had she felt helpless? Even for a moment? Brushing the thoughts and tears away, I whispered, "I don't know why I'm crying. If my mother's dead, she can't hurt me anymore. That was what she was planning. She and Robert. That's why she had him grab me from the car."

"What were they going to do to you?"

"My mother was going to get me tested for all sorts of things. Drugs, diseases, you name it. She was swearing up and down that I was some druggie. After my mother was killed, Robert planned to have his way with me before handing me over to Gustav." I focused on Haldrek. "Robert was sent here to kill me. Well, keep me from Lohikärra. But if that meant killing me..." I couldn't finish the thought.

"I'm glad he failed then." Haldrek squeezed me again, the weight of his embrace grounding me.

"Robert was working for Gustav. He is Hrothbere. He's related to the vampire man who attacked me in Aldinnvollr."

Haldrek stared at me in disbelief. "Our fathers weren't the only ones who knew how to move between this world and Lohikärra?"

I shrugged. "Rorik figured out how to create a vortex here with dragon souls. My dad was trying to figure out how to use the dragon stones, but that doesn't mean he wasn't the only one. I think other people in Lohikärra's past have tried to travel between here and there. Or even others outside of Lohikärra."

"The dragons would never abide those outside of Lohikärra using their powers."

"Rhaegos said the dragons accept anyone who wishes to serve or aid them. Not just those born in Lohikärra."

"She did?" Haldrek genuinely looked surprised. He exhaled, weariness beginning to creep into his expression. "Perhaps that is something to think about once we return to Lohikärra." He hugged me tight. "As for now, we figure out a way to return to Lohikärra. Safely. If anyone tries to hurt you again, they'll have to go through me."

I smiled. "I'm not giving up without a fight either. I may have given Robert a nasty facial injury before making my way here."

Haldrek laughed and pulled my hair away from my neck. "Then that blood on your neck isn't yours?"

I shook my head. "Robert captured me when I was spying on Gustav. He decided to rub his injury on my neck after he captured me."

Haldrek grimaced with confusion. "That's bizarre."

"I agree. I—"

The shattering of glass and a cuss word breaking through the quietness of the department store made me freeze. Haldrek reached behind him before grunting in frustration.

"I think Mattie might need some help after all." I slipped out of his embrace and turned toward the sound.

"Wait." He grabbed another flashlight from where he had been sitting—it looked like he and Mattie had procured a few resources when they had hidden in the store—and turned it on, placing it with the light facing up.

"That way we can find our way back."

"What if Blodnar guards see it and come investigate?"

"We'll hear them rattle the main chain door before they get to our camp. Or if they come through the side door like we did. I don't think they have their normal weapons either. If it comes to blows, I'll find something to fight them off with." Haldrek paused. "If Gustav or Robert comes around, I won't hesitate to kill either of them. Gustav is a traitor to Lohikärra, as is Rorik. The penalty for treason has always been death. As for Robert—the fact that he has tormented for so long in a way to give you nightmares... It would be more merciful for one of the dragons outside to destroy him than for me to face him."

I shuddered, surprised by the hardness in Haldrek's tone. As much as I loathed Robert, there had been enough death in the past few weeks to suffice for a lifetime. Haldrek gestured for us to start walking. He kept up with me as we made our way over to the dining wares area. As we got closer, I started to hear crying and I stopped Haldrek. If Mattie was crying... then I knew she was scared.

"Let me..."

Haldrek seemed to understand. "I'll keep watch."

I stepped around the corner and saw a dark shape huddled on the floor, soft weeping sounds coming from it.

"Mattie?"

The crying stopped and in a weak voice, she mumbled, "I'm an idiot."

I knelt next to her and saw a few small boxes laying haphazardly in front of her.

"You're not an idiot, Mattie. What's wrong?"

She looked around and lowered her tone further. "I don't know if I can do it."

"Reverse the vortex?"

She nodded. "I'm afraid if I don't do it right, I could mess things up badly. Shut down the portal accidentally, keep the dragons from returning to Lohikärra, kill people."

I sat there next to her, not knowing what to say. She was the smart, confident one. She knew Lohikärra like the back of her hand. Gingerly, I put my hand over her shoulder and leaned her into me for comfort. "What was your original plan?"

"Take four of these fancy glasses, pour some water into them and start enchanting them. I was hoping to maybe draw some of the dragons or dragon spirits into the water and use that to push the dragons into Lohikärra. But the crystals on our side need to be more powerfully charged than the ones Rorik has. I have no idea how powerful his crystals are. Just that they were powerful enough to open the portal. And magic isn't inherent in our world like it is in Sethys."

"Would the dragons be drained of some of their power by pushing objects and people into the vortex?"

Mattie shrugged. "It's a possibility."

"Do we have any other options?"

She shook her head. "Not that I know of. Gustav seemed pissed beyond belief I was still with that group. I think he thought Rorik was going along with *his* plans, not that he was going along with *Rorik's* plans. I got the impression he thought only the dragons would be flung into our world to stay. Not him or anyone else."

"That makes sense. Rorik betrayed him. But he's still trying to spin it around so that he comes out on top."

Mattie nodded. "Not that I feel pity for Gustav in the slightest. He's just as much a piece of work as his son."

We were quiet for a few minutes before I spoke up again. "You know who else is a Lohikärran here in Fargo? And expected to go back to Lohikärra at some point?"

"Who?"

"Robert." I sighed. "His real name is Hrothbere. Not only is he connected to Gustav, but also to that vampire who was hunting me. Supposedly Robert was sent to keep me away from Lohikärra until Gustav could use me. But that didn't work."

"Did you see him after your mother took off with you?"

I nodded. "She took me to the new hospital where she worked. Robert was waiting for us there. When the dragon that killed her zoomed by, I heard him say, 'By the dragons.' I pressed him and he admitted to being from Lohikärra. He's also the person who caught me here in the mall."

Mattie's eyes widened in surprise. "Your mother's dead too?"

I nodded again and sat against the shelves, locking my arms around my knees. "It's…I don't know what to think. Part of me is relieved she's gone, but part of me hates the fact that I had to watch her die in such a brutal way."

"It's because you're human, not a psychopath like her. You're dealing with a lot of stress." Mattie sighed, "We're *all* dealing with a lot of stress right now. I really want to make sure I can reverse the portal. Because if I can't…" She looked over my shoulder to where Haldrek was standing guard. "Along with all the other chaos going on, as long as Haldrek still has his dragon inside of him, it'll slowly kill him here in this world."

"What? Are you sure?" I stared at her as she returned her focus to me. My stomach clenched tight at the idea of Haldrek suffering here. "What about the other Lohikärrans who have been here before? Like our dads? Or Robert?"

Mattie shrugged. "I don't know. Your dad was here for about the same amount as my dad. Ten years. He could have been dealing with the symptoms and not known it. My dad, from the little I remember of him, always had some kind of chronic malaise until he died. Very different from the descriptions I read about him in Lohikärra. Part of me thinks it was because of the close ties that the House of Andrattür has to its dragons. As for Robert… for all we know, he was never a haldraga. He could have been a hired hit man. Even if he is part of the abthanry, he could have been on the lower rungs, so he never became a haldraga."

I inhaled, trying not to be overwhelmed by Mattie's fear. It wouldn't help for both of us to be anxiety ridden. And I believed in her. Even if I had fears about my capabilities, Mattie was competent.

"Mattie…" I caught her gaze and held it, trying to pour my determination and faith into her.

"Yes?"

"I believe in you. If anyone can reverse the portal, it's you. If you need any help, just let me know."

Mattie stared at me for a moment, then nodded. "I'll do my best. Even if it kills me."

Chapter Twenty-Eight

That night, I curled up next to Haldrek, soothed by his breathing and his body warmth. Mattie was still awake, scribbling down notes and standing guard as I fell asleep.

When I awoke the next morning, Haldrek still slept and Mattie was passed out in one of the chairs across from us. Dim light flooded in from the entrances. The store was silent, except for the dragons screeching outside.

Unwrapping Haldrek's arm from around my side, I snuck over to Mattie's side and looked at the notes on the floor around her. She had an open box of fancy crystal glasses next to her, a few of the glasses standing in a diamond shape. One set of glasses had a stormy gray liquid in it and had been taped together to make a large, almost pill-shaped crystal.

"Ugh. What time is it?"

I looked up to see Mattie rubbing her eyes. She glanced over at the crystal glasses that had been taped together and smiled. "It worked."

"It looks like it. Is that your plan?"

She nodded. "That gray fog in the glasses is what is supposed to attract the dragons. I saw it in the crystals Rorik had. If you look closely, it's what's covering the dragons outside. I was able to turn some of the water into it by channeling some of my life force into the crystals."

I widened my eyes at her. "Did that hurt you? I thought you said that magic wasn't inherent here?"

Mattie nodded again. "It isn't, but I figured I could use some of my innate ability to use magic to make it work. Apparently both of us have a little bit of magic from our Lohikärran ancestry." She shook her head. "It exhausted me, though. I had enough energy to put it on the floor and then pass out in the chair."

"And we've got three more to do."

"Yeah." Mattie sighed, then looked at Haldrek and at me. "You two could help me."

"How?" My throat tightened up at the same time as excitement and hope bubbled up inside me. We had a way home. But only if it didn't kill or weaken us too much first. Taking a deep breath, I forced myself to relax. Mattie needed our help and I wasn't about to leave her hanging.

Mattie eased herself from the camping chair she had been sleeping in and began creating the other three crystals. After she had poured water into the bottom cups and securely taped the top glass to it, she nudged Haldrek awake.

He opened one eye and looked around. "Where are we?"

Mattie rolled her eyes in annoyance. "Fargo. But I need your help to get back to Lohikärra."

He sat up uneasily and looked around. "Are we still safe?"

I nodded as Mattie placed one 'crystal' in front of each of us.

"I have a theory on how this works," she said as she gestured for us to place our hands on each of our crystals. "Since I was able to make another crystal last night, I'm hoping I'm correct. We each need to give a little bit of our 'life essence' to these crystals. Then we need to get them up to the roof where the portal is. That should attract enough attention from the dragons to get them to start coming for us and the portal. That will charge up the crystals and I'll toss the crystals into the vortex to change the direction and get things back into Lohikärra."

Haldrek groaned. "This is going to hurt, isn't it?"

"It's going to be *tiring*. Since when have you been a coward about pain?"

He opened his mouth as irritation flashed across his face. Being away from Sethys and Lohikärra was getting to him—Mattie's light teasing wouldn't have bothered him there. I grabbed his hand. "We're all tired and stressed. Let's just do this."

He closed his mouth and nodded, focusing on the crystal as Mattie began chanting and we repeated what she said. I gasped as I began to feel the inside of me pulled toward the crystal, much as it had when I had first seen Rorik while in the Realm of the Dead. It wasn't as painful, only uncomfortable this time. When Mattie finished, I looked up to see her pale and Haldrek sweating. But the crystals had begun to swirl with gray cloudy material and I sighed in relief.

Mattie grabbed the other crystal. "Now we just need to —"

The sound of rattling chain link and the metal gate opening made us all freeze for a moment.

Someone called out an order in the front of the store, but they were too far away for me to understand what they were saying.

Mattie and I looked at each other as we realized what was going on. Haldrek seemed understand our frantic looks and handed me his crystal before slipping backwards and grabbing a pair of golf clubs he had apparently found sometime last night. He crept away from us as I looked at Mattie. We snuck behind tables and shelving on our way toward the door.

The closest exit to the roof was just outside the door and down the sidewalk from this particular department store, so I guessed Mattie's plan was to use that set of stairs and make our way across the roof to the vortex. As we neared the door, we heard Haldrek shout on the other side of the room,

"Hey! Mattie! Ina! I was looking all over for you! What are you doing over here?"

I couldn't help but grin as I heard a dozen or so sets of footsteps run toward Haldrek's voice. He sounded like he was about to have some fun tangling with those soldiers.

"I wouldn't get too cocky if I were you. *Ina*."

I froze. Robert was walking toward us from the side door that we'd used last night. His face was partially bandaged where I had hit him, but his scowl was still prominent.

"Run, Ina!" Mattie pushed me forward and I began running for the front of the store, ducking underneath the metal grating as soon as I got to it, and making my way to the side hallway where another set of stairs to the roof would be.

"Grab them!"

A few of Gustav's warriors chased Mattie and I as we ran through the open door and up a few flights of stairs. We burst onto the roof and saw the vortex in front of us.

The clambering of footsteps and another push from Mattie sent me running forward to the very edge of the vortex. Mattie and I stopped as the crystals started to shake in our hands.

"I wouldn't do that quite yet. Not if you want Haldrek alive."

"Gustav," Mattie and I said in unison as we spun around. He stood a few paces behind us, Haldrek tied up behind him. Robert held the ropes in one hand, the other holding a blade to Haldrek's neck. Anger rose up inside of me, threatening to overflow.

"I was hoping you'd figure out a way to return to Lohikärra." He looked me over and smirked. "As much as I'd like to get rid of you right now, it seems I've got a more inconvenient problem back home. One I'd like to solve. But if all of us returned, I'd have to deal with you again. I'm not about to do that."

"What do you want?" I glanced at Haldrek. He was swaying, and I wondered if that tonic to let his dragon sleep was wearing off.

"I want the crystals. If you were about to jump into the portal with them, I expect they are the way to Lohikärra."

Mattie glanced at me. I nodded. Gustav had no idea how these worked. If he tossed one in, it wouldn't do anything. At least I didn't think it would do anything.

"What would you do if we didn't give you the crystals?" Mattie snapped. Her response surprised me.

"Simple. I would kill Haldrek. Then I would have my men kill you two. There's no way in Lyrroth I'm letting you two return to Lohikärra."

We looked at each other and my stomach churned with anxiety. Above us, dragons began to circle the vortex, howling and screeching. We'd gotten their attention as well.

"Don't do it!" Haldrek gasped. "He'll kill us all either way."

Gustav swung back, glaring at Haldrek. "I would shut up if I were you, *Thegn Andrattür*. You had plenty of chances to work with me. Now you get to die or stay here."

"What do you want, Gustav?" Haldrek shouted. It hit me that he was trying to buy time, but for what I didn't know.

Gustav cocked his head at Haldrek. "We're on a first name basis now? Why? Because I'm in control?"

Haldrek said nothing, but scowled.

"You should know by now what my intentions are, *Thegn Andrattür*. If you don't, you are too stupid for the title you wish to claim. You may be heir to the title of High King, but you won't be wearing it for long."

"You're planning on becoming High King?"

Gustav smirked again, glancing at Mattie and I. "As long as I'm alive."

Haldrek's eyes moved between us and Gustav. "As long as Rorik doesn't kill you first. Or pop you into another realm to die while he takes *your* title."

That was it. Haldrek was trying to distract Gustav while Mattie and I tossed the crystals into the vortex to reverse it. Already, the crystals had attracted the dragons' attention. More and more of them began circling above us. Gustav's men shuffled around, trying and failing to ignore the encroaching dragons.

"Rorik is not going to kill me. Nor do I believe he would ever try. He knows when I become High King, he will gain the title of aethling and thereafter inherit the title of High King."

"Are you so sure about that? Why did he send you here then? And without a way home? How do you know he doesn't plan on disposing of you as well as the rest of us?"

I stepped closer to Mattie and the sound of the vortex and the dragons increased. Despite the short distance between us, I couldn't hear what Gustav's response was, if any. Instead, I inched backwards along with Mattie and whispered, "Robert's going to be tossed into Lohikärra when the vortex reverses, isn't he?"

Mattie nodded. She looked at the dragons still churning above Fargo. "Once the crystals are in the vortex, it'll only be a few seconds before it pulls everything from Lohikärra in."

"Hey!"

We froze. Gustav took a few steps toward me, hand outstretched. "Give me the crystals. Now."

I hesitated, resting my heel on the roof, but ready to move at any moment.

He gestured for one of the makeshift crystals. "If it makes it easier, roll me the crystal and I'll release Haldrek."

I looked at Mattie anxiously. She nodded and I put the crystal on the ground, shoving it toward him.

Robert released Haldrek, but not without cutting him with the dagger. Haldrek stumbled forward, holding his hand to his face, then lurched toward us.

"I'm sorry... I..." Regret flooded over me as Haldrek reached me, grabbing my free hand.

"Run!"

Howling above us intensified as we ran the last few feet to the vortex. Shouts rose up above the noise, but I couldn't make out any words as Haldrek pulled us into the vortex with the three remaining crystals.

"No!" Gustav's voice boomed above the chaos.

I spun around, catching glimpses of him through the vortex clouds as he ran toward me, screaming in anger.

As soon as he jumped into the vortex and tackled me, I glimpsed the knife in his hand and we began wrestling for it as the winds spun us around. I went further into the vortex as the tip of it nicked my jawbone.

"Ina!" Haldrek's voice was hollow and distant in the fury of the vortex, despite being nearly on top of me. He tackled Gustav as I shoved the knife above Gustav's collarbone into the fleshy part of his neck. He gasped raggedly as Haldrek pushed him away. The blade cut across his neck, getting stuck as the wind and dragons pulled him further from us.

We sank further into the vortex for just a moment before the winds paused. As the vortex stopped shuddering, I wondered if we'd made a grievous mistake. Then the cacophony of dragon screams filled the air and I looked up to see the whole horde of dragons descending upon us.

This is going to look like one hell of a storm when this is all over.

The winds reversed, pulling us apart until I could only feel Haldrek's fingertips. I screamed, scrambling to get a better grip, but the sound was lost in the howling of the dragons sucked in around us. A boom and a crack made my whole body shudder and spin. Haldrek's hand was ripped from mine as I looked back and saw a wave of the gray ether pull him away.

The same wave pushed Mattie toward me. We impacted and suddenly I was in freefall, my body plummeting to the ground.

"*Suojaus!*" Mattie shouted just before we hit.

I gasped from the impact and watched as the ether fell over the side of the mall and consumed us. Just as my body went numb, I blacked out.

Chapter Twenty-Nine

When I came to, I felt something hard and leather-like brushing against my skin. Swatting at it, I realized it was much larger than I expected. Hot air consumed my hand.

Ina. Wake up, little one.

Opening my eyes, I saw one very large amber colored eye blink. I jumped.

Easy, little one. I am here to help you. We are bonded and you have helped my kin. But you are in a difficult place.

I was no longer in the parking lot outside of the mall. Instead, I was alone with Rhaegos in a brilliant white area. The space was shaped so I couldn't see any edges. I could see a faded rainbow on the edge of my vision, but as soon as I tried to look at it directly, it would disappear.

"Where am I? Am I dead again?"

Rhaegos made a sound like laughter, grayish smoke puffing from her nostrils into my face. She began to shift into a person, her scales transforming into a lavish earth-toned dress with sleeves draping to the ground. It shimmered with translucent green and purple as she moved. Her tail turned into a thick braided rope of hair cascading down her back.

"You are in the Realm of Dragons. Remember? It's a parallel place where my kind live between our hatchings in the realm where Lohikärra lays."

"Which is different than where Fargo lays?" My brain was still foggy, trying to grasp what was going on while also remembering what had happened.

Rhaegos nodded. "While we cannot live in realms outside of this one for more than a few millennia—by your reckoning—we have the gift to move between them with ease."

"Is that why the dragon stone sent Mattie and I between our world and Lohikärra?"

"And why Rorik—who seeks after the ways of Ryluth—could do so with our souls."

I nodded, still confused. Looking up at Rhaegos, I asked, "Did Mattie's magic work? Or work too well?"

Rhaegos laughed, but I couldn't tell if it was positive or negative.

"She did as she should. Most of Rorik's misdeeds have been repaired."

Most. I tried to think of what could have gone wrong. Or what still needed to be fixed. As I returned my focus to Rhaegos, she continued.

"You and Mattie are not fully of the realm of Lohikärra, nor fully of the realm of Earth. The magic could not place you in either place. Instead, you will each have to choose where home is."

I paused in surprise. As far as I was concerned, Lohikärra was my home. But I didn't know whether or not that was my decision to make for Mattie.

"Is Mattie here?"

Rhaegos shook her head, wisps of hair swaying around her head. "She has already made her decision with Sivath, though I do not know what that decision is."

I nodded. So she had already made her decision and mine was to be based on where I wanted to be. What home was for me.

"I know where I want to go."

"So quickly?" Rhaegos's eyes widened for a split second before returning to her normal stoic expression. Her tone betrayed a hint of approval, however.

I nodded. "Lohikärra. It's felt more like a home to me than Fargo ever did. Even if Mattie were to stay in Fargo, I belong in Lohikärra." My heart twinged at the idea of Mattie and I possibly being in two separate realms. But if I was going to be in a realm without her, I felt more at home in Lohikärra than I ever did in Fargo.

Rhaegos smiled and bowed her head once in approval.

"So be it, little one. Know this: there will be much for you to fix in that realm. Just because you've restored us to a more stable realm does not mean your life will be easy in Lohikärra."

I stiffened. I didn't expect it to be easy, but I hoped with friends and family like Haldrek, Aallotar, Thandes, Llamryl, and the others, it would be easier than staying in Fargo. "I think I can handle it. Especially if I have good friends and family around. Will you still be by my side?"

Rhaegos smiled widely and walked up to me. She hugged me tight and a feeling of love and acceptance flooded over me. I gasped, tears flooding my cheeks before I knew what was going on. The warmness and comfort of the feeling was foreign and intoxicating at the same time.

"Of course, little one." She paused for a moment and stepped back. Pulling a familiar oval-shaped scale from a hidden pocket in her dress, she handed it to me. "This will return you to Lohikärra when you are ready. But do not take too long. As I said, there is still much for you to restore—and reform."

I nodded and took the scale from her. It was identical to the one I had had in my room for years before. Just rubbing my thumb across the ridges on the scale calmed me as much as it had when I was younger.

"This doesn't hurt you? Getting rid of a scale, I mean?"

"Only as much as brushing your hair would hurt you." Rhaegos blew some steam my way, tousling my hair, and I laughed. "Now rest, little one, and I will return you to the realm of Earth."

I hugged her again, my head resting just under her ribcage and my eyes closed, holding firm to the stone with both hands. The air filled with a comforting smell, and I grew sleepy. In an instant, Rhaegos disappeared and I blacked out again.

This time, I woke up to the lazy beeping and humming of some machine in the background. The comforting smell had disappeared, replaced by a sterile smell, reminding me of rubbing alcohol. There was pressure on my left pointer finger and I could hear soft voices nearby. My right hand squeezed something hard. Memories of Rhaegos returned as I began rubbing the scale.

"What did the other girl say happened? Her supposed sister-in-law? Why they were on the roof in the first place?"

"They were trying to hide from the patient's mother's abusive boyfriend. One of our former security guards."

"Huh. Didn't know Sigyn was dating someone. Here or anywhere. What do the patient's test results show? Any reason for her being unconscious for so long?"

The sound of flipping paper reached my ear. "No. Nothing. Initially, we thought some kind of drug, because of the... well..."

"What Sigyn was always talking about. I know. But everything's negative?"

"Everything we tested for."

"Huh. Well, I'll go check on her and see if anything has changed."

The conversation went quiet and I quickly slipped the stone under my thigh as the nurse pulled the privacy curtain open.

Someone moved next to me and I turned to see Mattie waking up. She opened one eye for a moment, then both.

"You're awake!" Her voice got rough as she tried to blink away the tears.

"How are you feeling?" The nurse glanced over at me before plugging me into a rolling machine and checking my vitals.

"Tired. Hungry. Homesick."

"No aches or pains? No headache?" She started jotting something on her notepad.

"No. Not really. My back is a little sore, but nothing major." I rotated and stretched out my shoulders. The rolling machine began beeping and the nurse removed the wires from me.

"Okay. Well, your vitals all seem normal so I'll let the doctor know you're awake. I'm sure he'll have more questions for you. I'll go grab some water and some crackers for you in just a bit."

She disappeared, closing the privacy curtain, and immediately I turned to Mattie.

"How long have I been out? What do they know?"

"Only about a day. But it was still concerning. I told them I was your sister-in-law. Which is technically the truth. But I'm thinking I should have made up some story about being your sister, having the same dad, different mother kinda thing. I also told them we were escaping your mom's boyfriend. He had cornered us in one of the mall corridors and getting up on the roof was our only option."

"They're not curious why we were on the roof in the middle of a massive storm?"

Mattie lowered her voice. "As far as they know, there was no storm."

"What? What about the damage? And my mother being dead? Is my mother still dead?"

"Yes. As far as I've overheard, people were talking about her being in a car accident a couple days ago. But there's no damage otherwise. No broken buildings, no nothing."

I brought my voice lower. "Were you intending to do that with the magic?"

Mattie shook her head. "That was a happy accident."

Our conversation lulled for a moment as I tried to think of the best way to ask the next question on my mind. I fiddled with the dragon stone under my leg.

"Mattie…"

"If you're about to ask me about Lohikärra…" She pulled out a dragon stone of her own. "I already told Sivath that Lohikärra can't get rid of me that easily."

I smiled. "I'm glad you're coming back too. But what about…?"

"My inheritance? Everything here on Earth that I got from my parents?" Mattie sighed and shrugged. "Money isn't worth having if you're alone, or you have long lost relatives popping up to ask for or demand it. If I don't claim it by the time I'm twenty-one, it'll go to a bunch of charities my parents supported. So it's not like my dad's legacy won't be helping someone." Mattie's mouth quirked up into a smile. "I miss Llamryl. A lot. It might not pan out to anything, but for now I miss him. I wouldn't mind seeing him again."

I grinned as well. Nothing that could keep me from finding Haldrek as soon as we returned to Lohikärra, and not letting go for a very long time.

"Are we ready then?" I slipped the dragon stone from under my thigh as Mattie held hers in both hands. Glancing around us, I made sure the doctor wouldn't pop in right as we were disappearing.

"I'm ready as I'll ever be."

Without another word, we snapped the stones in half, and a bright light flashed over everything.

Chapter Thirty

Mattie and I tumbled face first into a grassy patch as we returned to Lohikärra. The weight of my sword returning to my belt made me roll to my side. Wherever we were, it was *crowded*. A few of the people where we had popped up stared at us wide-eyed, then hurried away.

One Hethurin woman ran over and pulled me up. "Thegn Svartån? You're really here? You're alive? Thank the dragons!"

I nodded, looking at her in surprise. We were in the courtyard of Svangendom. To my right was the plain stone structure the Priests of Tenelth called home. Focusing on the woman who had helped me, I asked, "What's going on? Why is everyone in the courtyard?"

The door to the priests' house opened, and the older priest I'd met on my first night at Svangendom stopped to stare at me.

"Rumors came from Drattüjert that you'd died," the woman whispered. "But you're here. In the flesh."

And with Rhaegos by your side. Tell the priests I know their thoughts.

I focused on the priest who stood just outside the door. "Rhaegos says hello. And that she knows your thoughts."

The priest turned pale and fell to his knees on the ground. "Forgive me, my thegn."

Dropping the woman's hands, I turned to the priest. "What did you do?"

"Thegn—the gesith came with tokens of your death. He said Thegn Etelaranikä gave them to him after you fought off the Blodnar in Drattüjert."

I opened my mouth to say something as Mattie ran over to me.

"Ina! We've got trouble." She gestured to a few men who followed her through the crowd. I turned to face them, hand on my hilt.

The warriors stopped as they came within a few feet of me. Their tabards bore the crest of Lansiranikä.

"Lemme guess. Hardbein is trying to take over my title again?"

The men said nothing, but stumbled backwards through the crowd.

Turning to the Hethurin woman, I asked, "What's going on? Why is everyone here? I'm assuming it has something to do with Hardbein."

The woman paled. "We were ordered here from the village by Lansiranikän warriors. There is a man inside the estate who says he is the new Thegn of Svartån. But we weren't told why we were all brought here."

I looked around to see more people in the crowd. Men, women, and children. A sick feeling started to twist in my stomach and I focused on the woman.

"Don't listen to any of the Lansiranikän warriors. Do whatever you need to do to protect yourselves, just in case. I'm still the Thegn of Svartån, no matter what the man inside says."

The woman nodded and others started to move, their attention shifting to Mattie as I turned to her. The mood of the group started to change, and the few Lansiranikän warriors still within my periphery began to fade away from the crowd.

"You know, for once, I'd like for someone not to try and take my throne and title from me. Specifically, I'd like Hardbein to stop trying to take my title. This is the second or third time, I think."

Mattie smiled grimly. "That's your life now. You technically have the authority to execute him now. If you chose to do so."

"Wouldn't that cause bad blood with Lansiranikä?"

"Probably, but given Bjorn's friendliness with Gustav, I doubt you ever had a chance to be buddies with him. You need to do something serious to keep Hardbein from popping up every time he thinks you are dead."

I groaned, knowing Mattie was right, and started walking with her through the crowd. The only comfort I had was that my armor and Freya's Menace had returned to me. That was an outward sign of who was the true thegn of Svartån. As much as Hardbein wished he was the thegn, he still couldn't claim the title while I was around.

As we stepped inside the main hall, I heard shouting and the clanging of swords on the main floor. Familiar voices erupted above the noise: Llamryl and the man attempting to take my title—Hardbein Hoskaldsson.

"You are *not* the Thegn of Svartån and until I see proof that the *true* Thegn of Svartån is gone, I will *not* stand down."

"You will let me take my proper place on that throne or else, half-breed." Hardbein swung his sword at Llamryl as we ran up the stairs. Llamryl easily defended against the parry. Behind him, Thandes stood in front of the throne, as if guarding it as well.

"Who said you were the Thegn of Svartån?" I called out.

All three of them looked over at me, and while Thandes and Llamryl began to smile wide, Hardbein snarled at me.

"You're supposed to be dead."

"But I'm not." I shrugged. "Still in the Realm of the Living, still the Thegn of Svartån. You seem pretty upset about that."

Hardbein sheathed his sword, but stood stiffly, not moving. I pursed my lips, annoyance growing inside me. He may have been my dad's age, but I felt like I was dealing with a little kid.

"While I can tell why you came here in the first place, what are you still doing here?"

"I do not recognize you as the Thegn of Svartån."

I frowned at him in confusion. "What?" The beginnings of laughter echoed around us from the few people in the thegn hall. "That doesn't matter. You are not a subject of Svartån. You are a gesith of Lansiranikä. Whether you recognize me as thegn doesn't matter." I pointed to the door behind me. "Get out. Take your men with you."

"Or what?" Hardbein put his hand on the hilt of his sword.

"Or I will have my warriors here force you out. As much as Bjorn doesn't like me, I'm sure he'd rather not lose more men because you're being stubborn. Now go." I paused and then added, "You are exiled from Svartån. You have twenty-four hours to reach the border and leave. If I or any of my men find you within Svartån after that, your life is forfeit. Understood?"

Hardbein stiffened up, his face contorted into an awful scowl. Without a word, he strode past me. Once he left the hall, Llamryl bowed to me and Thandes came up next to him, with a big smile on her face.

"It is good to see you again, my thegn." He looked up at Mattie and smiled from ear to ear. "Mattie."

"I'm glad to see you're feeling better." It surprised me to see him here and in full health so quickly. But good news was goods news. I gestured for him to get up. "Go on. I'm assuming you two want to at least hug."

Llamryl got up quickly and gave Mattie a big hug, lifting her off the ground as she laughed. I beamed for a moment before looking at Thandes.

"How long has Hardbein been here with his men?"

"Only a couple days. He came in announcing he was the new thegn of Svartån. That you were dead."

I grumbled and shook my head. "I'm here. For good. Have you heard any word from any of the other thegns? Or news of the dragons?"

Thandes shook her head. "Jaonos from Mirratoft did use the thegn stones this morning to ask if you had returned here yet." She nodded in the direction of the door. "Hardbein pushed Skuti away from the stones and demanded Haldrek talk to him as Thegn of Svartån or else."

I raised my eyebrows in surprise. "Hardbein was really pushing it, wasn't he?"

Thandes nodded. "Jaonos said nothing, but disconnected the stones so the liquid went black again. That sent Hardbein into a fury. Skuti tried to reason with him, but to no avail."

"Where is Skuti now, anyway? Is he alright?"

Thandes nodded. "He's probably in the library as we speak."

"I'm right here. I heard the noise and was glad to see Hardbein be ousted from the thegn hall once again." Skuti walked up next to me. "It's good that you told him he was exiled. I fear he'll try to make himself thegn if it's the last thing he does."

"Well, if he tries again, he'll lose his life." I paused. "What of Mirratoft? Is Haldrek there?"

Skuti shook his head. "I do not know. I assume so, if his *husceorl* Jaonos is calling on the thegn stones. But I would think Thegn Andrattür would try to contact you, unless something ill has happened."

Had Haldrek survived the return to Lohikärra? Perhaps Jaonos was contacting Svangendom to see if Haldrek was here once again.

"I should get a hold of Haldrek then, if I can." I felt for my pendant, surprised that the etching on the front of was now white. I hadn't noticed that before. "Haldrek. Mirratoft."

The glass in my pendant went inky black for a moment before returning to its normal clear state.

"Why would it do that?" I looked up at Thandes, who shrugged. Willing myself to not let anxiety get the best of me, I figured I could contact the thegn hall itself. Maybe I could get a hold of Jaonos.

"Mirratoft."

The water became inky black, but then cleared up with an image of the study alcove behind Mirratoft's main hall. At least that's where it had been in the games. I stared the ceiling before saying, "Hello?"

For a moment, there was nothing, then I saw Jaonos peek over the rim of the bowl and sigh with relief.

"Thank the dragons. You're alive. You need to go to Drattüjert as soon as you can, Thegn Svartån. Where are you?"

"I'm at Svangendom. What's wrong? Is Haldrek okay?" My stomach clenched with worry. How had returning to Lohikärra affected him?

"Physically, I think so. When he contacted me with his pendant, he was desperate to find you. He told me to block anyone trying to contact him, with the exception of you and Lady Mattie."

I sighed. "I'll head out immediately. If you can, tell him you talked to me face to face and that I *am* alive and back for good."

Jaonos nodded and the water went clear again.

Chapter Thirty-One

Llamryl and Mattie rode with me to Drattüjert. I wasn't about to break up their reunion and I wasn't about to ride to Drattüjert alone either. As we made it through the southern villages of Svartån and northern part of Svarhestån, we were met with a handful of warriors who wished to join us and return to Drattüjert. The travel was much quicker now with only a handful of people, versus the near five hundred I had had previously. Each night, I tried contacting Haldrek with my pendant, and each night I was met with the same inky black rejection.

As the days passed and we arrived at Aallotar's thegn hall, I heard news of what had happened since our disappearance. Hardbein had taken his men to Svangendom as soon as Bjorn had left Aallotar's thegn estate. According to the stories Aallotar's warriors regaled us with, Hardbein likely only made it to Svangendom because most of the Svartån men were still in Heidrunefoss fighting the Blodnar who had tried to attack Aallotar's thegn hall once more. However, when the dragons returned, they went after the Blodnar with a vengeance and drove them from both Drattüjert and Aallotar's thegn hall single handedly. No word on Gustav or Rorik's whereabouts, only that they had disappeared.

I had a sinking feeling neither would be gone for long.

In the morning, we headed out early. Even then, it was well into the afternoon by the time we reached the gates of Drattüjert proper.

In stark contrast to what I had seen last time, now people hurried around, repairing and rebuilding the walls and other defenses of Drattüjert. Priests of Tenelth were in force as we made our way up the outer stairs and over the drawbridge. The spirits who had covered the city and its streets were nearly gone, with the exception of a few Blodnar soldiers.

Riding along the main road, I had a detached sense of pity for them. The Blodnar had done awful things to Lohikärra and Drattüjert. They had killed my father and many of my men. They'd tried to kill me at the battle for Aallotar's thegn hall. But how many of them had been recruited by their leaders, the Blodnar version of thegns? If anyone had my anger, it was those men, and possibly women, as well as the Lohikärrans who had betrayed us. The majority of my rage was directed at Gustav and Rorik. They had done more damage than the Blodnar ever could.

Once inside the palace, my men having taken our mounts to a nearby stable, Mattie, Llamryl, and I could hear voices from the throne room echoing into the hall where we stood. The servants who bustled around us ignored them. Llamryl and Mattie weren't paying them much heed either.

"I never thought I'd find myself in Drattüjert. Much less the palace," Llamryl gaped. "It's bigger than I ever imagined. You think the roof is high so dragons can fly in here?"

"That could be a possibility." Mattie spun around slowly, taking in the whole place. "My dad recreated this place almost identically in the game." She focused on me and stopped. "You okay?"

I nodded. "Every time I've been here, bad stuff has happened. I'm afraid that's happening again." As I gestured to the throne room, a loud, deep shout made everyone stop.

Without thinking, I began running and didn't stop until I burst through the doors. Inside the throne room stood a handful of thegns—Aallotar, Hrimfax, Raynord, and Keldan. Their eyes all widened as they looked me over. Aallotar was to first to move and speak.

"Ina? Where have you been?"

"I... I've been traveling from Svangendom for the last few days. Why? Is Haldrek all right?"

"He's locked himself up in the High King's quarters and refuses to speak to anyone," Raynord snapped. "You've been traveling from Svangendom? How did you get there in the first place?"

I scowled at the return of Raynord's nasty attitude. He was stressed, it was obvious, but he didn't have to unleash it on me. "Rorik tossed me and Haldrek through a portal to Fargo. Mattie was able to return everyone but herself and me to Lohikärra. Rhaegos gave me one of her scales and it took me to Svangendom."

The rest of the thegns continued to stare at me, but Keldan cleared his throat. "Perhaps you can convince Haldrek to leave the High King's quarters. We assume he is grieving your loss, but if you can show him that you are not gone..."

I nodded. I wasn't sure where the High King's quarters would be. "Would someone being willing to go with me? I've never actually been in any part of this palace."

"I know where the High King's quarters are," Mattie said, standing next to me. "If the palace is the way...." She hesitated as she looked around at the other thegns. "If it's the way my dad described it in his notes, there should be a staircase off the other side of the garden."

She began walking through the door in the rear of the throne room and I followed, as did Llamryl and the other thegns.

After climbing a few flights of stairs and making our way down a long hallway, Mattie stopped in front of a rounded wall with two guards in front of the sole door.

"Apparently Haldrek and Mattie's father described the inside of the palace very well," Aallotar said approvingly.

I stepped forward and one of the guards shook his head.

"My apologies, thegn. We've been told to not let anyone pass unless Thegn Andrattür says otherwise."

"Do you know who she is?" Raynord snapped. I looked at him in surprise. He sighed. "If Haldrek seeing you allows us to move forward, I have no qualms. I'm merely frustrated by my nephew's stubbornness."

I turned to the guards. "I'm the Thegn of Svartån. Haldrek is my husband." It felt weird to say the word 'husband', like I was pretending or something. It barely felt real.

"I'm sorry, my thegn. We were given orders to—"

"Oh for pity's sake!" Mattie grabbed one guard's spear while Aallotar grabbed the other. In a moment of chaos, I ducked between them and pushed the door open. Running up the stairs, I tried to keep my distance from the guards who had decided to chase me.

I panicked until I saw dim light coming from a room where the door was ajar. Shoving it open, I saw a familiar person staring out a narrow window, his hands pressed against the stone frame.

"I thought I told you..." Haldrek stopped as he stared at me. At that moment, the guards ran into the room and one latched on to my shoulder, pulling me back.

"I'm sorry, my thegn. They—"

"Enough!" Haldrek kept staring at me, his eyes bloodshot. I struggled to keep my composure as my vision blurred. The guard tried to pull me back again and I shrugged him off roughly.

"Get your hands off of her," Haldrek snapped, taking a few steps toward me. The guard did as he was told. Haldrek whispered, "You've returned. You're here."

"I am. I am here." My voice broke as I jumped into his arms and he swung me around. His heart raced under his gambeson as he began to sob.

"I thought you were gone. Forever."

"No. I came back. I'm here. Forever." I laughed as his nose and facial hair tickling my neck. Tears fell on my neck but I didn't care. I wanted to stay in Haldrek's arms forever.

"I thought... I thought I had failed you. And you were dead. And..." He began kissing my head and neck eagerly. "Are you back? Forever?"

I nodded. "Lohikärra is my home now."

"What took so long? What happened when the vortex...? I got pulled in and dropped here at the palace, but you and Mattie got pushed out."

I squeezed him tighter. "Rhaegos talked to me. Mattie and I were half from that realm and half from this realm, so the magic didn't know where to put us." I laughed. "I woke up in the Realm of Dragons with her. She told me I had the choice to stay in Fargo or return to Lohikärra. It wasn't a hard choice. When I woke up, Mattie told me what had happened while I was unconscious and we decided to return here together."

Haldrek pulled away for a moment, staring at Mattie. "Were you sent to two different places? Is that what happened last time?"

"I had my own dragon stone this time," Mattie added. "Straight from Sivath's back."

"We both got tossed to Svangendom, though. Hence the delay. I kept trying to contact you. I even had Jaonos try to contact you."

Haldrek sighed. "Hardbein tried to contact me through the thegn stones. Demanded I acknowledge him as Thegn-heir of Svartån or else. After that, I stopped responding to my pendant. I'm sorry."

I nodded. "Llamryl and Thandes defended my throne. When I arrived, I kicked him and his men out. Exiled him under threat of death if he was found in Svartån after twenty-four hours was up. He was on his way back to Lansiranikä when I left."

Haldrek hugged me one more time and then said, "I... I should probably..."

"Go downstairs and start acting like the heir to the High King's title?" Raynord snapped. He grunted as a few people jabbed or smacked him.

"As joyous as this reunion is," Keldan walked over to Haldrek and placed a hand on his shoulder, "I think Raynord has a point. Though I wouldn't be so callous as he has been, given the situation."

Haldrek nodded and looked over everyone. "I think I'm ready. Not six months ago, the Vollr gave me three visions in this very room. One of them concerning the crown of the High King. I wasn't ready then, but now that I have someone by my side that I can trust, I'm ready."

He leaned down to kiss me and I savored the moment, despite the audience. In that moment, I felt well and truly at home.

When he stood back, I smiled and whispered, "Let's go restore Drattüjert and Lohikärra together."

Chapter Thirty-Two

The city slowly returned to normal as people picked up where they had left off, burying the dead and cleaning up the messes Rorik, the dragons, and the Blodnar had left behind. Though I wasn't technically High Queen yet, I spent my time helping the people of Drattüjert, particularly in sending the dead off to Mirroth.

The next few months was a time of both rebuilding and grieving—for both Haldrek and I. We sent off our relatives, including my father, to Mirroth. As I did his rite in particular, it was difficult to form the words. After his spirit slipped off to Mirroth, an emptiness I hadn't expected, hit me. I knew he was at peace and no longer at risk of becoming a zombie, but I also knew I wouldn't be able to see him again. The fact that our 'reunion' had been so short made my heart ache.

It was the first day of November by the time Drattüjert was in a position to hold a celebration. Exactly six months to the day after I became Thegn of Svartån, I found myself at the doors of the throne room in a much lighter, brighter palace. The hallway behind us was filled to the brim with people from the city and surrounding areas. The ceremony, held at first light, felt oddly ethereal as Haldrek and I were dressed in ceremonial robes specifically for this occasion. While not in our armor, I had Freya's Menace strapped to my side and Haldrek had an empty sheath, symbolizing our future at Lohikärra's rulers, both in peace and war.

The doors to the throne room opened and I was surprised to see it much darker than the hallway behind us. Instead of sunlight, it was lit with torches and candles. Looking at Haldrek in surprise, he nodded and took my hand, leading me into the room where Keldan stood between the High King and High Queen's chairs. On both sides, I saw several familiar faces—Aallotar, Hrimfax, and Raynord stood on one side and Mattie stood on the other with two less familiar faces: one of Haldrek's cousins Sigurd, Thegn of Nerthusån, and Gunner Braggisson, Thegn of Bragidrattür. Gunner had a piece of parchment on a wooden board in his hand alongside some kind of writing tool. An excited smile crossed his face as I passed and I was happy to see that he looked better than when we had first met in February.

"I've been looking forward to doing this ceremony for many months now," Keldan remarked. I turned to see him looking at me, then at Haldrek. "It will be good for Lohikärra to have a High King once again."

Haldrek and I nodded, kneeling before Keldan continued. "As First Priest of Tenelth, I invoke all the rights and privileges of kingship upon you, Haldrek Rodreksson of Andrattür. May Tenelth's descent guide you in wisdom as you rule over this land of ours and keep it ever free from those who would subject it. You have been called the Restorer of Lohikärra by the dragon descent of Tenelth and as such, from this time forward, you shall be known as High King Haldrek the Restorer."

Keldan took the staff he held, carved with a dragon's head, and tapped it on Haldrek's shoulders, then his head. Haldrek shuddered and inhaled, as if trying to hold a great weight. Keldan placed a crown from the king's throne on top of Haldrek's head, then looked at me.

"As First Priest of Tenelth, I invoke all the rights and privileges of queenship upon you, Maja Ingmar Svanunge of Svartån. May Tenelth's descent guide you in wisdom as you rule over this land alongside Haldrek the Restorer, and keep it ever free from those who would subject it. You have been called the Reformer of Lohikärra by the dragon descent of Tenelth, as well as one of the Mothers of Lohikärra—a rare and noble title. Epics will regal the descendants of these houses with your bravery and fortitude, much as they do of Freya, our first Mother. As such, from this time forward, you shall be known as High Queen Ina the Reformer."

Keldan tapped my shoulders and head with the staff. As he did, I felt a surge of electricity go through me and it felt as if Rhaegos was churning inside my body. After a moment, I felt the heavy weight of a similar crown placed on my head.

With that, Haldrek helped me up and we both looked at Keldan.

Keldan looked past us and to the crowd at our backs. "I am proud to present, to my fellow thegns and the people of Lohikärra, the new High King and High Queen of Lohikärra."

The other thegns clapped as the crowd in the palace and beyond began to cheer.

Keldan cleared his throat and raised his voice. "My fellow thegns, do you swear fealty to the new High King and High Queen of Lohikärra, for as long as you should live?"

A chorus of *yeses* and *ayes* was the response as Haldrek turned to me, squeezing my hand, and then to his uncle.

"High King Haldrek, as my final act as the First Priest of Tenelth, I bestow the Royal Staff of Tenelth upon you, as it was bestowed upon me a year ago. I believe the High King Kalle knew what would happen and did so in order to keep the staff safe. However, as the new High King of Lohikärra, it is your right and privilege to wield the Royal Staff." Keldan bowed as he handed the staff to Haldrek.

He stepped back, revealing a hole in the floor between the two thrones. Haldrek stepped forward and placed the staff in the hole. He gestured for me to sit in the Queen's Throne as he sat in the King's Throne. He twisted the staff until it clicked and said, "As High King of Lohikärra, I command the palace of Drattüjert to awaken!"

I gasped as all the lights in the room sputtered out, darkening it for a moment before bright beams of sunlight illuminated the room and focused on the thrones. Glancing at Haldrek and the other thegns, I saw most of them beaming widely. Only Mattie and I were looking around in surprise.

Keldan clapped me on the shoulder. "Drattüjert has accepted you and Haldrek as High King and High Queen. Congratulations."

I grinned weakly, still taking everything in. Looking over, I saw Haldrek take the staff and pass it to his right hand. Taking my hand with his left, he helped me stand, and we began walking back down the hall and outside for the final part of the ceremony.

The crowd parted for us as we walked to the small landing just outside the front doors of the palace. Fresh snow crunched under my feet as I held Haldrek's hand for support. We got to the railing and looked over the large square below us. Though Drattüjert was a large city, I doubted I had ever seen a crowd this large in Lohikärra before.

Haldrek looked over the crowd as he raised the Royal Staff of Tenelth. "As the new High King of Lohikärra, I have but one thing to say: To Lohikärra, now and forever!"

The people began to cheer and whistle loudly around us as we raised our hands in triumph. After a moment, we put our arms down and Haldrek looked over at me. He leaned in as I did and as we kissed, the crowd began to cheer again.

After many hours of eating, dancing, and mingling with our subjects during the celebration, I finally retired to the large and now sumptuous quarters designated for the High King and High Queen. Curled up on a window bench and holding a vial of purple liquid, I happily watched the festivities in the square below. People were still celebrating and the music made its way through the chill night air.

Footsteps came up the circular stairs that provided the main entrance to these quarters. Haldrek's head popped around the edge of the door and he grinned.

"*Mine drawing*. My queen. I wondered where you had gone."

"I had to go pee and when I got up here, I was too tired to go back downstairs. I've been watching the celebrations from the window."

"You're not cold?" Haldrek walked over and glanced out. The window was small and narrow enough that the cold air didn't bother me too much. In fact, it let in enough fresh air to keep this antechamber from getting too stuffy.

I gestured to the fur blanket on top of me. "I'm fine."

He sat across from me and began to pick at his fingers. I noticed stains on them, dirt or possibly some kind of dried sauce. "You look like you had too much fun with the finger foods today."

He glanced at his hands and laughed. "I guess so. I should probably clean them." After a moment, he looked up and asked, "If you're tired, why haven't you gone to bed? You know you don't have to stay up for all the festivities. These will be going on for at least a week."

I smiled, spinning the bottle in my hands. "I know. I just wanted to wait for you."

"Why...?" Haldrek smiled as he glanced at the bottle in my hand. "What's that?"

"It's technically a bottle of pee." I laughed.

"Then why is it... purple?" He frowned in confusion.

"Mattie has been working on her alchemy skills since we've returned to Lohikärra. She brought me a six pack of her most recent creation when she arrived for the coronation. It is a potion to see if one is with child or not." I raised an eyebrow and focused on the bottle to hide my expression. I knew if I looked up at Haldrek, my emotions would reveal themselves too quickly.

Haldrek's eyes widened. "How does it work? I mean...with the pee?"

I showed him the bottle again. "I pee into a bottle, add the potion and wait a few moments. If the pee turns clear, I'm not pregnant. If it turns purple..."

He looked up at me as realization hit him. "You're with child." He gaped for a moment. "How? How quickly does it work? How far along are you? When did you know?"

I couldn't help but grin at his expression. "It works fairly quickly. Less than minute until the color changed. I can only guess at how far along I am given how often we... um... enjoy each other's company..."

Haldrek smiled widely at my comment.

"But given that my period—my 'womanly time'—is usually as regular as the moon and it's been two weeks since it should have arrived, I may have asked Mattie about her experiments and had her bring some of this potion when she came to celebrate our coronation."

"How long have you known?"

"Since I came up here." I laughed. The giddiness in his voice made me smile. "I saw the potion and, given how I'd been feeling lately, plus my late period, I guessed I should check. And it came out purple." I sighed. "I'm both excited and terrified now."

Haldrek continued staring at the bottle as he bobbed his head in understanding. "You and I are the only ones who know so far?"

I nodded. "I'll probably tell Mattie, but I don't want it to be public news quite yet."

"Why not? If you're with child, I think that would be good news for people to hear. If there is an aethling on the way, it's a sign of stability for Lohikärra. Especially after everything that has happened this year."

"Because I took sex education in high school—as minimal as that was—and read books about pregnancy and there's..." I didn't want to say my fear out loud. As if doing so would make it come true.

"What?"

"Until a woman is about twelve weeks past her last period, there's always a high chance of her losing the pregnancy. In Fargo, most people do not announce they are with child until they are beyond that point. At least to people outside of close family and friends. I'm afraid what might happen if people outside our close friends and family knew. We took back Drattüjert, but Gustav and Rorik are still out there. So is Robert. What would keep someone from coming here and trying to hurt me and this child?"

"Neither Gustav nor Robert are a threat anymore. Gustav was dead as soon as he returned to Lohikärra, and Robert...is no longer a threat. I've made sure of that." He leaned over and kissed me tenderly on the top of my forehead. "You don't need to worry about either of them ever again. As for Rorik, I have warriors searching for him, with orders to kill him and bring me a token of his death. I will do everything in my power to keep you—and our child—safe."

Haldrek took the bottle from my hands and put it on a nearby table. He wrapped his arms around me, pulling me into his lap for a hug and a kiss. "As for other worries, I hope they amount to nothing, and I think...I believe this is an auspicious sign. Just as we're starting a new life as the High King and Queen of Lohikärra, so it seems you have new life inside you as well." He kissed me gently again as he scooped me up and carried me to the bedroom.

"Let us head to bed. It seems we have a bright, beautiful future ahead of us. I can't wait to get there with you."

The Lohikärran Chronicles

<u>**Visions of Lohikärra (Prequel)**</u>
A mysterious young woman, an elven invasion, and the tokens of the High King
Haldrek Rodreksson has known his entire life where his future lies and what is expected of him. But on the eve of battle, soothsayers show him three visions of a different future: a mysterious young woman, a new invasion, and theft of the High King's tokens. Visions which make him question his future and that of his homeland, Lohikärra.

When the capital of Lohikärra falls, Haldrek's world is thrown into disarray and he must scramble to keep the young woman from his visions safe.

Injured, weaponless, and with little support, will Haldrek be able to save the woman and change the visions he was given? Or will he, his homeland, and his loved ones fall to their enemies?

<u>**Heir of Svartån**</u>
Lohikärra was just a game. Until it wasn't.

Ina Svanunge lives in North Dakota, avoiding attention and counting the days until she's free of her abusive mother. But when she and best friend, Mattie, sit down to play the newest release from their favorite video game series, they find themselves in the game's world, Lohikärra. Only it's not the game - Lohikärra is real.

Once there, Ina finds out her long-absent father was a powerful thegn - and she's his rightful heir. Unfortunately, she isn't the only one claiming his title, and the others are more than willing to kill her for it. On a journey across Svartån, Ina must fight for her birthright or risk rejection from the world she has long wished to be part of.

Will Ina be able to claim her rightful title with help from Mattie and their handsome new friend, Haldrek? Or will she end up dying in a foreign, unforgiving land?

Thegn of Svartån
She will be Thegn of Svartån. If Svartån still exists.

Ina Svanunge is the rightful thegn-heir of Svartån, but she must fight to lead and protect her new homeland's people, even as she's still learning how to do both. Can she learn to lead and bring her people together before they are brutally conquered?

An invasion from the Isillas elves - Svartån's most ancient enemy - looms imminent and Ina's first priority is to prepare her new homeland's defenses. Which would be easier if not for the deep hatred held by many of her subjects against their half-elven neighbors. With the Isillas at their doorstep, Svartån is fractured and in need of a leader to unite it once and for all. Racing to improve not only her fighting and leadership skills, she finds herself out of time when the Isillas attack and endanger not only Svartån, but those closest to her.

Weakened and alone, will Ina be able to protect Svartån from the Isillas? Or will she both lose her hard fought title and risk the destruction of Svartån?

Queen of Drattüjert
Old enemies. New challenges. Ina is thegn, but can she be queen?

It's been almost two months since Ina Svanunge officially became the Thegn of Svartån. With the Isillas conflict behind her, she must now aid her fellow thegns against an even bigger threat: the Blodnar Empire from the south.

Lohikärra will never be whole without its heart: the capital city of Drattüjert still under Bloodnar control. Ina and her fellow thegns have a plan to take it back, but there are traitors amongst their ranks bent on obtaining their own power and glory. The last thing Ina's beloved country needs is the emergence of a necromancer bent on destroying both Lohikärra and its dragons entirely.

When traitorous calamity strikes, Ina and Haldrek are forced into a race against time to save their loved ones, Lohikarra, and even Ina's hometown Fargo. But the cost could be Ina's life.

Lady of Lohikärra
With great power comes great responsibility. And greater enemies.

Fully embracing Lohikärra as her new home, Ina has taken her place alongside Haldrek as High King and Queen. But Lohikärra is a broken country on the verge of civil war. Respected by some, despised by others, Ina must rebuild the capital city of Drattüjert while Haldrek rebuilds Lohikärra.

When Henry, an old friend from Fargo, arrives in Drattüjert offering a solution to all her problems, it'll either be her saving grace or too good to be true.

Will Ina figure out which before it's too late? Or will fractured loyalties cause her to lose everything she holds dear?

Heart of Lohikärra
Coming June 2023!

Love it?

Leave a Review!

Did you enjoy *Queen of Drattüjert*? If so, I would be delighted if you left a review. (If you already have, thank you so much!) As a new author, book reviews are golden. You can leave reviews wherever you purchased the book, Goodreads, or other places as well. Book recommendations on social media (Youtube, Instagram, Twitter, TikTok, etc) is also awesome.

Follow me!

Website: https://www.llnelsonauthor.com/
Newsletter: https://www.llnelsonauthor.com/newsletter/
Facebook: https://www.facebook.com/llnelsonauthor
Instagram: https://www.instagram.com/llnelsonauthor
TikTok: https://www.tiktok.com/@llnelsonauthor

About the Author

L. L. Nelson is a full-time librarian, history buff, and author of numerous stories and poems. In short, she is a word nerd with a passion for poetry, fantasy, historical fiction, and just a little bit of romance. She's been creating worlds and figuring out the 'what ifs' in her stories since she was old enough to read the words 'Egg Roll King' on a local Chinese restaurant sign in 1992.

In college, she took all the creative writing classes she could to feed her need to write. This gave her enough credits to graduate with a minor in English and the ability to second guess her work like a true writer. It also introduced her to a variety of genres and their tropes that she now uses in her stories and poetry.

As a librarian, L. L. Nelson has honed her research skills to a science. (A library science.) This has given her mad talent when it comes to finding obscure facts to use in her stories and poetry. (Like the fact that the Vikings used rap battles as a form of combat.)

When not dealing with her scripturient nature, L. L. Nelson is a mom, inventive cook, wannabe linguist, and dreams of being not only a 'word traveler' but a world traveler. Fortunately, she lives in Southern California with her husband and kids, so she can go to Disneyland once a year and pretend that she's actually traveling around the world, even when she isn't.

Acknowledgments

My utter gratitude goes out to a whole host of people, without whom this book would have taken a lot longer to write. Among them are the *many* friends I made at the 2021 20Booksto50k conference last year (especially Meryl Yourish and Cady Hammer), my editor for this book—Karie Crawford, my fellow mom writers, and of course, my family. Your support and help have been priceless.